DEATHBLOW HILL

**Books by Phoebe Atwood Taylor
available from Foul Play Press**

Asey Mayo Cape Cod Mysteries

THE ANNULET OF GILT
THE ASEY MAYO TRIO
BANBURY BOG
THE CAPE COD MYSTERY
THE CRIMINAL C.O.D.
THE CRIMSON PATCH
THE DEADLY SUNSHADE
DEATH LIGHTS A CANDLE
DIPLOMATIC CORPSE
FIGURE AWAY
GOING, GOING, GONE
THE MYSTERY OF THE CAPE COD PLAYERS
THE MYSTERY OF THE CAPE COD TAVERN
OCTAGON HOUSE
OUT OF ORDER
THE PERENNIAL BOARDER
PROOF OF THE PUDDING
PUNCH WITH CARE
SANDBAR SINISTER
SPRING HARROWING
THE SIX IRON SPIDERS
THREE PLOTS FOR ASEY MAYO

Writing as Alice Tilton

BEGINNING WITH A BASH
DEAD ERNEST
FILE FOR RECORD
HOLLOW CHEST
THE LEFT LEG
THE IRON CLEW

PHOEBE ATWOOD TAYLOR

DEATHBLOW HILL

An Asey Mayo Cape Cod Mystery

A Foul Play Press Book

THE COUNTRYMAN PRESS
Woodstock, Vermont

Copyright © 1935 by Phoebe Atwood Taylor
Renewed 1963

This edition published in 1993 by Foul Play
Press, an imprint of The Countryman Press, Inc.,
Woodstock, Vermont 05091.

ISBN 0–88150–262–6

Printed in the United States of America

10 9 8 7 6 5 4 3 2

DEATHBLOW HILL

1

I‌T was the hour when Suzanne Howes most enjoyed the
hill and the surrounding Cape scenery, the hour when
the sun began to dip beyond Weesit Harbor and the blue
rim of Cape Cod Bay, when the salt marshes took on a
golden haze, and the sea gulls swooped in ever widening
circles toward the ocean side and the crashing Atlantic
breakers.

A thousand—nearer, she thought, ten thousand times
in the last thirty years she had watched afternoons grow
into evenings from the hill, but they were always different. Sometimes the bay was green and smooth as velvet,
and sometimes angry little white caps bubbled over its
greyness. Sometimes the marsh was deep with snow, sometimes bright with mallow and goldenrod. And the bay
and the marsh were only two parts of the changing scene;
there was the sky to consider, and the long stretch of shore
line, the tides and the fishing boats, the jagged shadows
on the neighboring hills.

Now, in June, the panorama cheered her. The cloud-
less sky, the freshness of the marsh, the soft west wind,
they were all preludes to summer. And even though sum-

mer meant inestimable hard work with the boarders—
Suzanne bit her lip. Although she always thought of them
as boarders, her son Lance insisted on calling them guests.
Well, the guests meant drudgery, but at the same time
they made some things easier—

Unconsciously her gaze wandered to the ten foot chain-
link fence, with its four defiant top strands of barbed wire.
That fence did more than divide the hill neatly in two.
It separated the old Howes Homestead, with its abandoned lighthouse, where Suzanne and Lance lived, from
the gingerbread, fretwork and colored-glass monstrosity
that sheltered the other part of the Howes family—Abby,
the only daughter of old Captain Bellamy Howes, and
her husband Simon Keith. There was no gap the whole
mile length of that fence, nor any gate. There never had
been. Gales might blow the fence down, earthquakes might
shake it, but no power on heaven or earth could remove
or change what the fence stood for. As unconsciously as
she had looked at it, Suzanne gritted her teeth and turned
away.

An automobile horn tooted derisively from the marsh
road. It was Lance in the new station wagon, speeding
home from a day's fishing.

Suzanne waved, got up from her deck chair and started
for the kitchen ell. The west wind moulded her linen dress
to her slim figure, and over in the gingerbread house,
Simon Keith put down his binoculars and spoke to his
wife.

"Fifty if she's a day, and her shape's better than it
was thirty years ago—oh, Lance is coming." He changed

the subject hastily as he noticed Abby's lips tighten. Simon was just fifty himself, but Abby was over sixty, and he had to watch himself. "Lance is coming in that new car. That must have cost 'em plenty. They may cry poor, but, by God, they've got your father's money salted away somewhere!"

Abby jerked the lace curtain back from the bay window, and together they watched Suzanne until the kitchen door closed behind her.

"My father's money!" Abby's voice rose shrilly as she let the curtain fall back into place. "*My* money, you mean! Mine and yours! And we have to sit here and watch them squander it— Bellamy Howes's own money, squandered by that woman and that boy! Not even his own flesh and blood! The spawn of a Liverpool dock rat and a wench yanked from a New York gutter—"

Stifling a yawn, Simon sat down in the leather Morris chair. Every word of her tirade against Suzanne and Lance, and Eben Howes, old Bellamy's adopted son, was as familiar to him as Abby's scrawny figure and her ill-fitting clothes. He listened without actually hearing a word, yet as her anger mounted, he automatically checked her at his accustomed place.

"But old Bellamy did adopt Eben legally, Abby. We can't do anything about that. And Eben married Suzanne legally in New York. And Lance is their son. And by your father's will, they have half the land and that house—"

"But the money! Where's that money? Where'd it go to? Father had over a million. He told me so, time and time again! And what was there left in the bank when he died? Just forty thousand! Where's the rest? Of course Eben got hold of it before he died! Suzanne knows all about it! How else'd she bring up Lance, and educate him? I was schooled in Boston, and I know how it cost then, and it'd be more now! They can't live by those boarders. Eben died twenty-six years ago, just before Lance was born, and you can't say, Simon Keith, she's lived by boarders ever since! She—"

Abby broke off and grabbed the binoculars from Simon's hand.

"Lance has packages," she continued eagerly. "And a bucket. Been fishing, I guess. He's just dropped a letter. That's a new shirt he's got on— Simon, what are you smiling about? Where are you going?"

"Out to feed the hens." He patted her bony shoulder. "Cheer up, Abby. I've been thinking of an idea, lately."

"Idea!" Abby sniffed. "Idea indeed! A fig for all your ideas. You've had those before."

"But this one," Simon informed her softly, "is different. This one is going to work."

She was too interested in watching Lance to notice the glitter in Simon's eyes, and the ironic smile that played around the corners of his mouth. Lance had finally retrieved the letter, and Abby found herself wondering, as she always did, what that tall, broad-shouldered boy was really like, and if he was really engaged to that blonde girl in the yellow roadster, the one whose father owned that factory in Detroit.

Lance dumped his miscellaneous armful on the kitchen table.

"Hi, Mud. Morning paper— Little Annie's on the loose again. Morning mail. Bucket of flounders outside. Sorry I'm so late. Met Broody Mary, and she wanted to know when you'll want her."

Broody Mary, who had been christened Jerusha Sekells, lived in Weesit Centre, and during summers helped Suzanne with the boarders.

"I told her," Lance continued, "to pop over and see you tonight, because I thought that mail looked promising. Gape at it while I get the fish."

He was grinning when he returned.

"Abby's in a dither. Probably itching to know if it's flounders or clams in the bucket. So damn silly of 'em to park in that bay window where the sun always catches their glasses. What's the New York one?"

"Very business-like letter from a woman who signs herself J. House. Wants me to wire her in Boston tonight if she can come tomorrow. Doesn't give me much time, does she? Names her employer and three banks for references—who's Benjamin K. Carson, Lance? Sounds familiar."

"Tycoon. See 'Time,' under Business. He was on a cover a few weeks ago. What's J. House to him?"

"Secretary. Saw our ad in the 'Tribune.' Wants a room in the lighthouse for a month. House—that's going to be very confusing. Every time someone calls her, I'll probably answer—"

"Don't give it a thought," Lance said heartily as he emptied the pail of flounders. "If she wants a room in the light, you should care if she was named Petunia. God bless that light! They may have called it Bellamy's Folly when granddad put it up, but don't the guests love it! Well, J. House'll be forty-five and look twenty-eight, and give us market tips, and tell me I'm wasting my life away. And that I shouldn't let adverse economic conditions get me down, ha-ha, there are plenty of jobs for lusty engineers —what's the matter? Isn't the crested one from good old Tab?"

"Lance, what's today?"

"Monday, June third. All day."

"This is from Tab—Mrs. Newell, I mean. I do wish, Lance, you wouldn't get me into the habit of calling her Tab! She wants a lighthouse room, too—"

"That fills the tower," Lance nodded. "Yup, that's swell. Tab'll pulverize the tycoon's girl friend, and there won't be a dull minute. Tab hates new rich—"

"Lance, be helpful! Tab says she's coming Tuesday, June third. And—"

"And there isn't any. She's either coming today the third or tomorrow the fourth, and probably not either. Remember last year? We expected her the nineteenth, and she crashed in the twenty-eighth. Lost her list, but she knew the digits made ten. Mud, you don't think the old war horse's coming tonight?"

Suzanne shrugged. "You'd better drive up to Yarmouth in case she should. I'll wait dinner for you, and I'd better phone Broody Mary. Thank Heaven, the light's all ready! And," she hesitated, "and your clothes are ready. In your closet."

Lance's smile faded.

"Okay," he said briefly.

Fifteen minutes later he stalked into the kitchen, his dungarees and sweat shirt replaced by a tightly fitting, blue drill jacket and stiffly-starched white slacks.

"Fauntleroy the bellhop. Mud, this collar's shrunk or something. You'll have to let it out. Be seeing you."

Suzanne sighed as she watched the station wagon bounce over the marsh road. Weesit villagers often wondered how, with that fence, and the feud, and her long widowhood, her face could be so curiously unlined. They said that no one and nothing could beat Suzanne Howes, and they had said it so often and so loudly that she was beginning to believe it herself.

The truth of the matter was that though the barbed wire and Abby and Simon were sufficient to wear anyone down, Suzanne had always been faced with other things that worried her more. At first there had been the major problem of survival—grocer's bills, coal bills, the inevitable repairs on the old house, equally inevitable taxes, and Lance's education. Now that she had built up a well-to-do clientele, wealthy dowagers like Mrs. Newell, wealthy men like Howard Smail, the book collector, the survival problem wasn't so pressing.

It was the problem of Lance himself that worried her now. Two solid years back in Weesit were beginning to leave their mark on him. The bellboy, chauffeur and man-of-all-work rôle was sheer torture for him. He tried not to show it, but Suzanne knew. And then there was Clare Chatfield. If Lance had a real job and more contacts with the sort of young people he had always known away at school, Clare would never appeal to him as she did at the moment. Because Lance felt she was something utterly beyond his grasp, she began to loom as an unrealized ideal.

There was a knock on the door, but before Suzanne could open it, the tall angular frame of Jerusha Sekells filled the doorway.

"Broody Ma—oh, Jerusha! I was just going to telephone you. I—"

"Don't," Broody Mary said firmly, tossing her Boston bag on a chair, "try to call me J'rusha. You can't, more'n five minutes, no matter how hard you try. I must say that marsh road's worse'n ever. Hear about John Nickerson? He's got the mumps, and him eighty-five! I seen a cord an' stake out in the yard—now don't you tell me you gone an' got another cat?"

Suzanne shook her head. "No. Lance had a puppy offered him, but I put my foot down. I—somehow, I couldn't forget Pooh."

Pooh was the little black kitten that in some way had broken the long length of cord that secured it to the stake, and crawled over, or dug under, the fence. Lance had heard a shotgun that afternoon, and the next morning the mangled little ball of fur was flung over the fence.

"Beasts!" Mary said savagely. "Beasts! I'd take a shotgun to them two in a minute, if I got half a chance! Them an' their ole money-money-money! Fools! They think you'd all but slave yourself to death, if you had ole Bellamy's money hid away in a sock somewheres? F'you ask me, they got it themselves! That Simon, with his leer an' his oily ways—why, them black eyes of his undresses you with a look! The ole—Lance said maybe Mrs. Newell was comin' soon."

"Tonight or tomorrow. You know how she is."

Mary permitted herself a dour grin. "Her an' her lists. Lot of poppycock. Her mem'ry's as good's yours or mine, only she pretends she has to use lists, an' then she pretends to lose 'em, an' everythin's at sixes an' sevens. Huh. Clever. Then she ain't never tied down—" she broke off and turned to the door. "Didn't you hear someone out there just then? Thought I heard a step on the walk—"

"Come away, Mary." Suzanne's hand moved toward the table drawer. The revolver there wasn't loaded—none of the half dozen Lance had scattered about the house were loaded, but Simon Keith wouldn't know. "Is it—"

"T'ain't Simon. Yessir, there's somebody, though—just run behind the barn. Maybe 'tis—"

"Mary, don't go out! Mary, come back here—"

But Suzanne's orders fell on empty air. Mary had raced out into the gathering dusk. In a few minutes she was back, panting, brandishing a long silk handkerchief of bright yellow.

"Run like a deer, he did. Got away from me. But he dropped this. Funny thing for a man to be havin', ain't it? Got a little knot tied in one end. Huh."

Suzanne looked at the scarf. "Probably some stray tourist, or summer person who hasn't been here long enough to know of the Howes feud—I thought I caught sight of someone walking across the marsh this afternoon. Well, it's no matter, Mary, as long as it wasn't Simon. Throw the thing away. Look, Mrs. Newell may or may not come tonight, but a woman from New York is coming tomorrow. It's time I wired her that she's expected. You needn't stay tonight, if you don't want, but if you could plan to come tomorrow—"

"Needn't stay tonight? Expect me to walk back to town across that marsh, with some strange man lurking around on it? Not much. Not so's you'd notice it. Leave you here alone? Nosireebob. Go send your telegram—wait up. Simon bothered you lately?"

"Not since February." The color rose in Suzanne's cheeks. "Lance was in New Bedford. Simon was drunk. I outran him to the house and locked the door. Mary, you're the only one who knows about that—you mustn't ever, ever let Lance know, or even suspect! If Lance ever dreamed that—that I'd had any trouble with Simon, he'd tear him apart, limb by limb, within ten minutes, and probably throw Abby into the bay for good measure! It's better he should go on thinking this whole hideous affair something to laugh at and bear with—"

"He won't know nothin' from me," Mary assured her. "Now, git along. Might's well have one night of leisure. An' don't worry. Simon Keith knows I'm here, an' he won't dare edge round this place long's I am. He ain't forgot the kettle of boilin' water he got in the face last summer. Not much! Broody I may be, but I'm dangerous when I'm roused."

Suzanne laughed in spite of herself.

"You almost scare me, sometimes—oh, Mary, I'm so glad you're back! Even if you didn't do ninety-nine percent of the work, I'd be just as glad. It's such a relief to feel safe from Simon all day long—"

Alone in the kitchen, Mary looked at the yellow scarf and smiled grimly.

Not for nothing had she spent the first twenty years of her life on her father's schooner. She knew a thing or two.

Fitting the knotted end of the scarf between her little finger and her fourth finger, she wound it over the back of her fourth and third fingers, carried it to her palm between her second and third fingers. Then, holding the unknotted end in her left hand, she extended the scarf to its fullest length.

"Guess," she muttered to herself, "you better be glad I *am* back, Sue Howes! If someone wasn't goin' to garrot someone else, I'm Lydia Pinkham! All creased. All ready. An' Simon ain't bothered her lately. Just a summer visitor, fiddlesticks! Huh!"

With a quick motion she pulled down the kitchen window shades. No sense in advertising all she knew. She lifted the stove lid and clanked it, but the yellow scarf never saw the glowing coals. Neatly folded, it was thrust into the farthest corner of the topmost shelf of the old preserve closet. No one but Mary ever bothered with that top shelf; no one else could reach it.

Back in the kitchen, she pulled a folded cambric nightgown from the bottom of her Boston bag, and from one sleeve she extracted a tissue-wrapped box. From that she quietly removed six blunt-nosed bullets, and those she fitted with a practised hand into the chambers of the revolver in the table drawer.

"There," she said aloud. "There! That for you, Simon Keith, or your hired thugs! Or anyone else that wants to scare folks and make trouble! Come along, the whole caboodle of you!"

With a sniff of satisfaction, she stalked over to the sink.

Broody Mary was prepared to repel boarders.

2

Lance Howes shivered in the Yarmouth Station, for the wind had shifted and the air was damp with fog. While he huddled over the wheel and damned Tabitha Newell with amiable intensity, the lady herself sat on a platform, a hundred odd miles away, with eleven other trustees of the Wolverton Orphanage, and interestedly scanned through her lorgnettes the faces of two hundred orphans.

To them she was a large, over-upholstered old lady with a lot of white hair, more fun to watch than the others because her diamond rings glistened so pleasantly whenever she moved her eyeglass around.

They all knew her as the only trustee who had retained her equilibrium the day the mice were let loose at assembly, but only a few of the naughtier ones gave her full credit. They knew her habit of driving up in her limousine from time to time and requesting a couple of the worst offenders on the problem-child list. No one demurred, because Mrs. Newell's son-in-law was a well-known psychologist, and it all seemed perfectly logical. The problem children so requested, moreover, always returned in the best of spirits, with, as the director often said, an entirely new point of view. No one had ever thought to ask the children any pointed questions about their outing, and the children, delicately primed by Mrs. Newell herself, never volunteered the information that their supposed psycho-analytical afternoons began with a thumping big lunch at the Parker House, continued with a good lurid movie, and ended with as many chocolate marshmallow fudge sundaes as each little problem child could hold.

Mrs. Newell smiled at Annunciata de Marco. Annunciata had shrewdly inquired what Mrs. Newell intended to say on the day she was caught. Would she lie? Mrs. Newell told her serenely there were always her lists, and if the list that said "Psychologist" got mixed with the one that said "Lunch, movies, tea," certainly Mrs. Newell was not to blame.

The speaker, a dull fellow from some experimental school, wound up to a polite salvo of applause, and Mrs. Newell, declining an invitation to remain for refreshments, went out to her car. She had too many things on her mind to dally with orphans.

Marvin, her chauffeur, helped her unnecessarily down the steps.

"That guy's still here," he informed her in a low voice. "Least his car is. Run past the gates a couple times, but I guess he didn't dare come inside. Honest, Mrs. Newell, this is screwy! Can't I call a state cop? It's a lonely road home, an' if he wanted to gang us, I couldn't do much. This is the first time he's trailed you out of Boston in all the two weeks he's been followin' you—"

"And I must say," Mrs. Newell said cheerfully as

Marvin spread the blanket over her knees, "that he's been led a pretty chase! Beginning to look haggard, I thought this morning. He's so silly, Marvin. The whole thing's so silly! Fancy any man in his right mind marching around, day after day, with a bright yellow handkerchief in his pocket, while he was presumably trying to make himself as inconspicuous as possible!"

"But s'pose he means to kidnap you? You—"

"Certainly I've given him every opportunity," Mrs. Newell interrupted crossly. "Don't worry, Marvin. You can protect me. I've every confidence in you. After all, you were nearly heavyweight champion—"

"Welterweight," Marvin corrected.

"Well, whatever it was, you can fight. See if you can't lose him on the way back. Take that road past the Bailey's estate, then speed up and pull into one of the bridle paths and snap off your lights. We'll be near the outer lodge, near enough to howl if any help is needed. If he lets himself be tricked, turn around and come back on the turnpike. Oh—I'm not going home tonight. Take me to Miss Atterbury's."

"The—you mean, that sort of boarding house on Beacon?"

"Exactly. I had a bright idea, Marvin. This business has gone on long enough. I'm going to stay at Miss Atterbury's tonight, and tomorrow I'm going to the Cape, down to Weesit. Then there'll be no need to worry over all this nonsense, whatever it means, because I telephoned Asey Mayo from the orphanage, and he's going to take charge—"

"Asey Mayo?" Marvin, sounding happier than he had in two weeks, stuck his head into the tonneau. "That Cape detective?"

"Yes. He got Levering's forty-footer back from those bootleggers while Levering was abroad. Really a splendid fellow. Combination of Euclid, Scheherezade, and David Harum. That is, I mean he's a jack-of-all-trades, Marvin. You'd like his Porter sixteen roadster. He worked for the Porters—what's that?"

"Can I go too?" Marvin asked. "Can I come with you? Does he look like his pictures?"

"You? Well, maybe later. Yes, Asey does. Tallish, blue eyes. He's a native Cape Codder, looks it and talks it. Better get along, Marvin. Old yellow handkerchief—Archie the Cockroach, or whoever he is, will get suspicious if we chat too long. I'll tell you more of Asey later."

Shortly after midnight, Marvin pulled the limousine to the curb in front of Miss Atterbury's.

"Splendidly done," Mrs. Newell said approvingly as she got out. "Go back home now, and have Jane pack my things. Don't bring anything here, but have all the luggage put on the Cape train tomorrow morning. See to it yourself. Then—Marvin, what's the matter? You're white! You're—why, you're shaking!"

"Mrs. Newell," Marvin controlled himself with difficulty, "you see the front of this car? You—"

"A new bumper and—and things, and it'll be as good as new. Don't worry about it, Marvin. Really, that was magnificent driving, and I'm proud of you. That cockroach had no right to try to force you into Bailey's stone wall, and you did absolutely right in ditching him. Served him right. And he wasn't hurt. I saw him slide out. And don't worry about me, either. I wasn't jarred a bit, really."

"But—"

"I doubt," Mrs. Newell continued serenely, "if any policemen come asking you questions about leaving an accident but in case they do, refer them to Steve Crump. Good night, Marvin. I'll write you all about Asey Mayo."

Leaning weakly against the car, Marvin watched his employer mount the brownstone steps to Miss Atterbury's.

"Like a leaf, I was," he told his mother later. "Like a leaf. Trembling all over. Think of it, ma! I'm goin' around tomorrow an' sock that doctor! Tells me to find some quiet outdoors work, like drivin' for an old lady, because of my heart! Quiet! Say, Spider Maloney was a cinch compared to workin' for her! An' I bet," he added with a hint of admiration in his voice, "I bet you, ma, the old girl sleeps like a top!"

Descending the stairs into Miss Atterbury's dining room the next morning, Mrs. Newell appeared to have slept, if not like a top, at least like a log.

She beckoned to the trim negro maid.

"I wonder if you'd be good enough to telephone the South Station and find out when the Cape train leaves? And if I have to change for Weesit Centre, and what time I get there? You call information, or something. I personally never understand a word they say."

"It leaves at eight-thirty-something, and gets into Weesit around twelve-thirty—"

Mrs. Newell swung around and surveyed the girl, sitting at a small table in the corner, who proffered the information.

She was a good-looking girl, and young, and the combination startled Mrs. Newell. Youth and beauty were comparative strangers in the Atterbury ménage. And—Mrs. Newell reached for her lorgnettes. Topping the girl's soft brown sweater suit was a scarf of the shade of yellow that had haunted her for two weeks!

"I couldn't help hearing your question," the girl went on apologetically, "and as I'm on my way to Weesit, I—"

Her words trailed off under the searching gaze behind the platinum-rimmed lorgnettes.

"It's the shock," Mrs. Newell said slowly, "of seeing anyone under sixty-five in this dining room."

The girl laughed. "A friend of my mother's gave me a letter to Miss Atterbury years ago. She said it would be entirely safe for a girl travelling alone, and she seems to have been entirely right."

"Any changes?" Mrs. Newell inquired.

"Any—oh, the train. Not mornings. My," the girl hesitated, "my name is House. I'm going to spend some of my vacation at a place called Deathblow Hill. Where there's a lighthouse built into a boarding house, or the other way around, or something. Perhaps you'd have breakfast with me, and tell me something about it and the town?"

Mrs. Newell did some quick thinking. Miss Atterbury's guests, while not picked from the social register, had to present references. Suzanne Howes was careful, too.

Probably the yellow handkerchief scarf was just an accident. After all, there were probably hundreds of factories which did nothing else but manufacture yellow scarves, day in and day out. And if, by any rare chance, the girl was connected with Archie the Cockroach, it wouldn't be a bad idea to investigate.

"Thank you, my dear." She sat down at the little table. "As a matter of fact, I'm going to the hill myself. I've known Suzanne Howes for a number of years. Charming woman. Her husband, who was much older than she, was the adopted son of Captain Bellamy Howes, of Howes and Company. And he knew my grandfather, of Newell and Company. All in the China trade. Her son's a nice young fellow, and their maid-of-all-work is a delight. As for Weesit—well, you'll have to see it for yourself. It's not nearly as infested with what Lance Howes scornfully refers to as the tourist trade as some of the upper Cape towns."

"Why Deathblow?" the girl asked. "Why the light?"

"Old Bellamy built the light in the days when his packets and barques all came into Weesit Harbor. As for the name, I don't think anyone really knows why. Some say it's because of the way the wind blows there, and some lay it to the Indians. Poor Indians, always getting the blame for everything! But there's never been any death blow on it that I know of, though—" she started to say that there might well be, in view of the Howes feud, and then thought better of it. The girl didn't look like the sort to be prejudiced by the feud and the fence, but one never knew.

She turned to the maid.

"More porridge, if I may. Thank you."

The swinging door had barely closed behind the girl when a man darted in between the portières leading to the stairs. He was panting furiously, his clothes were mussed, and blood streamed from a cut in his cheek.

"Miss Joan—quick—"

The girl jumped to her feet.

"Bates! Bates, whatever are you—what's wrong? Has Mr. Carson—is he all right—"

"Miss Joan—"

As he stood there, silhouetted against the portières, two arms shot out from behind him. There was the flash of a yellow scarf, then Bates, his hand tugging helplessly at his throat, was jerked back through the curtains.

Mrs. Newell and the girl stared at each other for a dazed half minute. Both admitted later that they wondered if they had actually seen a man whisked away before their eyes, or if they'd dreamed it.

Mrs. Newell found her voice first.

"Was he," she inquired quizzically, "a friend of yours?"

"It was Bates—I don't understand! Come! Hurry— we've got to do something!"

They reached the door at the head of the brownstone steps just in time to see a cab swerve wildly around the corner.

"That was Bates! Bates, Mr. Carson's butler! Mr. Benjamin Carson. I'm his secretary! Oh, I don't know what to do!"

"Might telephone Mr. Carson," Mrs. Newell suggested, "and find out what the matter is."

"But I can't! He left New York last night on some freight boat. I don't even know what boat. He's taking six months' vacation, and not a soul knows where he's going. Not even I know!"

"Quite sure that was Bates, the butler?"

"Sure? But of course! For the last three years, ever since I began to work for Mr. Carson, Bates has been the butler! Why, he took my bags out to the cab yesterday, when I left for the airport! Of course it was my Bates!"

"Well," Mrs. Newell observed drily, "he may be your Bates, my dear, but he was my yellow handkerchief. Come along. It's after eight."

"You don't think I'll go tooting off to Cape Cod, leaving Bates like this! I didn't see the number plates on that taxi, but—but this is awful! This—"

"Yes," Mrs. Newell agreed thoughtfully, "this is ceasing to be funny. I felt so last night, and now I'm convinced of it. We—"

"We've got to *do* something! There must be something we can do!"

"There is," Mrs. Newell told her cryptically, "and we're going right straight to him."

3

ASEY MAYO, his broad-brimmed Stetson at a rakish angle, shot the streamlined roadster along the sandy ruts of the Weesit turnoff. His keen blue eyes were fixed on the wavering curves ahead, but he hardly saw them. The sheaf of telegrams in the pocket of his flannel shirt presented a situation which occupied his thoughts to the exclusion of everything else.

Yellow scarves, yellow handkerchiefs—if he didn't know Tabitha Newell as an exceptionally keen woman with an irreproachable family behind her, he'd think the old lady had taken to drink. Men chasing her with yellow hand-kerchiefs! He laughed to himself. There was, she even admitted it herself over the phone last night, something pretty silly in a woman of her age being ruthlessly pursued by a man and a yellow handkerchief. He conjured up a picture of Tabitha Newell and her lorgnettes dashing up Beacon Street, closely followed by a man—what was it she called him? Followed by Archie the Cockroach, waving yellow handkerchiefs.

His chuckle died away. Ahead at the foot of the Bay road, a woman was waving something yellow at him.

"Plague of 'em," he murmured. "Huh—oho!"

He eased the car to a gentle stop, and grinned.

"Hi, Broody Mary. I mean, hi, Jerusha—"

"Mary'll do. It has to. Asey, I was just this minute settin' out for town to telephone you. Wanted to have a little talk with you."

"Hop in." Asey opened the door. "I'm on my way to meet the noon train in Yarmouth, but I got ten minutes."

Mary clucked her tongue. "Ten minutes, you—you scorcher you! Lance left twenty minutes ago to meet that train!"

"But he ain't got that buggy of his broke in yet," Asey observed. "Wait'll he does. What's on your mind, Mary?"

She looked at him searchingly before she answered. People said that all the to-do about him, and all the newspaper talk hadn't changed Asey a bit; if the outside was to be trusted, Mary thought, people were right. She nodded to herself and cleared her throat.

"Asey, they call me Broody Mary because they say I never see nothin' but the dark side of things. But you know I seen enough of this world to know it's the dark things that mostly happen. I ain't often fooled. An' you know, too, I kind of put on a lot of it, because folks sort of grown to expect it, an' it sort of seems to give 'em a certain amount of what you might call pleasure. The gloomier I get to some of the boarders up to the hill, the bigger tips they give me. You know how 'tis. But that ain't gettin' on to what I got to say. Asey, you knew father. You cooked on the 'Belle of Weesit' back there in the eighties. You've known me all my life. I guess, anyhows, you know enough to know that if I come to you an' say I'm scared about somethin'—"

"You," Asey finished for her, "are scared. Yup, I get your point. There's fire behind the smoke." He turned off the motor. "Tell me—"

"You better not stop here. Drive on to the other side of town. I'll walk back."

A few minutes later he parked the car at the entrance to one of the wood roads beyond the centre.

"This do? Y'know, Mary, 'f you're in any sort of trouble, I—well, don't know's I can settle it, but I'll have a try—by the way, where'd you get that yellow thing?"

Mary passed it to him.

"That," she said, "is what you might call the jist of the whole matter, Asey. Feller that had it tried to get into Sue's yest'day. Run off b'fore I could lay hands on him, but he dropped this. 'Member that Frenchy, the bearded little coot we took on in Marseilles once? 'Member what he done to that German carpenter? Well, just you stare at that scarf an' see that knot in the end."

Asey examined it, then wound the scarf through his fingers as Mary had done the night before.

"This," his eyes narrowed, "this is queerer than you can guess, Mary. Tell me, what about friend Simon Keith?"

She stared down at the floorboards. "What about him? You know all there is to know about that man. B'sides, I promised Suzanne I'd never say a word."

"My, my," Asey returned in his blandest tones, "an' there you went an' did! Mary, I'm s'prised at you, to get taken in like that. Thought you was sharper. Yes—yes. So Simon's been botherin' Suzanne, has he? An' she ain't told Lance, for fear the kid'd go off half-cocked, which he would. An' you—"

"Asey Mayo!" Mary sounded exasperated, "Sometimes I think you ain't human! Father said they called your grandfather David Razor, an' sometimes it seems to me they could call you Asey Razor without stretchin' the truth a mite!"

"Nothin' inhuman about addin' two an' two an' makin' four," Asey told her with a grin. "It's the fellers that get five that you want to be scared of. How long's Simon been makin' passes at her?"

"Only the last couple years. Seemed to come over him all of a sudden that Abby wan't so young as she once was, an' Suzanne—well, you know her."

"What you make of Simon?" Asey asked.

"I'd be ashamed to tell you." Mary clamped her lips firmly together.

Asey pulled out his pipe. "He married Abby for her money, all right. Huh, I could feel sorry for her if she'd only acted nicer toward Eben. After all, Bellamy adopted him before she was born, an' Eb turned out lots better'n some of the boys that Cape Cap'ns picked up hither an' yon. Eb was a nice r'liable feller, but I always felt that bein' adopted give him a false notion of mankind. Bellamy done so much for him that he sort of b'lieved in Santa Claus. Wa-el, I—my golly, I got to hustle! First, take a peek at these wires."

Mary went methodically through the sheaf of telegrams, and as she read, the furrows on her forehead deepened.

"It's English," she admitted grudgingly at last, "but it don't make sense. What's wrong with Mrs. Newell?"

"She's bein' p'sued," Asey explained, "by a cockroach wavin' a yellow handkerchief, an' a girl named House come into her life, an'—"

"They's a woman named House comin' to the hill today."

"Same one, I gathered. Anyway—" Asey went on and told about Bates and his mysterious disappearance, and all the rest.

"Glory be!" Mary shook her head. "What's it all mean, all this yellow handkerchiefin'? I thought 'twas Simon or someone he sent, up on the hill, but what's it got to do with all this up in Boston? I—why, it's crazy!"

"Sure 'tis," Asey agreed. "Anyhow, I'll be hangin' round the hill for a time, to see 'f I can straighten out Mrs. Newell, if she's still goin' to be p'sued, so I can keep an eye on Simon for you, at least. Meantime, Mary, I'd sort of stick around Sue."

Mary nodded. "Smalley's there now, fixin' some sills. But I'll stay around."

"You better. When two people like Simon an' Abby've waited an' wailed around for money more'n twenty years, they're like to do most anythin'. I got to get goin'—"

"Ain't it queer?" Mary asked as she climbed out of the roadster. "Honest, Asey, ain't things queer?"

"Queer? M'yes. Only thing is, when you stop to think

it over, it's queer that things ain't queerer. Be seein' you—"

The roadster slid away, and Mary turned back toward the centre, and on a hillock above the wood road where they had been parked, Simon Keith tucked his binoculars into his leather blouse.

"Asey Razor, eh?" Simon murmured with satisfaction as he walked toward his truck. "Well, Asey Razor, I've got the jump on you, and it'll take you some time to figure it all out."

He whistled softly as he kicked at the starter, and when the engine finally began to splutter, he burst into song.

It was only a nursery rhyme, and off-key at that, but the words would have given Asey cause for reflection.

> " 'Will you walk into my parlor,
>   Said the spider to the fly—' "

Simon turned the truck off on the main road, and headed up the Cape.

> " 'Dum-de-dum-dum-dum-de-dum—
>   So he wove a subtle web, in a little corner sly,
>   And set his table ready, to dine upon the fly—' "

4

Asey Mayo wrinkled up his nose at the "Detour" sign near Dennis, which would add at least five miles to his route and without doubt prevent him from reaching Yarmouth in time to meet the Boston train.

He beckoned to one of the road gang.

"No chance to get through?"

"Not a chance, brother. Both sides torn up. An'—oh, boy, pipe that, will you?"

An enormous oil truck with an equally enormous trailer lumbered up behind Asey's roadster and rumbled off on the narrow detour. The driver's thumb was not to his nose, but it might as well have been.

"I couldn't get by him in that lane, not in a thousand years," Asey said disgustedly. "He knows it, too. I frittered away six minutes passin' him on the straightaway b'low here. Oh, well," he grinned philosophically, "'parently Heaven don't mean for me to meet that train. Fate's agin me. Prob'ly the stars is mixed up in it too."

He switched off the motor and settled back comfortably against the grey leather cushions.

"Spendin' the day with us?" the road worker inquired genially.

"Folks I'm after can be met here just as easy as at the station," Asey returned.

Actually he was rather glad of the opportunity to consider the yellow scarf situation and its various ramifications before Tabitha Newell arrived. The stranger on the hill whom Mary had chased might have been Simon, but the cockroach who pursued Tabitha obviously couldn't have been. Perhaps there was some connection between the two, perhaps it was just a series of silly coincidences. If Mary's yellow scarfer wasn't Simon, it might well have been someone sent by him. Not a Weesit man, for Suzanne was too popular, and Mary would have known. There wasn't any such thing as an entirely unknown stranger in Weesit.

A state police car drew up beside the roadster, and Bob Raymond, one of Asey's trooper friends, jumped out and lounged over to the door beside Asey.

"Was it for this you burned up the King's Highway, Asey? I saw you—at least, I had a vague feeling it was you who scudded through Brewster a few minutes back. What's the idea?"

Asey told him about the oil truck. "So," he concluded, "I'm just settin' an' waitin', like ole Sebub Higgins. Sebub an' the rest of his Holy Rollers climbed them elms back of Eldredge's when I was a kid, an' set an' waited one solid week for the end of the world to happen. On the eighth day a good stiff no'theaster come up an' sort of c'nvinced 'em the world was as normal as ever, an' like to wabble on for a good spell yet. What's news?"

"News?" Bob made a face. "Don't be funny. I could

have been put on ice last October, and no one'd have missed me. News—say, I'd pay money for a good clean murder. Say—you know all I've had to do the last two days? Investigate the plaintive wails of Obed Young, over in Weesit Neck. He's all wrought up because someone's swiping his eggs and milking his best jersey cow."

A sudden gleam appeared in Asey's eyes. "Over in the neck, huh? Find out who done it?"

With some heat, Bob remarked that egg and milk thieves didn't leave calling cards.

"Probably just someone who wanted a nice fresh custard. I think it's some of that worthless Corregio tribe up the road from Obed's, but how the hell could I pin anything on them?"

"You couldn't," Asey said slowly, "b'cause Lina Corregio an' her brood don't steal. They lie just as easy as rollin' off a log, but otherwise they're honest. Seen any strangers lurkin' about, Bob, in your wanderin's?"

"Strangers? Say! Sure, there's been regiments of strangers, come to Weesit Neck for the express purpose of swiping Obed Young's eggs and milk, with eggs, as he told me mournfully, at thutty cents—what's the frisky yellow scarf in your pocket for, Asey?"

"Y'know, Bob," Asey said, "I wish you took these minor chores like Obed's eggs an' milk a mite more serious. Great oaks from little acorns grow. Lots of action comes out of eggs. Think of C'lumbus."

Bob started to laugh, but somehow didn't. When Asey made suggestions in that tone, he meant what he said, and Bob had a healthy respect for the evolutions of Asey's brain.

"Okay, I'll tramp back and see what can be done— only why, Asey?"

"See this?" Asey waved the yellow scarf. "This is sort of puzzlin' me, an' they's a crazy chance Obed's missin' eggnogg might clear it up."

To him it all appeared logical enough; if there were a stranger lurking around Deathblow Hill, and no one had spotted him in the village, he might very likely be camping out by the Neck, living on Obed's jersey milk and thirty-cent eggs. But all that was not so crystal clear to Bob, who stuck his thumbs in his Sam Browne belt and teetered back and forth on his toes.

"Happen to know, Asey, the qualifications for committing an individual to a psychopathic institution in this Commonwealth? Well, just stick inside the law, and I shan't say a word."

Asey chuckled. "Run along an' hunt eggs, trooper, an' let me know if you happen on anythin'. I ain't makin' no promises, but I got reason to b'lieve I might maybe perhaps provide you with a little excitement."

It was only a matter of seconds before the police car was speeding away in the direction from which it had come. As it disappeared from sight, the station wagon, with Lance at the wheel, and Mrs. Newell and Joan House behind, turned on to the main road from the detour.

Tabitha had the door open and was on the running board before Lance stopped.

"How d'you do? Lance, that's an excellent vehicle of yours, and very likely station wagons have their part to play in this world, but—should you be terribly hurt if I finished this ride with Asey?"

"Lane sort of bouncy?" Asey asked as he helped her into the roadster. "But you shouldn't of felt the bouncin', not with all Lance's knee action an' fancy springin'—"

"It was neither the bounces nor the fancy springing that bothered me," Tabitha announced. "It was the lack of coöperation between the two. We bounced, and then sprung. Then there was that oil truck—but we won't go into that. When I die, just open my heart and you'll find 'Oil Truck' engraved on it. Lance, you and Joan trail along."

Once she and Asey were on their way, she dropped her bantering tone.

"I'm worried, Asey. This sort of thing is entirely outside my experience. I don't know how to cope with it. In fact, I don't even understand with what it is I'm supposed to be coping. It's nothing I can quell by sheer personality, nor anything to jape at, or reduce to absurdities—did you make anything of those telegrams I sent you this morning?"

"Uh-huh. 'Cept where they got 'carrot' an' 'garret' for 'garrot.' That sort of c'nfused me. Yup, I see where you might feel scared, Mrs. Newell. But wait'll you hear the rest of the story. We been havin' the yellow peril right here on Cape Cod. Listen."

Mrs. Newell shook her head at the conclusion of Asey's recital.

"So—dear me. If I read it, I shouldn't believe a word. Mary's man and mine can't be the same. Simon—there's a tidbit about him, by the way, that I've been pining to divulge for two years, but I never found the right moment. Simon's eavesdroppings aren't as vain as they seem to be. He can read lips."

Asey slowed down the car, turned and looked at her. "He—huh. Can, can he? Whee! Sure?"

"Sam Blair up at the store told me something Simon had told him. About my grandfather's company—"

"Newell's, in the China trade? But—"

"But Simon told him something I'd told Lance, something old Houqua said, that Simon couldn't possibly have just read. And if he had, he'd never have phrased it as he did. Now, Lance and I were talking out in the garden. We were the only ones on the hill at the time, and no one could have overheard. Obviously Lance wouldn't have told Simon. They don't speak. Lance was the only one I told. The whole thing puzzled me till I thought of lip reading, and I dismissed the idea. Too silly. Then I proved it. Pretended to yell things at people, actually only whispered, but made my lips form the words. Those words flounced back. On dozens of other occasions, too. I never told Suzanne or Lance. It seemed to me they had enough to worry about, and if they knew that Simon practically overheard every syllable they spoke, well—"

"It'd be pretty last straw-ish," Asey agreed. "An'— oh, my!" He chuckled. "Think of the things that man's read about himself. But in the light of—huh. God A'mighty—I wonder! When Mary an' I was talkin' this mornin', it seemed to me I heard a car stop. Sounded like a truck. I wonder if that scurvy critter followed us from the marsh—well, it must of tickled him consid'rable if he did. But glad's I am to know about that, we ain't gettin' any forrader on this scarf business—where's the girl come into it?"

"Secretary to Benjamin Carson, the tycoon—such a nice, descriptive term, that! Worked for him since her mother died. Carson left New York last night, and she couldn't raise anyone at the house, or his office. This Bates, who was so oddly whisked away, was supposed to be having a vacation too. She can't make it out at all. Does Lance know about the scarf business yesterday?"

"Not a word, an' I'm inclined to think the less he knows, the better. He's a nice kid, but a lot like his father. Sort of—who was that guy that used to fight windmills?"

Mrs. Newell nodded. "Don Quixote. Yes, he is. If he had any idea that Simon—hm. Yes. Lance would have been one of those dauntless early Christians who unhesitatingly and with a certain amount of pleasure offered his head to the jaws of the nearest lion. I freely confess," she added as Asey laughed, "that I have a sneaking admiration for that type, too. Because I should have turned pagan all over again before I got to the arena. And you," Tabitha smiled at him, "you would have told the lion funny stories about a couple of Phoenician cap'ns you knew, until the poor beast was completely disarmed, and then you'd have pricked his jugular vein with neatness and despatch. Yes, Lance is a problem. This girl—I'm sure she's genuine enough,—she should do him good."

Something of the sort had already occurred to Lance himself. When you expect a hard-bitten, hard-boiled, middle-aged spinster, and when she turns out to be as good looking as Joan House—

Lance put his finger on the horn and held it there.

"Sheer ebullience," he told Joan. "That's the thanksgiving in me coming out. You and Tab and I are going to have fun. I was sure of her, but willows wept for you! Know how to fish?"

"No."

"Row a boat? Dig clams? No? Cheer up, you will."

"They're things I always meant to do," Joan said, "but I never—you see, I had a funny sort of bringing up—why are you stopping?"

"Mine also," Lance informed her blithely, "was a curious childhood. It's hard to drive and reminisce well both at the same time. Now you take the time I blew beans at Simon. You'll love Simon. First cousin to the Arsenic family. And then there were my bright sayings—why, mother bought groceries for years with the dollars earned by my brilliant lispings! At the age of five there was definite proof that I'd become the world's greatest bridge builder. I was always a fool for blocks. Yes, Miss House, you may quote me directly on that. 'I always felt,' said Lancelot Howes, 'that I was a man of destiny—'"

"Lancelot!" Joan said delightedly. "Not really—not really Lancelot!"

"Father had a romantic streak," Lance explained, "and always planned to call his first son Lancelot. Mother was all for something solid like John, or Thomas, but father died before I was born, and—well, I'm Lancelot. That's that, and now it's your turn."

Joan looked out over the distant dune and the blue patch of bay before she answered.

"I like this Cape of yours," she said. "I—you want to know about me? It's nothing much. My father died when I was a baby, and mother went to work in a department store in Chicago, and got to be a buyer. Gift buyer. She boarded me out till I was fourteen, and then I trailed along with her. I—oh, I can't even tell it well, I'm afraid. I've lost the light touch in the last three years. I've helped buy carved wooden boxes and bad jewelry in every tourist port in the world. I did all her letters and stuff. After she died, I got this job with Benjamin Carson. Dumb luck. He lives in a row of old brownstones on the Drive. I was going to another place in the row to see if I could get a nurse-maid's job, and mixed the numbers. Never really got it through my head for a day or two that I was secretary to him, and not a maid to some children named Dusnick. Funny, I've always remembered that name. Anyway, Carson's grand. I live in the brownstone and manage the house. And now I've got six months off. First vacation in three years. First time I've been farther away from New York than Jackson Heights since. It's awful, now I think of it."

Lance watched the curve of her chin, and the way her brown hair curled at the back of the neck.

"I bet," he said, "it was pretty drab at first, wasn't it, after all that kiting around?"

Joan drew a long breath.

"Hideous. I'd never been in one place much more than a month in all my life. Funny that I've never been to New England before. Mother hated it. Said the weather was too unspeakable. But I've been thinking since I got to Boston yesterday, that I seem to know this part of the world. Odd, because I never happened to have that seeming-to-be-here-before-feeling about any other place. I—"

She stopped short and looked curiously at Lance. In ten minutes she had told him more about herself than—why, than Ben Carson had found out in three years! It wouldn't do. She changed the subject.

"I—tell me about Mrs. Newell. I don't know what to make of her."

Lance threw back his head and laughed.

"Tab? Oh, she's just not of this earth. There's no one like her. Wait till you see her and Broody Mary together. There's a pair!"

"What's Broody Mary? A dog or a cat?"

"Neither. We can't have 'em because of Simon—oh, that louse has come up again! Look, I might as well tell you that Deathblow Hill contains a feud within its borders. Not the good, lusty, rousing sort you find in the South, but a passionately restrained, Eugene O'Neill business. Very thin-lipped. All about money of my grandfather's, which never turned up. Both parties involved feel that the other had or has it. There," he wound up cheerfully, "now you know about that, thank God! Always a hard thing to explain, that feud. Don't look so puzzled. The loopholes'll fill in all by themselves."

Joan said plaintively that she hoped they would.

"They will. And don't fidgit. We'll start along. Only, first, how do you feel about the unemployed? 'Yes' or 'no' will not be considered adequate answers. It's rather important that I know, too."

"Why? I mean, what—"

"State your answer concisely," Lance said, "giving reasons."

"Well," Joan hesitated, "I feel about 'em, if that's what you mean. I've been unemployed myself. I have even," she bit her lip, "even been on the dole. In a nice way, of course. They gave me cash instead of flour checks. That was before I got to be Carson's secretary—why d'you want to know?"

"Purely personal reasons." Lance started the car.

"Oh. Oh, I'm sorry. But—"

"You needn't be. Personal, but no deep secret. I'm unemployed, you see, and your reactions to the unemployment situation are vital to my well-being. They loom. I mean, suppose you had some firm conviction that the man you married should be able to support you. In that case, I could never propose honorable matrimony. That sort of thing. See?"

Joan stared at his clear-cut profile.

"See?" Lance repeated. "My, you're a thoughtful creature. What're you brooding about now?"

"Thinking," Joan told him with a dazzling smile, "that Tabitha Newell is not the only amazing person in New England. And I had such—"

"Preconceived notions? Everyone does. Cotton Mather,

Paul Revere, Desire Under the Ellums, Blessings on Thee, Little Man, Barefoot Boy—and so forth. But don't put me in Tab's class. I'm a simple soul. So simple I openly admit that Lancelot wants his lunch—we've got to make time— Tab and Asey'll be just about home by now."

As a matter of fact, they were walking up the oyster-shell walk to the side door.

"Open," Tabitha commented, "but no sight of Suzanne. Usually she's out to meet me, and that fanfare of yours should have wakened the dead. Does it seem to you," she sniffed, "that something's burning? It is. Perhaps she's in the kitchen. Let's go around."

The kitchen door was open, and Asey stood aside to let Tabitha precede him.

On the threshold she turned and gripped Asey's arm. Every drop of color had drained suddenly from her face.

Lying on the kitchen floor, one hand to her throat, was Suzanne Howes.

5

"SHE's alive," Asey said a few seconds later, "she—yup, she's comin' to, but even so, Mrs. Newell, you hop to the phone an' call Doc Cummings anyway—"

"Thank—here—" Tabitha fished in the depths of her gargantuan pocketbook and brought out a tiny flask of smelling salts. "Use these—always wondered what to do with 'em. Nephew Levering always sends me a bottle every Christmas. With a lavender lace shoulder throw—"

Her voice trailed off as she hurried into the front of the house.

Asey bent over Suzanne again, and whisked the flask under her nose.

"Ugh!" Suzanne made a face and then coughed. "Water—"

"Water comin' up," Asey said, filling a tumbler at the tap. "Don't try to chatter—plenty of time to tell us things. No, nor don't get up. Just stay there an' take your time. You get the doc?"

Mrs. Newell's poise was badly shattered.

"It seems," she cleared her throat, "that he's already on his way here. Mrs. Cummings said a man called up about ten minutes ago and said for him to come at once. Asey, ca—can you honestly grasp that? And you should see the house—it's a mess!"

Suzanne tried to speak, but Asey stopped her.

"Wait up—you ain't ready to talk yet. How d'you mean, mess?"

"I mean ransacked, despoiled, rifled, pillaged—take your choice! You never saw such a hodgepodge! Absolutely indescribable! What is it, Suzanne? You want to see it? Well—Asey, carry her in on the couch. I'll clear it off first—"

The long living room, which ran across the south end of the house, had probably never seen such turmoil in all of its two hundred years.

The rugs were rolled and rumpled; the pictures hung crazily, tilted at all angles, as though someone had been peering behind them. Flower bowls were spilled over, and rivulets of water ran disconsolately along the cracks of the punkin-yellow floor and ended in a puddle by the window, where one chintz curtain swung drunkenly in the wind.

Chairs were up-ended, the bric-a-brac from the walnut whatnot in the corner was scattered everywhere over the room, the old Governor Winthrop desk was a sea of papers and spilled ink. The five-masted schooner-in-a-bottle, which ordinarily stood on a rack on the mantelpiece above the fireplace, leaned on its side in an emptied wood box, next to the spilled brass jug of the fire lighter.

Suzanne looked at it all, and an expression of infinite despair came over her face.

"It ain't so bad," Asey briskly set to work replacing

the carpets while Mrs. Newell mopped up water. "Nothing busted only that little luster cup, an' I can fix that as good as new. He messed things around, but he wasn't out for up'n down, out an' out d'struction, 'parently. Might almost call it the aftermath of a feller huntin' a collar button. More pettish than mad—wonder what about upstairs, an' in the light?"

The bedrooms and the lighthouse rooms gave evidence of having been examined, but the damage was confined to rumpled bed sheets and half-opened bureau drawers.

"Had more time up here." Asey thought outloud. "Nice an' neat—huh. Here's the doc, steamin' along in that ancient an' hon'rable cradle of his—"

Dr. Cummings, panting slightly, strode into the living room and planted his inevitable little black bag on the table.

"For the love of Heaven, what've you been doing here, breaking up housekeeping? Suzanne, you—Asey, were you the fool that called and said Mrs. Howes would die if I didn't get here in a hurry? What's—really, I'm speechless! What's been going on?"

"Someone," Suzanne spoke with difficulty, "came up from behind me and nearly choked me to death. I don't know any more that happened till Asey and Mrs. Newell came. I'd been outside in the deck chair, and I thought I saw someone pass by the window—he must have been here for hours—"

Dr. Cummings opened up his little bag, surveyed the little vials, frowned, and cast a professional eye at Suzanne.

"Glass of water, Asey. Oh, you two needn't stay here—"

With an easy hand, the doctor shook some powder into the water, watched it dissolve, and presented the glass to Suzanne.

"Thirty years I've known you, Sue, and this is the first time I ever felt you needed any of this stuff. Go ahead and drink it—go easy, but finish it."

He wandered around the room, picked up a Toby jug and a blue, Sandwich-glass hen, returned them to the whatnot, and tidied up a pile of magazines. Suddenly he swung around and confronted Suzanne.

"Thirty years is a long time to know anyone, and never speak your mind. Unusual for me, anyway. But I think, at this point, we'd better drop pretense. Was it Simon?"

"I honestly don't know. Somehow, I can't think so. Simon—well, he wouldn't have called you."

The doctor pulled out his pipe.

"No, no, that's true. He wouldn't. You know, Sue, I've met a lot of people in the course of my career whom I'd unhesitatingly describe as rotten eggs. I don't know anyone, however, who more honestly deserves the title of worst egg in the basket than Simon Keith. I've heard the things he's said about you in town, I can imagine that you've had more than one personal encounter with him, and I know perfectly well that Lance doesn't know. I—"

"Doctor, he mustn't! Please—won't you call Mary? I think I heard her voice just now—she's got to clean this up, so that it'll be all right when Lance gets back. Truly, he mustn't—"

"It's just about time," the doctor said grimly, "that Lance knew and appreciated this situation."

"But not now! Can't you see, with Mrs. Newell here, and another guest coming—I can't, now. I—maybe Asey can explain to him, later. But I—God knows what he'll do to Simon! And it's perfectly possible that Simon's not to blame for any of this. But if you let Lance know now, he—oh, he mustn't know, now!"

The doctor hesitated. "All right. I'll call Mary, and officially, you fainted. But I promise you this. If you don't have Asey tell Lance, I'll tell him myself. And if Simon happens to be at the bottom of this, I'll run him out of town, or see that he's run out, and I'll personally provide tar and feathers and a rail. Now, lie back and relax. You've got to, or Lance *will* raise the roof. I'm going to see Asey—hey, Broody Mary!" he raised his voice. "First aid here!"

Mary, her jaw something hewn out of granite, came in and began deftly setting the room to rights. Suzanne lay back on the couch and closed her eyes. After one look at her, Mary quietly drew the shades and worked away in the dimness.

Out in the kitchen, Asey finished the recital of the yellow scarves for Dr. Cummings's benefit.

That gentleman snorted.

"Asey, if I didn't believe in you as firmly as I believe in Plymouth Rock and the Eiffel Tower, I'd call you an unmitigated liar. But—God in Heaven, man, what's behind all this? Why should what's-his-name's butler be spirited away, and Suzanne nearly choked to death, and her house ransacked? Of course, the fellow showed a humanitarian spirit in calling me. Apparently he didn't intend to kill her, but just put her out of the way until he made off, but even so!"

"She must have spotted him," Asey said thoughtfully, "as he went to work in the living room. He went after her, and then finished up. Huh. What'n time did he expect to find? Whyn't he pinch a Currier an' Ives, or that ole Sandwich plate, if he was after somethin' portable that'd bring in a few dollars? An' Suzanne's purse was right there on the desk, an' it wasn't even touched!"

Broody Mary returned to the kitchen.

"There, that's tidied up, an' the poor lamb's asleep. Well, Asey Mayo, that wasn't Simon Keith's work, anyway. That's one thing I can tell you."

Asey wanted to know why she was so positive.

" 'Count of a twenty dollar bill, right there in plain sight in a pigeon-hole of the desk. Oh, if I hadn't stopped to talk with Lyddy! I'd been home an hour ago, an'—oh, dear!"

Mary's annoyance was more nearly complete than any of them guessed. She had always wanted a chance to try out those bullets.

"Prob'ly," Asey told her, "there'd just been two of you choked instead of one. If that feller went over everythin' upstairs as careful as he went over the livin' room, an' put everythin' pretty much back in order to boot, he's been there some time. Wonder if Carrie'd know about who phoned—"

"Carrie's the girl at the phone office, isn't she?" Tabitha asked the doctor as Asey left. "She charms me. First time I used the phone down here, I looked up the number, got the number of rings straight, and then rang the box bell, and felt so proud! And ten minutes later Lance came in, and rang, and said casually, 'Say, Carrie, gimme Barley Snow—oh, he went by toward the Neck? Try him at Joe's.' I've often wondered what type of ambulance they'd send in the city if you said, 'Say, Mabel, find old man Smith'—did she know, Asey?"

Carrie, it seemed, only knew that it was a man with a deep voice. She'd never heard it before, but she'd know it again, and would let Asey know at once if she did.

"Now," Asey said, "I'm goin' over to see Mr. Simon Keith. Come with me, Mrs. Newell? I like a witness when I talk with the Simons of this world. Doc, you stay here an' make up a story for Lance. Hot stove an' a faint, or what you will. You can also figger out just what that feller was after, if you've got a mind to."

To get to the gingerbread house, it was necessary to drive back over the marsh and take the road which ran on the other side of the fence.

"You look," Tabitha commented, "as though you were about to present the world with a great discovery, or rob a bank—anyway, you seem awfully cheered, and I'm just quaking—look, there's Simon, behind us. Just coming home in the truck. What are your tactics? Tell me quick—"

"D'pends on his." Asey stopped the roadster and waited for Simon to come along.

"Morning, Asey." Simon drew up beside them. "Good morning," he smiled what Broody Mary had called his oily smile at Tabitha. "Coming to see me?"

Asey nodded. "Simon, there's been what you might almost call a tragedy on the other side of your hill this morning. The old place was ransacked, and Suzanne—"

Simon leaned forward anxiously.

"She—she wasn't hurt?"

"She was garrotted, but she's all right now. Lance an' Mary was away. I wondered if maybe you or Abby might of seen any strangers, or anyone, around?"

"I left around ten-thirty," Simon said. "Drove over to Orleans, came back and spent the rest of the time till now up with some of the boys on Main Street. Abby went to spend the day with Annie Clark. They're going to Provincetown. She left before I did."

Asey thought for a moment. "At the risk of makin' myself real unpopular, Simon, an' with no legal right in the world—"

"I know," Simon interrupted easily, "you want to know if I can prove it. I can. Swede Johnson, one of the boys from the government camp, went to Orleans with me, and came back, and was with me up on Main Street till I started home a few minutes ago. Annie Clark can vouch for my wife. But I have noticed a strange man around the hill several times lately, Asey. A short, thick-set man in a brown suit, with a yellow tie, or hand-kerchief. I thought he was one of Suzanne's guests."

Neither Asey nor Tabitha blinked an eyelid at the mention of a yellow handkerchief. Both thought of the lip-reading, and wondered what was coming next.

"And," Simon added, with every appearance of ear-nestness, "believe me, Asey, that whatever I may think of Suzanne Howes and her son, I should be the last to wish either of them any bodily harm."

Asey started the roadster.

"Thank you kindly, Simon. I'm glad you feel that way, an' I hope you'll c'ntinue to. No, don't move your truck. I'll back up to the turn."

"And what," Tabitha asked when they were on the other side of the road again, "and just what do you make of all that?"

"Simon," Asey said, "may be, briefly speakin', one of the shoddiest, scurviest fellers that ever cluttered up God's green footstool, but I never was a one to under-est'mate his brains an' their workin's. 'Count of he's got a brain, an' he uses it. Huh. I wish he'd bellowed. Lots easier to deal with folks that bellow an' rant than the smoothy kind."

"You believe this Swede Johnson business?"

"Simon would never lie about anythin' so easy to check up on. Here's Lance an' the girl, just comin' over the marsh behind us. They took their time—"

Lance accepted the doctor's explanation of his mother's indisposition without any question.

"She's working too hard. I do my best to take care of the heavy work, but that stove—" he shook his head, "I wish I'd got her an electric stove instead of getting this car, but the other was shot, and—Doc, can't you— oh, I guess it's no use to ask you to persuade her to take things easily. She won't. But Mary's here, and she'll help. Can I see Mud? Better let her sleep? Okay. Joan, I'll show you your room and take your things up. Tab, how many trunks have you?"

"Two, I think. Marvin was to get them on the train, but it's possible he didn't, though my cases turned up. We just," she smiled at Joan, "just barely caught that train, as it happened."

"Okay. Come on, Joan—"

"Wait, Lance. Don't forget Mrs. Newell's telegrams, after that poor man ran miles trying to stop you, up-town—"

"Golly!" Lance pulled two envelopes from his coat pocket. "Sorry—here they are, Tab. And if you're playing the market, you ought to be ashamed of yourself. Or is it the ponies you're dallying with again?"

"All that," Tabitha told Joan, "because Marvin once knew a lovely horse that always won, and I bought an occasional two dollar ticket! Run along, Lance! I've seen you buy sweepstakes tickets from an Armenian rug peddler!"

"Open 'em quick," Dr. Cummings urged when Lance and Joan were out of earshot. "Maybe it's more yellow perilling—"

Tabitha scanned the telegrams.

"Only yellow is the paper. Look, read 'em, will you? Maybe you can make sense."

Dr. Cummings put on his glasses.

"Hm. Marvelous writing, that new station master. Who's James?"

"My psychologist son-in-law."

"Hm. 'Everything all right don't bother have a good vacation now don't worry.' What's he mean?"

"I gather he's trying to tell me that everything's all wrong, I should bother, and undeniably will worry a lot. Read the other. That's from Evalynne. Evalynne," acid entered into Mrs. Newell's tones, "is my sister-in-law. My brother has excellent taste in etchings, but when it comes to—oh, read it!"

"'So sorry dear Tabitha. Am sending Levering in car with Marvin. Feel you will need them. Call on me for anything. I think it is perfectly disgraceful.' Hm. What's Levering?"

"My nephew. He—how can I say it without rending family ties? He didn't have sufficient vitamins in his diet as a babe. Well, James distinctly says not to worry, and Evalynne is sending a limousine, a chauffeur and her son to help me recover, and she thinks it's disgraceful. Wouldn't it be nice to know the size and shape of the disaster?"

Mary came out to them as they sat in the garden.

"Long distance, Mrs. Newell. Boston."

Fifteen minutes later, Mrs. Newell returned. An odd little smile played around the corners of her mouth.

"In my case," she announced, "the wall safe in the

library was forced. I'm so glad, because the combination's been locked inside it for ten years at least, and I've always felt it would be a nice thing to use. And they cut up the best hair mattresses. All done while Jane was away. Marvin says Jane's checked with her inventory lists— amazing woman, Jane. Keeps lists and remembers 'em. Nothing's missing. But frankly, don't you call this outstripping the bounds of mere coincidence?"

6

Later that afternoon, Suzanne and Asey sat out in the garden and watched the quohaug boats chugging home across the bay.

Snatches of hymn tunes and a comfortable clatter of pans issued from the kitchen, where Broody Mary was starting dinner. Down by the inlet, Lance was painting his sailboat while Tabitha and Joan looked on and offered suggestions.

"It's all so peaceful and ordinary and normal, now," Suzanne said to Asey, "and yet this day has—how can I say it?"

"If I was you," Asey returned, "I'd just say I was shook to the foundations. I've had a couple of minor twinges, like, myself."

"A quarter of a century," Suzanne went on, "I've known that on the other side of that fence lived two people who would dearly love to harm me. But I never felt I was in any real danger. Their fence kept us from trespassing, but it kept them off, too. Of course it may not have been—Asey, you'll stay here for a while, won't you? I'll feel better if you do."

"Wa-el," Asey puffed out his cheeks and adopted the impressive tones of Weesit's only lawyer, Jabez Hoke, "I have been pers'nly r'tained by our good friend Mrs. Newell to—golly, Jabe must stuff his mouth with oatmeal. I can't keep that up. Sure, I'd like to stay here, but have you got room for me, with this chauffeur an' nephew that's comin'? Know either of 'em, by the way?"

"Marvin's a dear. He's driven me in Boston. The nephew I've never seen, only heard Tab's scornful references to him. Yes, there's room, if you'd not mind being with Lance—he's coming up from the shore now, Asey. I suppose the doctor's right. He's got to know about everything—only make him promise on his honor not to lay hand on Simon. He won't, if he promises."

Asey stood up. "I'll see what can be done. Doc an' I talked it over an' kind of worked out a speech—"

His smile faded as he crossed the garden. "Sure," he muttered to himself, "just tell him everything! Like your mother bein' near killed, an'—heigh-ho!"

Of course it had come to the point where Lance had to know, and get things straight as far as anyone had them straight; still—Asey drew a long breath.

"Lance!"

On the whole the interview passed off more smoothly than Asey had anticipated. Lance was breathing heavily at the conclusion, and there was murder in his eyes, but he gave no indication of leaping the fence and starting for Simon with a club.

"So." Lance said. "So. That's all?"

"Ain't it enough? An' right now let me say this all over again. Simon's bothered your mother, but that's no reason for you to bust loose an' cause her more trouble than either of you ever dreamed of. She can manage Simon. An' for the time bein', with Mary here, an' your guests an' everythin', it's okay. An' it's perfectly clear, at least to me, that Simon didn't come here himself this mornin', though he might of had someone else come for him. Anyways, we don't know. An' until we find things out, don't you even look cross-eyed at that fence!"

Lance smiled and pitched a pebble at the top strand of barbed wire.

"What a fool you think I am! Let me see if I have the facts. One," he ticked his forefinger, "one, Tab pursued by stranger and yellow handkerchief. I'm going to call it Y.H. for short. Two, Y.H. tried to stop her in her car. Foiled. Three, Mary finds a Y.H. here. Can't be the same gent. Four, a Y.H. causes Bates, butler to Joan's boss, to float off into space. Five, garrotting technique leads us to believe that one Y.H. or another ransacks our house, thoughtfully stopping short of killing my mother. Six, ditto for Tab, but no casualties. Say, did either Joan or Tab feel she was being followed today?"

"Nope. They snuk out the back door, but that don't mean their whereabouts ain't known. They said in the radio news this afternoon that Mrs. Newell was here, while her home was entered."

Lance dug a little hole in the turf with the toe of his sneaker.

"What's your idea, Asey?"

"Someone," Asey said briskly, "wants something either you an' Suzanne, or Mrs. Newell, would seem to have."

"That's what I—but how about brother Bates?"

"He," Asey said, "is the piece of jig-saw puzzle you look at an' say, that's sky—no, it's water! Nope, it's the pool, no it ain't, it's the apron—"

"And find it's an eyeball or a new kind of rosebush. Uh-huh."

"Just so. Howsumever, I been thinkin'. Your grandpa had a lot of money, Lance. For his time he was an awful rich man. An' it didn't turn up in cash."

"You've thought 'Jewels.'" Lance juggled a paint brush and smiled. "So did I. I figured that out when I was a kid. Mother doesn't know, but I've dug and prodded and hunted every inch of this hill. I've tapped miles of beams. At one time or another, I've had every wall and floor and ceiling apart. I've pried into furniture. I've gone through Bellamy's old suits up in the attic—the stuff that was sent home after he died in Hong Kong. I've taken his sea chests apart and put them all together again. Yes, I thought jewels."

"You're goin' too fast youngster. I hadn't got to that part. I was just tryin' to make c'nections. Ole Bellamy was in the China trade. So was Mrs. Newell's grandfather."

Lance looked at Asey with admiration. "I get it! But Bates—that man just won't tie in anywhere!"

"Mebbe," Asey said, "an' mebbe not. You go get Joan, and ask her to come here."

Bates, he knew, didn't tie in directly, and couldn't even be cut to fit. Joan had said he was a small, ordinary little man who did his work well, and who had been very decent to her.

But Joan herself—that had been the solution which came to him after luncheon, as she sat 'in the corner of the living room where all the old tintypes hung. He had all but forgotten the Howes ear-marks, for Lance of course was a Howes by name only. But those pictures, even though they were faded and blotched, brought back what was known in Weesit as the "Howes" face.—A higher than average forehead, a long upper lip, a full yet firm mouth. And the girl, as she sat there, might well have been one of those Howeses of another generation come back to life. If House were, or might have been Howes, at least they would have some hazy connection between all the crazy events.

Joan smiled up at Asey. She liked the twinkle in his eyes and his long face with its network of wrinkles, and the deep tan which so successfully concealed his age. She wondered how old he was, not knowing that Asey's age was a point on which his best friends bickered. His stride was as springy and jaunty as Lance's, and yet he must be lots older than Suzanne, she thought. Of all the amazing people she had met in the past twenty-four hours, she liked Asey best. Suzanne was a dear, Lance was fun, Tabitha and Broody Mary were in classes by themselves—but Asey was all three. Somehow he seemed to her a real Cape Codder, the sort of person she had expected to find. And she felt at home with him, just as she had felt at home with the dunes and the gulls and the scrub pines and all the rest.

"Mind if I delve into your past?" Asey asked her.

"Not a bit. Tabitha has, and Lance did, and Suzanne made some subtle inquiries. I'm used to it."

"Good. It's your name. House. Wasn't, by any chance, Howes, once, was it?"

Joan stared at him. "Why, I don't know. It might have been, but I—why, I don't know, I never thought of it! I learned to write House, and I suppose it always was. Why?"

"Tryin' to get some sodderin' done. What was your father's name?"

"William."

Asey looked his disappointment. "Huh. Y'see, ole Bellamy Howes had a raft of brothers an' sisters. Fifteen. Twelve of 'em died within two weeks of each other, in one of the plagues of fever they had down here in them days. The two oldest that was left was lost at sea, an' the third was the baby. Wasn't he the one that went off to the Civil War, Lance?"

"Yes. He never came back here, but Bellamy heard from him. He went out West. That was Dency—"

"Dency?" Joan said excitedly, "why—that was father's middle name! D—d'you s'pose father was the son of this Dency? It—oh, it's too fantastic!"

"Don't see why." Asey pulled a pad and a pencil from his pocket. "Where you born, Joan? 'Frisco? Okay. I know a lot of folks in 'Frisco. Mind if I use the phone, Lance?"

Lance gulped. "You—are you by any chance considering calling 'Frisco, Asey? Because if you are, just cast a passing thought at our budget. Not that I want to curtail your brilliant thoughts, you understand, but—"

Asey patted him on the shoulder. "There, there, remember I'm bein' paid to invest'gate. It all goes on the expense 'count. Y'know, this may work out!"

He strode away, humming under his breath.

"Wonder," Lance said, "he doesn't summon Wiley Post, or someone, and take to the stratosphere. I—what you say?"

"I said," Joan repeated happily, "if my father turns out to have been Dency Howes's son—why, I'm a Cape Codder, aren't I? No wonder—why, of course! That's why I understand Asey, and the place, and everything! I'm a Cape Codder. I—"

"As far," Lance observed drily, "as anyone could be a Cape Codder, having been born in 'Frisco, having spent a few minutes on the Cape itself, and having a mother from Texas. Yes—as Asey would say, yessireebob, you're a real native, Joan. You're also cousin to Abby and her asp, and you're related to me. Second cousin by marriage adoption. Sounds remote, doesn't it? And Bellamy's mother, and Dency's, was a Swett and a Higgins. Hm. I'd say you could stand on Main Street and yell 'Cousin,' and ninety percent of the population could rightfully answer. Well, we're related, but—oh, that works out, doesn't it? It would've been sheer tragedy for us to turn out real first cousins, but second in such a casual fashion makes it all right. Was Bates in love with you?"

His abrupt change of subject startled Joan.

"In—no! What ever put that in your head, Lance? Bates looks like a retired jockey, and I remind him of his daughter, who went into burlesque and was never seen again, or something."

"Good. What about Carson, the gold plated? Smug laddie, from his pictures. About forty, isn't he? Is he in love with you?"

Lance's comments and questions were jauntily impersonal, but they annoyed Joan.

"Don't be flippant about Ben Carson," she said quietly. "He's a grand person. It's hardly his fault that people call him a tycoon. After all, he's been successful, and he's made a great deal of money, even with the depression. Just because a lot of smart-aleck reporters and columnists take cracks at him doesn't matter a whit. As Ben says, if they had more than two cents to rub together in their own pants pockets, they wouldn't waste time panning him. It's not successful business men who do any cracking about him. Nor has-beens. Just want-to-be's-but-can'ts."

She regretted the last few words as she spoke them, and a look at Lance's face convinced her that they had hit home even harder than she intended they should.

"Touché," he said lightly. "So you're in love with him. Sorry. None of my business."

Before she could stop him, he swung around and started for the house. At the same time a viciously stub-nosed, canary-colored roadster shot up the road and stopped in a cloud of dust before the garage.

A small girl with a shock of blonde hair leaped out from behind the wheel and dashed toward Lance.

"Dar-ling! Lance, you dear! I made daddy come three days early and never let you know a thing, for a surprise! Still love me?"

Apparently Lance still did, Joan thought, for he picked her up bodily, tossed her into the air as though she were a feather, and kissed her soundly before setting her down on the ground. Joan quickened her step.

Over in the gingerbread house, Simon passed the binoculars to Abby.

"She's sore," he said. "Sore as a boil. I told you to wait until that blonde showed up before you made any predictions! Lance Howes knows which side of his bread has the butter on it, let me tell you!"

Abby peered through the glasses. "She dyes that hair, Simon. It's even brighter than it was last summer, I think—"

Mrs. Newell closed her book with a snap as Joan entered the living room.

"Is that chrysanthemum-headed creature back again? That goes to show how little stock you should take of gossip columns! And I was so sure!"

"Does she get into gossip columns?" Joan asked.

"Well, when it says, 'What blonde daughter of what super-streamlined auto czar will angle for what blue-blooded dookums this summer in England,' I just naturally concluded that Clare Chatfield was going to follow up that pasty-faced Englishman who tagged her around all last summer. Is Rupert with her?"

"The Englishman—"

"No, child, no. Her marmoset. What I think of marmosets," Tabitha announced grimly, "is only exceeded by my opinion of supposedly normal females who keep marmosets."

Just as she was fairly launched on the subject of marmosets, their habits, manners, mannerisms and owners, Marvin appeared in the limousine with Levering Newell.

Marvin was beaming from ear to ear; he touched his cap to his employer, delivered a handful of letters, and then retired to a position two feet behind Asey. He had once stood as near to, and gazed as admiringly at Max Baer.

At the sight of Mrs. Newell's nephew, Suzanne suppressed an exclamation of surprise. She had pictured him as a frail, bespectacled youth with a high voice, someone who would complain about the coffee and want glasses of hot milk before retiring. And here was a fine-looking young fellow as tall as Lance. His shoulders weren't as broad; in fact, he rather made Lance look bulky. But he was pleasantly sunburned, and beautifully dressed, and his manners were excellent.

He kissed his aunt, bowed to Suzanne, smiled graciously at Joan, and Clare Chatfield, and shook hands with Lance and Asey. Mrs. Newell, who watched him with one eyebrow raised, would have been amazed to know that Levering had instantly recognized Clare as her father's daughter and as instantly rejected her because of her dishevelled hair and shrill voice, and made up his mind that Joan was the most worthy object of his attentions he'd met in some time.

Although Asey's first telephone call had netted him a former reporter friend who was willing to undertake the investigation of Joan's family, it was long after dinner before the complete information finally arrived from San Francisco.

"That's settled," Asey said with a sigh of relief. "You're Joan Howes, daughter of William Dency Howes an' Mary Averill, an' William Dency's father was Dency, son of Abijah an' Patience, an' also a brother to Bellamy. Got some from your birth c'rtif'cate, an' the rest from old Dency's death certif'cate. Anyway, that's an end to phone ringin's for tonight. I told Carrie it seemed to me she'd spent the evenin' pushin' our bell. I had all the charges switched to my 'count, Lance. All six calls, either way."

"I'm sure it's very nice," Tabitha said, "to know that Joan's name is Howes and not House. But at the risk of appearing slightly wet-blanketish, what of it?"

"Not much, I guess, if you figger the expense," Asey said, not in the least disconcerted by the question, "but it's a connectin', if sort of thin thread. Boiled down, someone tried to find somethin' here, an' they tried to find somethin' in your house, an' they snatched Bates away b'fore he could tell anythin', or mebbe even warn, Joan about somethin' else. Your grandfather had dealin's with Bellamy Howes. Lance an' Suzanne an' Joan is all r'lated to Bellamy Howes. Why Simon an' Abby ain't been picked on, I don't know. P'raps they got ransacked an' never noticed, or maybe they didn't. But somehow it seems more sane'n it did. We got somethin' to begin on, an' maybe t'morrow it'll be clearer. Lance, I'm goin' to bed. Any place I can store my car? It's goin' to rain bye an' bye, an' I'm real proud of the finish of that car of mine—"

Bye and bye it did rain, and the wind howled around the ells and the chimneys of the old Howes place. The shutters rattled, and a loose shingle flap-flapped steadily on the roof, and in the top lighthouse room, Joan Howes listened to all the noises and shivered.

She was used to all the traffic sounds, like busses and taxis and drays and trucks. She understood automobile horns and ferry whistles and the squawk and rumble of trolley cars. But there was something sinister in these country noises. She gritted her teeth as the wind swept again around the light. It was, she thought, like an early radio version of Massenet's Elegie as a cello solo, with lots of static.

Finally, with both hands tightly pressed against her ears, she ducked her head under the sheets. It was after daylight before she fell asleep, exhausted.

In Lance's box-like room by the eaves, Asey too was awake, trying to fit pieces together. But even his keen ears failed to note the slight scraping of the kitchen door as it opened, or the soft stealthy footfall of the man who slid inside.

It was left to Broody Mary to inform the household of the stranger's visit.

Shortly after six the next morning, she tapped at

the door of Lance's room, entered and closed the door behind her.

"Don't you dare git out of bed," she said in a low voice. "No, neither of you, not till I'm gone! But you two get dressed quick's ever you can an' come take that corpse out of my kitchen!"

"Who—what corpse?" Lance sat upright in bed.

"That fellow on the magazine cover, I think. The one Joan works for."

A few minutes later Asey tossed the magazine on the kitchen table.

"That," he said, "would seem to be the end of Benjamin Carson, tycoon. Offhand, Lance, who would you say strangled him?"

7

LANCE looked down at the still figure and shook his head.

"Yes, he *was* smug," he said almost to himself. "Poor fellow. Asey, this is awful, isn't it? What do we do? Mud—oh, this'll be terrible for her! And Joan! What'll we do?"

"Call Bob Raymond an' the doc. Whole business is theirs, now. I'll go phone."

When he returned, he brought in a light blanket and covered the body.

"That's better," Mary said from the doorway, "but ain't you goin' to move the poor soul? I got to get to work, an' I couldn't dream of doin' anythin' with him there. Don't seem right for him to be lyin' in a kitchen. Can't you move him, Asey?"

"Not now."

"I sort of hate to say it, Asey, but how'm I goin' to get breakfast?"

"When's it due?"

"Nine or so," Lance answered for her, "and—Mary, how *can* you think of breakfast? How *can* you?"

"Murder or no murder," Mary returned, "folks has got to eat, an' things has to go on."

Lance said with a touch of anger that Mary would make her bed and eat her breakfast and wash the dishes if she knew the world were ending ten minutes later.

"An' why not?" Mary demanded. "Why not? I s'pose the chances is no one'll want much breakfast, but land's sakes, Lance, folks got to eat, even at funerals! Well, I'll make up some coffee on the laundry stove, but you needn't ask me for any, Lance!"

"Wait a sec an' I'll make up your fire," Asey said. "Tell me, he lyin' there when you come down?"

Mary nodded. "Right there where he is in front of the door. I stared five minutes—" she swallowed and then stoically went on, "b'fore I could make my feet walk enough to come tell you."

Just for a second some of her self-control appeared to leave her. Only Asey noticed, and realized how near she was to hysterics. Lance had made up his mind that Mary was carrying her indifference to a point of callousness, and he showed his resentment. He was fond of Mary, but because in all the years he had known her, he had never seen her display her emotions, he more or less took it for granted that she had none.

"Tell you what," Asey said, "let me make the coffee. You run up to Suzanne's room an' look after her. Don't wake her, but when she does wake, tell her what's happened. Let her get herself settled an' used to this b'fore she has to come down an' face it. I'll lock the entry door, an' Lance an' I'll see to everythin'."

Mary nodded abruptly. "Poor lamb—yes, I'll look after her."

"Now," Asey said briskly after she left, "now, Lance, pop into the laundry an' start the fire an' the coffee. An' just sort of think twice b'fore you size up Mary as an unfeelin' shell. Diff'rence is, she knows somethin' you ain't found out yet, that there's a time to weep an' a time to make coffee, an'—you ever happen to notice how women that weeps at emergencies is always the lazy, unsettled ones? Everyone has to stop what they're doin' an' wave spirits of 'monia—"

Lance, his ears fiery red, was already out in the laundry.

Asey smiled grimly to himself. Lance Howes was a nice young man, kind to his mother, and dogs and children liked him, but he was just about due to be jolted out of his rut.

"Mite selfish," Asey thought, "an' he don't know it. That's the trouble with him. That Leverin' feller, he's selfish, but he knows it an' loves it—oho!"

He whistled as he looked closely at the kitchen door. The heavy, wrought-iron bolts had both been lifted out, and hung to one side in their rack. The door was unlocked, and the key on the inside.

"Oho!" he repeated. "So, Mr. Carson, someone let you in, did they? We'll see—"

Methodically he examined every window and door on the ground floor. All were securely locked. Then he went out of doors and walked around the house. Every window was screened, and the screens were screwed in. Asey tried one experimentally.

"Let in," he murmured. "That's a cinch. Well, well. An' Joan's the only one that knew him."

Certainly, he reflected, no one in that house would have let any strangers in the previous night without telling him, or someone in the household. He rather doubted if any of them would have considered the bare thought of opening a door.

Within a few minutes Dr. Cummings arrived, and before he had time to set down his little black bag, Bob Raymond, followed by another state trooper and a man in civilian clothes, entered the kitchen.

"Petrie," Bob explained the civilian to Asey. "Photographer from headquarters. He was down visiting Hamilton here, so I dragged him along. He took pictures for the old 'Item' when Ham was a cub. I made him come. Listen, Asey, before things get started and while Petrie's busy, let me give you a happy piece of news. Hanson's really got appendicitis, and Markham told me to boss this, and to snare you in on it too. Giovanni and Mike Leary are on the Gierstein business and he says he can spare 'em if he has to, but to worry along if we can. He'll send anyone and anything we need. Good old Hanson. Isn't it swell?"

Asey looked at him reflectively. "Seein' chevrons or bars on your coat?" he inquired. "I wouldn't, yet a while. This has all the ear-marks, Bob, of a nice juicy mess, an' if you ask me, Giovanni an' Mike'd have trouble doin' any solvin' if they was quintuplets an' had a couple of miracles happen for each quint."

It was half an hour before Petrie and the doctor were through.

"And I can tell you right now," Petrie said, "that I think you're going to draw a blank on prints, Asey."

Asey nodded. "I thought so. Everythin' so nice an' shiny. Oil, I'd say. Oh, well, somethin' might turn up. How 'bout it, Doc?"

"Nice, neat job," the doctor announced appreciatively. "He never knew what hit him. Got him from behind—bing! And that was that. Found anything that might have been used, like one of your yellow scarves?"

"Nary a one. Be so much nicer if we had. Bob, did you find out about Obed's milk an' egg thief?"

"I nearly got him last evening," Hamilton said. "I missed him by a hair. He had his car parked on the back lane, and mine was on the neck road, and I didn't even see his plates. He's short and thick-set. City man. At least, he wore a felt hat. He'd sneaked through the underbrush up to the barn. Obed didn't spot him, though he was sitting right there with a shotgun on his knees. Stealthy chap. Melted right into the dusk. I took a shot at him, and so did Obed, but he got away."

"We'll get him, though," Bob promised. "I've got Obed's sons posted—say, don't they know?" He nodded his head toward the locked door, as a murmur of voices came from the dining room.

"Only Mary does. Just a sec, before we get to them, Bob. You got anythin' to help us, Doc?"

"Not a thing. Oh, that girl's picture, Joan or whoever she is, is in his wallet. Notice that?"

Asey already had. "Yup, an' with all that money—hundred dollar bills. Fun bein' a tycoon, up to," he amended, "a certain extent. Okay, Bob, we'll go tell 'em, only just don't let on that someone let him in. An'—wait. Gimme Carson's wristwatch. Thanks. Ham, you an' the Doc see about takin' him away? All right, Bob. You're the boss. I'll give you moral s'port."

Bob hesitated. Now that he was in a position of full authority for the first time since he had been in the force, he began to waver. He grinned at Asey.

"Son-of-a-gun! You know damn well I'm so scared of making a mess of this right now that I can't even think straight! Run it yourself! They know you here, and you've got some things already thought out, and—don't tell me you haven't got a trap up your sleeve for someone! I know that cat and canary look of yours!"

Asey grinned back. "I would sort of like to break the news here. And I tell you what I'd like you to do. Call Jimmy Porter—you know him, in New York, an' get ev'ry scrap of dope you can from him 'bout Carson. He'll know. Here's his house number, an' here's his office. After that, see if you can find out where Carson come from. If he was stayin' here in town, or where, or what. An' then, pop over to Keith's, an' bring Simon here. An' then—"

"There's only one of me," Bob said, "and you can't tell what might be happening week after next. Okay, I'm on my way. Oh, sort of keep an eye on everyone here, won't you? Don't let 'em stray too far unless you're along."

Asey found Tabitha and her nephew in the dining room.

"I'm agog," she said. "Agog. Police cars, Dr. Cummings—Asey, has the yellow peril broken out again?"

"B. Carson, tycoon," Asey said, "was choked to death in our kitchen sometime early this mornin'. I'm not breakin' it to you gentle, b'cause I know you won't fly into no hysterics. That's the story, boiled down."

Tabitha leaned back in her chair. "Carson, Joan's boss? Good God, Asey! I can't say that I feel more than impersonal grief for him, but how hideous! How awful for Sue! Does she know?"

"Mary's with her. Mr. Newell, you happen to toil or spin for Newell and Company?"

Levering smiled. "I did, after college. Then they had to cut down the staff, and I left."

"Probably," Tabitha observed, "the only gracious gesture he ever made, Asey. His salary meant keeping on a couple of hoary old book-keepers who'd been there since the Pilgrims caught sight of Race Point."

It had occurred to Asey that Mrs. Newell might be prouder of her nephew than she dared let anyone suspect. He was sure of it, now.

"But I know quite a lot about the company," Levering said. "I've got together all of great-grandfather's papers, and I had some notion of writing a book about him and the business. Not," he added honestly, "that I ever shall, but it's a good excuse."

Asey sat down, and Tabitha noticed that he sat on the edge of his chair. But his tones were casual enough.

"Happen to know if Newell an' Company had many big dealin's with Bellamy Howes?"

"You know," Levering, too, leaned forward, "that's half the reason I jumped at the chance of coming down here. Great-grandfather was an odd duck. Kept his books himself for years. He had a shorthand system of accounting that would make hieroglyphics out of buying a barrel of molasses. There's one book I found only this last winter where he made a lot of mention of Bellamy. It's curious, Asey. For some reasons or other, best known to great-grandfather and God, Bellamy Howes paid him the sum of eight hundred thousand dollars, cash, and I absolutely cannot find any reason why."

"Eight hundred thousand—and you never told me!" Tabitha said accusingly.

"I never told anyone. It was after the 'Jon Newell' and the 'Sara Newell' were wrecked, and the company was in a state. Dithering for cash, I'd say. Howes's money saved the company. But what he got out of it, I don't know. That was in 1880, and—"

"Bellamy died in '81," Asey said. "Abby was fifteen or so, Eben was a lot older. The feud here began after Bellamy died. Eben give Abby his share an' went to New York, an' worked in the shippin' business till he married Sue in 1907. He was near twice as old as her. He died before Lance was born, an' Sue come back here with the boy. Eben hadn't left her a cent. Then, somehow, with Simon around, the feud flared up worse'n ever. All on account of the money Abby an' Simon kept hopin' would turn up, an' it didn't, an' they thought Sue had it, from Eben, who'd somehow snatched it, an' all the time—"

"All the time, apparently," Levering said, "Newell and Company had it. Sure of all the dates, like Bellamy's death?"

Asey, who had pumped Lance dry the night before, nodded. "He died in Hong Kong. Plague. Huh. This sort of opens up vistas, don't it? Wonder what Carson— Mrs. Newell, come upstairs with me. I'm goin' to try an experiment. I'm wonderin' how much that girl knew. D'you suppose, somehow, he might of found out, an' put two an' two together, an' figgered that—oh, it's too dum crazy. But—"

"But if," Tabitha started to wonder outloud, "if she and Carson were conniving about some mysterious something or other that old Bellamy may have got from my grandfather in return for eight hundred thousand dollars, she—why, come to think of it, if anyone knows what that might have been, they don't know whether Howeses or Newells have it—"

"Come to think of it," Asey said, "our pal Simon might of done some figgerin'. But I see your point. If Carson an' the girl was connivin', an' the girl finds out she's a Howes, she might balk—let's go up."

It took several lusty bangs to wake Joan.

"We want to come in," Tabitha called. "And Asey's with me. Put on something to receive visitors in."

Joan, with a dark blue silk dressing gown sleepily clutched around her, let them in.

"Oh!" she rubbed her eyes. "That wind! Kept me awake—Asey—is anything wrong?"

"Yes." Asey glanced briefly at the rumpled bed-clothes; Joan hadn't slept well. And there was a picture of Carson in a tooled-leather frame on the maple bureau. "Yes. It's goin' to be hard to tell you. Goin' to be hard for you to take. You all waked up?"

"Something—tell me!"

"It's about Mr. Carson."

"What? Oh, Asey, tell me quickly! It's always so much easier to know than be kept waiting. What's happened?"

Asey looked at her and smiled. "You're doin' it well, but it ain't quite good enough. You know better than anyone what's happened to Carson."

"I? I—what d'you mean?"

"You knew Carson wasn't on any freight boat, didn't you?"

"I—"

"Didn't you?"

Tabitha, who had never heard Asey's quarterdeck voice, drew in her breath. This man, this stern, cold, erect figure—this couldn't be Asey Mayo! Instinctively she knew Asey had something up his sleeve, but what? And why was he trying to force it from Joan?

"I—that's not your business, Asey."

"So you knew," he said quietly. "An' you lied about it. Why? Were you actin' under Carson's orders?"

"That's not your business either, Asey."

"So you were. What d'you know about these hench-men of his? Short thick-set feller, and the small one? Paid 'em off, didn't you?"

"Asey, I don't know what you're talking about!"

"Yes, you do!" Asey said. "You know, all right! They're the boys who threw smoke screens for his little tricks. Well, if they acted under Carson's orders, like you, they won't act no longer—"

"What's happened to Ben?" Joan's face was white, but even Tabitha marvelled at her composure. "Are you trying to tell me that—that he's dead?"

Asey ignored her question. "So you knew your name was Howes, all the time, did you? Carson knew. Nice, smooth openin' wedge. My, yes."

"Mrs. Newell," Joan appealed to Tabitha, "is he mad? Has he gone crazy? Will you tell me what's hap-pened to Ben?"

"Go ahead an' tell her," Asey said. "Tell her the whole story. Tell her—but how can you be told anythin'? You let him in."

"He—Ben's not here!"

"Mr. Carson," Tabitha was beginning to feel more than sorry for the girl, "was—he came here last night, and this morning, Mary found him in the kitchen. He had been killed."

Joan sat down on the bed. Not a muscle of her face had moved since Asey began questioning her, and even with the news of Carson's death her expression did not change. Inwardly Asey gave her full credit; he did not in the least enjoy his rôle, but he had begun it, and he had to play it to the end. Besides, he had found out two things which sympathetic questions would never have brought out. Joan knew Carson had not left the country, and she had been ordered not to tell.

"Now," Asey said, "why'd you let him in?"

He walked over toward the window. Carson's watch was in his pocket, and he intended to palm it, put it in the girl's open suitcase, and then confront her with it. Perhaps if he could anger her sufficiently, he might extract some further bits of information. Her color was mounting, now. She was going to lose her temper, and if she was as much of a Howes as she looked, she would lose it very thoroughly.

A telegram on the open suitcase caught his eye, and without apology he picked it up and read it. He read it through again, and then dropped Carson's watch back into his pocket. There was no need for it.

His lips curled as he read the message aloud to Mrs. Newell.

"'House, care Atterbury, Boston. See you Tuesday—Wednesday. Still incog. Ben.'"

8

Asey folded the telegram elaborately and thrust it into his pocket.

"That," he said coldly, "is just about all I want to know right now. You said last night you was proud of bein' a Cape Codder. Well, here's one Cape Codder standin' right here in my boots who ain't so proud of you. Lots of quaint ole habits in this neck of the woods. One of 'em's stickin' to your own kin. You're the first Howes I ever seen that turned against her folks. Even Abby Keith, an' she's a Howes, she never done anythin' like you done, for all her talk. Ready to go, Mrs. Newell?"

Tabitha wavered. After that telegram, she had no desire to be very kind to Joan. But the tears were running down the girl's cheeks, and Mrs. Newell hated to see people cry. And Asey had been almost unnecessarily hard on Joan. He had browbeaten her. At the same time, with that wire—

"Comin'?" Asey repeated. "I sort of need you. An' as for you, Joan, please to stay on this floor. Someone'll bring you breakfast, an' there'll be a state trooper to see you don't wander—"

"A—you mean, a policeman?"

"This is a murder case," Asey said quietly, "in the hands of the p'lice. All right, Mrs. Newell."

Tabitha, thrusting a small and rather useless handkerchief into Joan's hand, followed Asey downstairs and into the living room.

"I know what you're goin' to say," Asey told her, "an' you're right. Funny, two women may be mad as hatters at each other, or pretty much strangers, but the minute a man talks harsh to one, the other ups an'—you think I'm a mean pig, don't you?"

"Well," Tabitha said, "well, after all, why'd you go at it that way?"

"She either knows a lot, a terrible lot, about her late boss," Asey filled his pipe thoughtfully, "or else she don't begin to know anywhere near as much about him as she thinks. She's too thumpin' loyal to come out in the open an' spill any beans they may be about Carson, anyway. You can get her mad, but she don't explode in the good ole-fashioned Howes manner. Just gets stubborner. They's a lot of things I think she's willin' to tell me about Carson, but he's give her her lines to a certain extent, an' he's her boss, an' she wouldn't dream of tellin'. Only thing left to play on is her pride. An' she's proud of bein' a native here. Asked fifty billion questions last night. I kind of hope she'll come clean after she's had time to think it over. She's reas'nble. But if I'd just gone at it easy, she'd carry her loyalty to Carson to her own grave. An' b'sides that, you got to r'member that wire. An' that someone in this house let Carson in."

Bob Raymond knocked at the door.

"Busy? Asey, I yanked Jimmy Porter out of bed, and after he cooled off, and woke up, he admitted to knowing Carson. Said he was a bad actor, and you'd know all you need if you read that magazine article. Said he knows Carson's brother—"

" 'Nother tycoon?" Asey inquired.

"Nope, he's a porter for Porter, believe it or not. Jimmy was coming down Friday, but he said he thought he could get off to fly down this afternoon and he'd bring the brother with him. And Markham's arranging with the New York men to do some digging into Carson's things, and he's sending a couple of our men over this afternoon. Now I'm going to see if I can find where Carson stayed, if he did. Here's that article. Read it and weep."

Asey offered the magazine to Tabitha, but she shook her head.

"I've read it, thanks. Have you?"

"Uh-huh. Nothin' in it he could sue the editors for. Just three columns d'voted to not quite accusin' him of everythin' from robbin' the treasury an' stealin' the mint to kidnappin' the King of England an' drivin' under the influence. Kind of a Get-Rich-Quick Wallin'ford air about it."

Tabitha nodded. Not for worlds would she have admitted then to Asey, or anyone, that she had been taken in and neatly swindled in an aviation company that Carson promoted.

Asey studied Carson's picture. " 'Back to ingenuity,' " he read aloud the squib underneath it, " 'his depression cure.' Huh. Sort of unwise to come out an' admit you make your money out of ingenuity. Wooden nutmeggy—"

Levering came in. "I say, Asey, the ambulance is here, and the doctor's going, and Hamilton wants to know if you're cherishing any more ideas. Funny thing, I've seen Carson before, though I can't remember where, and it was an odd place, too. Odd for a man like him, anyway. Peculiar part of it is that I practically never recall faces, though I always recall names."

"Snob," Tabitha said. "Snob. Not a name that means anything that you don't know. He's a sort of combination walking Blue Book, Social Register and Debrett. Asey—oh, dear Heaven! Here's that ragged chrysanthemum! Levering, exercise your fatal charm, will you? On that Chatfield thing? I couldn't bear to—oh, she's coming in!"

Levering smiled. "Dear aunt, there are lengths to which I cannot be flattered." He walked to the door. "Anything I can tell Hamilton, Asey?"

"Tell him to go clump up an' down the hall upstairs for a while, outside the first floor landin'. Little experiment."

Clare Chatfield, with Rupert the marmoset on her shoulder, burst in the room as Levering slid out the side door. Mrs. Newell took one look at Rupert, sighed, and picked up the Old Farmers' Almanac.

"Oh—whatever's the matter? Mr. Mayo, what's the matter? Where's Lance? Who's that darling looking trooper? He must be new. I'm sure he never stopped me for speeding! Is anything wrong?"

Asey looked at her the way a St. Bernard might survey a frolicsome kitten.

"Lance," he said, "is busy. He is, or was to make some coffee out back. But—"

"But Levering," Tabitha didn't look up from the almanac, "was looking for you."

"Isn't he the best looking thing? Where is he? I've got to go to Boston, and I want someone to drive with me. Maybe if Lance isn't too busy—but if he is, maybe Levering—"

"Levering," Tabitha said with a wicked gleam in her eye, "would love it. Tell him I said to go with you and bring back all the papers he spoke of. Hurry—"

Without further interest in anything that might be going on, Clare dashed out to the back of the house.

"I always enjoy," Asey said, "someone whose first impulse's to obey orders. I wonder if it 'curred to her to wonder why she should hurry? We could do with those papers, but ain't it hard on your nephew? An' he ought to sort of hang around—"

"It'll serve him right," Tabitha said. "Everyone should eat his peck of dirt. And those papers are connected with all this mess."

In a few minutes Clare's roadster shot away.

"Quick work," Asey said with a chuckle, "but—huh! Not goin' to Boston today, Leverin'?"

"Levering!" Tabitha said as he sauntered in the room. "You wretch—what about those papers? How'd—did she take Lance?"

"I hope you don't mind," Levering kissed his aunt serenely on the forehead, "but I asked Marvin to go and get the papers for me, though Ham yelled out the window he shouldn't go. Clare thought Marvin was an awfully nice looking boy, too. Asey, there's an odd little man with a walrus moustache outside. I mean, he's outside. He wants you—"

"Syl!" Asey laughed. "That's Syl Mayo, cousin of mine. He pract'cly s'ports the detective story industry. Buys murders by the gross, in packin' cases. Likes to hunt clews. Finds 'em, too. Got an eagle eye."

"Is that the one," Tabitha asked, "who uses the horse theory?"

Asey nodded. "'I thought,'" he imitated Syl's nasal drawl, "'where I'd go if I was a horse that strayed, an' I went there, an' he was.' I'll go see him, an' see if I can find what's become of Lance an' that coffee he was to make hours ago. What's up, Hamilton?"

"Girl upstairs says she's come to her senses, and can she come down and talk."

"Good. We'll leave our breakfast till lunch. Tell her to come down, Ham. Tell Syl to grub around, Leverin', an' see what he can see. An'—I don't s'pose *you* could maybe get breakfast, could you?"

"Get breakfast!" Tabitha scoffed. "D'you expect lilies of the field to fry eggs?"

"I once boiled an egg," Levering said cheerfully. "I might try it again."

Joan, dressed in the soft brown sweater suit she had worn the morning before, came quietly into the room and sat down in one of the straight-backed chairs. All the traces of her tears had been carefully removed, and only the redness of her lids remained to recall the earlier scene.

"I've finally understood," she said to Asey, "why you went at me that way. Of course I shouldn't have told, even now, anything he asked me not to. Silly of me, but I —well, go on and ask me anything. I've never broken a promise before, and I don't like to now. But that trooper's clanking around brought it home. This is something too big for me to—to—"

"Throw monkey wrenches. Okay. You knew he was in this country, didn't you? Why'd he mean to be incog? Why'd he come here? What d'you know 'bout his business, an' him? Did you know he was in town? D'you know anythin' 'bout any of his other employees, not just Bates an' the house servants? Has he any en'mies? Was he engaged in any p'ticular sort of—" Asey smiled, "of ingenuity, right now, that you know of? Tell us the answers to all them, an' anythin' else you can think of. An' did he know your name was Howes, an' did you ever hear him speak of Howeses, or Newells, an'—"

"That's enough," Joan held up her hand, "to keep me talking for years. Lucky for you I've got a shorthand mind by now. I may mix the order, but I've got 'em all. Here goes."

She knew that Carson was in the United States, and that he had not gone away on any freight boat vacation. But he had asked her to tell the freight boat story if she were asked about him; several times before he had made similar requests.

"That was when he had some deal or another on, and

he didn't want to be bothered, or else things were coming to a head, and he wanted them to take their course, or he just wanted a rest, or—well, any number of reasons. So of course I did as he asked."

The telegram Asey read had been delivered to her the night she arrived in Boston, at Miss Atterbury's. The very fact of his wiring her there had amazed her, since she had not told him anything at all concerning her vacation plans, except that she thought of going to New England. But the servants had known, and might have told him.

"At least, that's the only explanation I can think of. Why he might come to see me—I simply know no reason for it! I can't figure it out. I didn't know he had any intention of coming to Cape Cod, now or any time. Because he wired, I more or less expected him to turn up, but I didn't know why or when. I didn't know he'd actually arrived here. I don't know when he came."

"Now, 'bout him an' his business, an' ingenuity, an' en'mies," Asey suggested.

According to Joan, Carson was a brilliant man, a good business man, pleasant to work with and for.

"It's hard to enlarge on that. His business—well, he helped promote companies, took over companies and made them pay, and he was a director of a lot of things. I suppose he has as many enemies as any other man in his position. More, possibly. He could always see through things and solve them, usually in a clever way others didn't think of. For the most part he did his work in the library at home. He had an office downtown, but he used it only for conferences, went there perhaps two or three times a week. I usually went, too, took dictation and all. He had things arranged so that office calls came up to the house when we weren't down there."

"How about Eastern and Seaboard Transport?" Tabitha inquired.

Joan shook her head. "Eastern and Seaboard? I never heard of it, Mrs. Newell."

"I have in my desk at home," Tabitha fingered a paper knife, "some five hundred shares of that company. Stunning looking shares. Purple and sort of mauve. Any time you want a hen house papered, Asey, let me know and I'll give 'em to you. I'd practically guarantee that any hen would produce a dozen eggs a day, just from the inspiration of those lovely purple and mauve certificates. Very inspirational company, by and large. Carson was president."

"Ben? But I never heard—are you sure of that?"

"I wish I weren't, Joan. I bought them last year. First mistake I ever made. Remember Lance's jibes about the market when he gave me those telegrams yesterday? Most of the wires I got last summer were about Carson's stock. I looked into him, after the E. and S. flurry. That is, Steve Crump did the looking, while I gnashed my teeth and got as purple as the certificates every time I thought about it. He promoted Stedman copper, a couple of copper products companies, some silver mines—oh, really, Joan, some engraving company must have paid extra dividends, just from the purple and mauve ink."

Joan sat very still in the straight-backed chair.

"Of course," she said at last, "you know what you're

saying. I—but I didn't know. Of course, Ben was away a lot. He might—but I can't believe he was a crook!"

"I don't want you to," Tabitha said promptly. "I don't, and never did for an instant think you knew about that side of him. I wanted Asey to know, that's all."

Asey smiled. "Asey," he observed, "had pract'cly almost guessed. Forget the purple certif'cate part, Joan, an' go on."

"I've been thinking about Bates, Asey. He never seemed as fond of Ben as he did of me, but he was always efficient. So were the others, Beulah the cook and her daughter, who was maid. Ben used to give them Irish sweeps tickets, and once Beulah won a consolation prize and got in the newsreels, and they both adored Ben. Apparently, that is. And, Asey, as far as I know, Ben didn't know my name was Howes, or anything much about me at all. He took me on the recommendations of the business school where I went, and some letters from mother's department store friends. He may have picked up bits of information about me, but only the things I may have let drop. And— why, I didn't know till you found out, about the Howes part, myself! And you spoke of henchmen of his. Bates, and Beulah and Violet were the only ones he employed besides me. And I don't know what business he may have been engaged in now. Before I left, most of the important things had been wound up. I supposed when he asked me to say he'd gone away on a freight boat that he might have some loose end left over, or possibly even that he just didn't want to be bothered with anything new. When he said 'Incog' in that telegram, I was more or less sure that he wanted to be just himself, and not—"

"Not Carson, tycoon. I see. I—for Heaven's sakes, Syl Mayo!"

Syl, his walrus moustache drooping, pushed in a tea wagon on which there was a loaf of bread, an old-fashioned agate coffee pot, a hunk of butter, an electric toaster, a package of shredded wheat biscuits and a varied assortment of kitchen china.

"I know!" Asey said. "I know! You look at it for two minutes by the clock, an' then you turn 'round an' try to r'member what's on it. Syl, for Pete's sakes, what you doin' with that hodgepodge?"

"Breakfast," Syl said mournfully. "He told me you said I was to get breakfast b'fore I started any huntin', an' I never seen a kitchen so neat in all my born days! I couldn't find nothin' attall!"

"He told you I said—who told you?"

"That tall dark feller with the ice cream pants an' the broad 'a'. Asey, take this stuff an' feed 'em, will you? I wan somethin' man-size to do!"

Asey laughed till tears filled his eyes. "So Leverin'— y'know, Mrs. Newell, you don't give that boy credit! I didn't—what's he doin', Syl?"

"Him, Asey? Oh, he's out huntin' clews, he is." Syl sounded a little hurt. "Seems to me, Asey, when you know I—"

"You got bamboozled," Asey told him, "by a city slicker. I told him to get breakfast, an' for you to hunt. Run an' hunt. I'll coör'nate—ain't it wonderful the words the gov'-ment learns us these days? I'll coör'nate this stuff here. Seen Lance?"

"No, I ain't," Syl returned, "an' I sh'd think if there was any breakfast gettin' to be done, he'd be the one to get it. Here's that feller now, the one that—"

"That made a slaver out of you. Leverin', from now on, d'you mind if I call you Buck?"

"Why?" Levering asked. "Is it my rough and ready air? I thought I looked quite well this morning. I thought my manners were excellent—"

"They be," Asey said succinctly, "an' you look like a fool tailor's dummy. But I'm goin' to call you Buck, on account of you pass it so often. What you glowin' about?"

"I toil not," Levering said coolly, "neither do I spin. But they also serve who only stand around and pass bucks. See what I found in the garden—"

He held out a large white handkerchief, which had been folded crossways into a triangle, then rolled and folded till it was not much more than an inch wide.

"Nice for a garrot," he continued. "Helpful initials neatly hemstitched on it, too. S.K."

"Simon!" Tabitha, Syl and Joan spoke all at once.

"Simon!" At first it appeared to be an echo, and then Abby Keith appeared in the doorway. "Simon—where is he? He hasn't been home since supper last night!"

9

"IF YOU," Broody Mary waggled her finger in Syl Mayo's face a few minutes later, "if you, nor anybody else, ever come up an' told me that Abby Keith'd be in this house—*this* house *here!* Here, with Sue Howes puttin' her best imported cologne water on her forehead, I'd of phoned straight to Taunton an' told 'em to get a padded cell ready! The idea! Why—why, the idea!"

Syl took a more reasonable view of the situation.

"Wa-el," he drawled, "when someone comes moanin' an' wailin' an' weepin', all sort of bedraggled an' tearful, an' upset, an'—an' half crazy, an' all, all over your doorstep, like, you got to do somethin', Mary. Can't throw her out. It ain't like she was goin' to spend the rest of her natural life here. An'," he added piously, "'If thine en'my hunger, feed him. If—'"

"I never was a one to heap any coals of fire on mine en'my's head," Mary announced with heat. "Not if I thought he was just waitin' for a chance to trick me! It's all a trick, that's what it is. Lookin' at Suzanne like that, an' everyone fawnin' around an' sayin' 'Poor Thing!' An' that Simon—"

She broke off abruptly as Asey came into the kitchen.

"Syl," he said, "take a ladder an' hop over that fence, or else walk around an' take a look about Keith's place. Abby's all worked up about Simon. Says he come from the post office last night an' brought in the paper, an' then went out, an' she ain't seen him since. His truck's home, though."

"R'minds me," Syl said, "how'd that Carson man get here, anyhows?"

"Seven league boots, for all I know. I've called the doc again. Abby's in an awful state. He'll have to get the district nurse to come an' take her home an' look after her. She wants to go home now. Got a cryin' jag—what on earth you got on that tray, Mary?"

"Hot tea, spirits of ammonia, an' whiskey. An'—"

"An' you," Syl laughed, "you was the one that was so mad—"

"I still am," Mary returned, "I'm mad as hops. But land's sakes, what'd folks say if Abby Keith had a fit or somethin', an' died here? What'd she say? Make up some yarn that no one lifted a hand to help her. I'll take this tray in an' stick it under her nose, an' then there won't be no talk!"

"Okay. Syl, you go nose around Keith's. Chances is that Simon strayed off an' made a night of it with some of his friends, but I'm goin' to try to locate Bob an' have him make sure. Simon's got some explainin' ahead to wriggle out of that handkerchief of his bein' here. Oh, Mary. I'm goin' to wait for the doc, an' then I'll take the other two women off to town with me. While Bob's after

Simon, I'll look into where an' if Carson stayed. An' you make Sue take it easy. Leverin'll be here."

Mary murmured something about a stuffed shirt.

"Uh-huh. Only he's more of a shirt with less stuffin' than I thought. An' for Pete's sakes, where's Lance? You see him?"

"He was runnin' down to the boat house an hour or two ago."

"Huh. Well, Syl, hunt up that kid while you look for Simon. An' send him home. He's goin' to get a nice piece of my mind, Lance is. If Jimmy Porter comes—oh, but he won't get here till later."

The doctor and the district nurse took Abby Keith home, and after some manoeuvering, Asey managed to get Suzanne upstairs, Tabitha and Joan in his roadster, and Levering settled in the front room.

"Your job, Buck," he said, "is to keep r'porters an' waifs an' strays out. Bob's got a man at the road entrance, but that don't mean there won't be folks millin' around just the same. It won't come out formal till the aft'noon papers, less they put it over the radio, but you keep your eyes open."

Before Asey and the two women left, Bob Raymond returned.

"Ham says that Abby—"

"Yup. I want you to find Simon, an' Lance. I'll take over your end. Get anywhere?"

Bob mopped his forehead with a khaki handkerchief.

"Not a thing. I went to all the overnight camps, and

overnight guest places, and the hotels that were open, and the—what are you looking so chuckly about, Asey? I suppose you'd have gone to the post office and asked?"

"You go find Simon an' Lance an' ole yellow hanky, if you can," Asey suggested soothingly, "I'll be seein' you."

Tabitha wanted to know how Asey intended to proceed in his search for items concerning Carson.

"Spit-an'-chatter club," he answered promptly. "That bunch that hangs around Main Street. They're usually there till midnight, an' they come back as soon as someone's fed 'em in the mornin'. Nothin' nor no one that passes by that they don't know about, or see, or anyways guess. Great guessers, they be. Joan, I been thinkin' about Bates."

Joan remarked that Asey had thought no more of Bates than she had.

"Mebbe, was he tryin' to tell you somethin', or warn you, or what?"

"All I know or am sure of is that it *was* Bates. He seemed half crazy."

"You don't think—now, mind you, don't go off the handle at this, but you don't think it might have been Carson that yanked him away?"

Joan considered for a moment before she answered.

"Personally I don't think it was Carson. I'm sure of it. But it could have been, I suppose. I mean, it's possible. His wire came around eleven Monday night, from New York, but he could have taken a plane over and got to Boston Tuesday morning. All I feel about the whole thing is that Bates must have started after me Monday night. He won't ride in planes, so he must have taken a train. He doesn't drive."

"Lookin' at it one way," Asey said, "Bates might of found out somethin' d'rectly you left, an' then took a train an' come rompin' after. An' then Carson sent that wire, an' started after—huh. Well, we'll talk to the boys."

He slowed the car and called to one of the half dozen men leaning up against the paper store.

"Hi, Tim. Say, seen a smooth-faced stranger around last night? Tall feller, heavy built, light suit, blue tie?"

Tim listened, then cocked his head and stared blankly into space.

"Tall, heavy, light suit, blue tie," Asey repeated helpfully.

Tim held up a finger. "Wait a sec, an' I'll see."

He turned around and walked back to his friends.

"Look at them heads bobbin'," Asey commented. "Crows on a phone pole. Well, soon's they figger out why they think I might want to know about any such feller, an' make sure he ain't someone they know that's in trouble, maybe they'll break down an' impart a little inf'mation. Don't think," he said to Joan, "that these is typical of your new-found rel'tives. They ain't. These is the kind you always find—well, Tim?"

"Would he of been drivin' a coop?"

"Yup," Asey said without hesitation. Carson might well have been at the wheel of a baby Austin or a ten ton truck, but if Tim and his friends knew anything about a man in a coupe, he might as well have the benefit of the information.

"Then it was him, I guess. I didn't see the plates, an' Sol says they was covered with dust anyways. Yup, he come by here around nine last night. He said he wanted a room."

"Tell him any special place?"

"Told him he had our p'mission." Tim laughed uproariously. "Get it? He said, 'I want a room,' an' Sol come right back at him, Sol did. Said, 'You got our p'miss—' "

"I get it," Asey told him. "I got it about forty-five years before you was born, Tim. Weaned on it, as you might say. What happened then?"

"Oh, he drove on, an' the car went around the corner. Ain't seen him since."

"Ain't seen Simon Keith, neither, have you?"

"Not since mail time last night."

"Thanks."

Asey drove along Main Street, turned the corner and then stopped.

"Huh," he said, "smacks of Syl an' his horse idea, but I think—yup. Let's go in an' see Emmaline Snow—"

He turned in the driveway of a neat yellow Cape Cod house.

Mrs. Snow, buxom, red-faced, bustled out to the car.

"Why, Asey Mayo, I ain't seen you since before Christmas. Real glad you stopped in. How do, Mrs. Newell, nice to see people come back. Why, Asey, she looks like a Howes, that girl."

"It's just been discovered that I am," Joan said pleasantly. "You don't know how nice it is to go somewhere and have yourself recognized as belonging to a family."

"Heavens on earth!" Mrs. Snow clucked her tongue, "no one that's ever seen a Howes, or a picture of 'em, but what'd know you was one. Asey, you know that picture of Bellamy's mother that hangs in the Ladies Aid parlor—why, she's the spittin' image of it! Want me for anything in particular, or will you come in an' visit a spell?"

"I'm huntin' a feller I think come to town last night," Asey told her, "an' I know he got as far as Main Street, an' I know he was huntin' a room, an' seein' that 'Guests' sign out there, I wondered—"

Mrs. Snow told him that was exactly what happened.

"It's the Moorland Inn folks's sign, but the bottom broke off, an' you don't know how many folks come in here, thinkin' it was my sign, an' wantin' a room for the night. New coat of paint on the house that does it, I guess. Well, I told Sara that the next time it happened, I was goin' to give 'em the spare bedroom an' make a dollar, so I did. You want the feller? He's still in bed, the lazy thing. Guess he's a travelling man. They work hard, an' probably the poor fellow needs sleep, so I didn't wake him, but I got some lunch for him."

Asey got out of the car.

"He's still—did he have a car?"

"Yes, it's right out there in the barn—why, my goodness gracious! Asey Mayo, why that car's gone! An' 'twas here when I went out to the barn this mornin'! Don't that beat—well," she sighed lustily, "I guess Sara was right. She said, you go lettin' strangers have your best spare room, an' they'll muss your house up, or go away without payin', an' I guess that's what this feller done! Must of taken his car an' run while I went up to the store."

"Let's see your spare room, will you?" Asey asked. "Mebbe—let's take a look. An' say, did he look like this?"

He passed over the picture of Carson he had torn from the magazine.

"That's the one," Emmaline said. "Benjamin Carson, tycoon—land's sakes, Asey, what's a tycoon? I thought it was a kind of storm."

"Guess," Asey said, "that's just about what the feller turned out to be, a kind of storm. Let me see the room, will you? Mind waitin' here, you two?"

As Asey anticipated, the best spare room was immaculate and undisturbed. A locked suitcase lay on the candlewick spread.

"B.C.," Emmaline read the initials. "Guess it's your typhoon all right. Why, he ain't even dirtied a towel! Huh. This is my first an' last experience with any overnight guests, let me tell you that! What was the matter with my best room that he goes an' spends the night somewheres else, an' then sneaks back the minute my back's turned, an' gets his car, an' goes away as if the house had a—a smell, or a disease, or something!"

"Sit down a sec," Asey said. "An'—nope, guess I'll have to get a chisel to that suitcase lock. Look, Emma, tell me everythin' that happened from the time he come till you seen him last, an' then I'll tell you why I'm so anxious to find out about this typhoon."

Carson had knocked at the side door a little after nine the previous evening, and asked for a room. He had apparently been delighted with the spare bedroom, for he had commented politely on the wax funeral wreath and the other wall decorations, and then asked if he could use the telephone.

"I listened," Emmaline confessed, "from the dinin' room, because after I said he could, I thought to myself maybe he'd phone Boston or some far off place an' maybe saddle me with a bill. But he—oh, 'twas kind of funny, Asey! He didn't know about ringin' up. Kept askin' the operator what was the matter with the fool line. Finally I tiptoed out to the woodshed an' come back heavy, an' knocked on the door an' told him you had to ring. Then I had to close the door, but I banged it so tight it popped open again. Say, Asey, by the way, is that girl in the car a real Howes from around here?"

"Bellamy's brother Dency's granddaughter," Asey told her. "Let's see. Bellamy's mother was a Swett. She'd be some relation to you, Emma, but I ain't got the spirit to figger it out. Who'd Carson call?"

"Why, he asked for Deathblow Hill. Right then I decided to ask him two dollars for the room instead of a dollar, because Sue Howes up at the hill, why, Broody Mary told Sara that Sue got as high as a hundred dollars a week for one of the rooms in that old light! A week, mind you! Well, after he rung, I heard it thunder, an' I went right out to put the milk away, an' when I come back, he was about through, said he'd be over, an'—"

"He said—listen, Emma, this is important. You're sure he spoke to someone at the hill, an' told 'em he'd be over?"

" 'Course I'm sure. That's why I asked you about that girl in your car. He told her he'd be over, an' just as she planned."

Asey bit his lip. "Look, Emma, how'd he say it, just like that? 'I'll be over, as you planned?' "

"Let me think. No, it was like this. He said, 'I'll be over. Yes, just as you say. If you're sure that's the best plan, Miss Howes.' "

10

Asey leaned back in his chair and fitted his fingertips together.

If Emmaline Snow said that Carson had called and made a date with a Miss Howes at the hill, without any shadow of a doubt he had done just that. There were some people who couldn't lie if they wanted to, and Emmaline was one of them.

"Sure it was Miss, an' not Missis?"

"Positive."

Miss Howes. Still, at the same time, Asey believed Joan was telling the truth when she said that she hadn't known that Carson was even on the Cape, that she had no word from him except for that telegram.

He half closed his eyes and visualized the little entry way between the dining room and the living room at the hill. The phone was on a small mahogany table, and the slim Cape phone book was covered by a leather folder. Next to that was a three by six pad of bright blue paper, and an automatic pencil was tied to it by a blue string. Next to the table was a cane-seated chair—the back legs were rickety, and he'd have to fix them for Suzanne sometime when this was over with. There was a print of one of Bellamy's ships on the wall, and a tiny silhouette.

So much for the entry. Now to fit the people into it.

Between seven and ten, that phone had rung at least fifteen times on the 'Frisco calls alone; McMichael had called him, and he had called back, and there had been easily half a dozen false alarms when Carrie, practically overcome by the excitement of coast-to-coast calls, had rung by mistake. He had directly answered most of those calls himself, but some had been taken by whoever was nearest the phone.

Now, who exactly had called him? Lance, and Levering, and Mrs. Newell, those he was sure of. At one time, when Mack said he'd call back after an hour, Levering had seized the opportunity to call Boston, Suzanne had talked with a friend in Chatham, the doctor had called the hill to inquire about Suzanne, and Mary's cousin had called about the church fair. Well, it all amounted to the fact that everyone in the house but Marvin, and Joan, had come to the phone. And yet, Carson had spoken to Miss Howes. Of course, Joan might have gone into the entry, but he couldn't seem to place her there.

Asey looked up to find Emmaline regarding him patiently.

"I was so busy broodin'," he said, "I most forgot you. R'mark'ble woman, Emma. Don't know's I ever seen one that'd let a man sit an' think without askin' him what, an' why, an' wherefore."

"You," Emmaline returned, "didn't live thirty-one

years, four months an' twenty-seven days with Leander Snow. I did."

Asey grinned. He had known the late Leander, a dour soul who spoke perhaps two words a day.

"That's so," he said. "Well, now I'll tell you my side of this, Emma. Only don't spread it over town for a while yet."

"That typhoon got killed, did he?" Emmaline nodded sagely. "I guessed so, you seemed so sort of broody, an' that girl'd been cryin', an' Mrs. Newell wasn't nowhere near's chipper as she usually is. Sort of subdued, like. Well, take his bag, Asey, an' I'll just put my overnight guest business down on the books as a flop. I wasn't much impressed by that Carson, anyway. He had the same sort of look that feller that started the fish cannin' business a couple years ago an' tried to sell stock in it had, if you know what I mean."

Asey looked at her a moment. "Y'know," he said admiringly, "they may be folks that don't put much faith in fem'nine intuition, but I'd bow down to it any day in the week. He was a fish-canner-stock seller on a big scale, Emma. Most folks didn't guess. Well, I'll be gettin' along, an' thank you kindly. You've raised a real nice little puzzle."

"You mean," Emmaline said as they went downstairs, "he didn't call her, huh? Asey, why don't you go see phone office Carrie? She might help."

"I'm goin' to her," Asey said, "just's fast as I can get there."

But Carrie couldn't help.

"I did nothing but plug in Howes's place for four hours, seems to me," she told Asey. "Seems to me I do remember a local call or two, but with all the long distances coming in, I didn't bother to pay any attention to 'em. Sometimes I remember calls later, but honestly, with all the rest going on, I don't think I'll remember any calls from town. And all the time you were talking with that man out west, that Chatfield girl was talking to some man in New York."

Asey thanked her and walked out to the roadster.

"I gather," Tabitha said, "that you got nowhere, though I don't pretend to understand what this is all about anyway. Asey, if Carson's automobile was at Mrs. Snow's this morning early, and it isn't there now, where is it? And if it was there this morning, then he didn't use it to come to the hill. How'd he get to the hill?"

"How old is Anne?" Asey shrugged. "His boots was clean, so I figgered he come in a car. But then, the kitchen was clean, too. No footprints. Maybe the same person that wiped off fingerprints, wiped off the boots an' the floor. Maybe Carson walked to the hill. Maybe he flew. Maybe he roller-skated. Maybe, oh, deary me, I never was a one to like loose ends, an' I never seen more."

"We've been listing them," Joan said, "just to while away the time. Items like who followed Tab—I mean, Mrs. Newell—"

"Go ahead and call me Tab, if you want," Mrs. Newell said resignedly. "Lance began it by privately calling me 'Good Old Tab,' as though I were a faithful collie. He's a great name-maker, that boy. He started Broody

Mary, you know, Joan. Now no one remembers she's
—Jerusha, except the minister."

Asey chuckled. "He once made an announcement from
the pulpit, an' said a church supper was to be run by our
Sister Jerusha Sekells, an' lots of folks wondered who she
was."

"How'd he pick out Broody Mary?" Joan asked.

"Mary Queen of Scots always appealed to him," Tabitha
said, "but he always called her Broody Mary. Probably was,
poor woman! Anyway, go on with the lists, Joan. Asey will
love 'em."

"Well, who followed Tab, and who removed Bates,
and why was Bates, and where'd he go to, and who scared
Mary and Sue, and who ransacked both houses, and why.
Those are just preliminaries. Then, who let Ben in—"

"An' who answered his phone call," Asey added, "an'
p'ticularly since he called her Miss Howes."

"Oh!" Joan cried, "oh, Asey—did he really, or are
you trying to trap me, or something?"

"He really did. An' who killed him, an' why, an' what
was he doin' here anyways, an' where's Simon, an' how'd
his hanky happen in the garden, an' where's Lance, an'
who stole Obed's milk, an' what about them yellow hankys
anyway. Yup. Sounds like a recipe for goulash. Well, we'll
go back to the hill. Carson call you Joan, or Miss?"

"Usually Joan, except when we were at the office. Asey,
I've racked my brains, but I can't think of a single thing
that would ever connect him with the Cape."

Asey grinned. "I don't expect you to. I don't expect
anythin' to connect ever again. I knew a feller in Sydney

once that b'longed to some order or r'ligion or other, an' he was always talkin' about cosmic int'ference. I think that's the trouble here. Static straight from Heaven."

Levering came out to greet them on their return to the hill.

"No reporters, no trace of Lance, or Syl, or Simon. In fact, there's nothing to report. Hadn't we better do something about Lance? Mrs. Howes wants him. At least, she wants to know where he is, and she seems to have doubts about his clew hunting, as Mary and I assured her he was."

"She's connectin' Lance an' Simon," Asey said. "Huh. Say—there he is, down at the boat house! Go tell her he's here, an' let me know if she wants him."

Asey strode off down the long slope of the hill to the boat house by the small wharf.

Lance, pipe in hand, sat dangling his long legs over the water.

"You, my son," he murmured to himself prophetically as he watched the determined swing to Asey's shoulders, "are going to get what-for in no uncertain terms. But it's worth it. I done my duty as I seen it, like a brave and valiant Howes—"

Asey stopped some six feet away from Lance and stood and surveyed him till Lance grinned and held up his hands.

"I surrender. I'm a thoughtless, useless boy, and—"

"You're all that," Asey said briefly. "An' then some."

He continued to stand away and focus his searching gaze on Lance, and Lance could feel his cheeks grow red. His ears got uncomfortably hot. His feet began to wind and unwind about one of the barnacled wharf piles.

"Oh, stop, Asey!" Lance stood it for five minutes. "Stop your old X-raying and say it! Get it over with!"

Asey didn't stop. "An' I ain't got no intention of stoppin', neither. I'm makin' more impression this way. You look like a ten-year-old kid that's delib'rately gone out an' got mud on his dancin' school clothes so's he'll have to stay home. You act like a ten-year-old kid, right now. You think I'm goin' to give you blazes for wanderin' off when I asked you to do somethin', an' when I wanted you. Then you think I'll f'get an' f'give. I would, if you happened to be ten years old."

Lance tapped out his pipe. "I had a story all made up for you," he said, "but I'll tell you the truth, and I don't want to, and you won't believe me. But honestly, I—I just couldn't go out there and start a fire in a stove and make coffee. Not after seeing Carson! Those horrible eyes! Honestly, I had to get away. I'd never seen a—a corpse before, in all my life! It—well, you and Mary were so matter of fact—I just cut and run. I came down here."

Asey said nothing at all. Knowing Lance, he rather believed what he said, but he wanted the boy to grasp an idea.

"That's true, Asey!"

Deliberately, Asey sat down on the edge of an overturned rowboat. He was so deliberate that Lance wanted to scream.

"Asey, that's the truth, I tell you!"

"Heard you the first time."

"But—say, I can't help the way I'm made!" Lance kicked at the barnacles.

"Dear boss," Asey said ironically, "I hear the bridge toppled. I couldn't bear to stay an' see it, on account of never seein' a bridge topple b'fore. Awful. Too horrible for words. I'm sorry, but it's my nature. Huh. Was it you or Joan that answered the phone at nine-twelve last night?"

Lance stifled the angry retort on his lips and mentally kicked himself for letting Asey rile him. The old fox, getting him worked up, and then sliding in a question. Well, he might as well be hung for a sheep.

"I did," he said. "So that's what you think of me, is it? Can't take it? Let a feud roll on without doing anything, letting my mother be—I get it. The old fact dodger."

"So you answered the phone, did you? One of my calls?"

Lance thought quickly. "No. Cummings for mother. At least, I think so."

Asey knew otherwise. He had taken the doctor's call himself. So Lance was lying to shield Joan, was he? For the first time, Asey remembered that it had taken Lance and Joan nearly two hours to get back from Yarmouth. Lance had never even cared for the idea of Carson. What was it he had said that morning, something about Carson being smug?

Reflectively, Asey puffed at his pipe. Lance, Joan and

Carson. That was something he hadn't even thought of considering. But Lance couldn't have left the bedroom the night before without his knowing.

"That all?" Lance, now that Asey's words had begun to sink in, was thoroughly mad. "I'll go back to the house."

"All, 'cept," Asey looked at the jagged rents in Lance's trousers, "when'd you go over the barb fence? Just now, or earlier?"

"Those rips? I caught myself on a nail right here on the dock. I haven't been stalking Simon."

He stomped up the winding path to the house. As he disappeared from sight, Syl Mayo dashed over the hill.

"They said you was back," he panted when he reached the wharf. "Say, Asey, I found a lot of funny things. No, I ain't found Simon. But first, I been lookin' at the fence. I started by that clump of pines, 'cause it seemed to me a good place for anyone to go over. Wouldn't be seen attall. I begun there an' worked to the marsh, an' when I come back to go from there to the bay, see what I found!"

He held up two little pieces of white duck.

"Lance." Asey said.

"Just so. He must of gone over that way this mornin'. Then, up at the far end by the beach, I found these." He pressed five little pieces of red wool into Asey's hand. "Them's from Simon's red sweater. Abby says he had it on last night, an' it was whole 'cause she'd just darned it. N'en, while I was lookin' around Keith's, I looked up, an' see what was out on the roof, in plain sight, outside Simon's room. Just out on the flat part of the roof, near the gutter—"

"Syl, your wife'll butcher me with an axe if you fall off roofs huntin' things! An'—say, wasn't she expectin' you to fix that g'rage floor for them folks in Eastham today? If she—an' say, how'd you happen to know about this, anyways?"

Syl confessed sheepishly that he'd seen Bob Raymond's car shoot up Main Street, lickety split, and turn to the beach road.

"I wanted to follow, but I didn't, an' then half way to Whitin's, I come back, an' Marty Bowen said he'd seen the car come this way—"

"So you thought if you was a horse what'd you do, an' you did—"

"You won't laugh when you see what I found on that roof," Syl said staunchly. "Look!"

With a triumphant gesture he pulled a bunch of keys from his pocket.

"An'," he said, "they fit ev'ry door an' padlock at Suzanne's. I tried 'em. An' then there was this piece of wire. See how it's bent? I bet you could push back even them heavy bolts on the inside of Suzanne's doors, with this. See how it's curved? Yessir, I bet you that Simon Keith's been in the Howes place many's the good time, with these."

If Simon could get in, Asey thought, he might have let Carson in the night before. But Simon didn't know Carson, and besides—

"Say," Syl said, "you don't s'pose Simon's dead, somewhere, too, do you? Say, wouldn't that be—oh, shucks! Look!"

Asey followed the line of Syl's finger, and made out the figure of Simon, walking along the beach.

11

"Shucks!" Syl said. "He's alive! An' it'd been almost like a story, if he'd been dead. It—"

"It'll be almost like a story," Asey said, taking Syl's elbow, "to listen to his expl'nations. Let's go get 'em started."

Simon's shirt and trousers were dripping wet, and his canvas sneakers oozed water with every step he took, yet his greeting to Asey and Syl was entirely amiable and unconcerned. Rather, as Asey commented later, as though it was his invariable custom to stride along the beach, looking like something the tide had washed up.

"Morning, Asey. Hullo, Syl. I hope, Asey, that your presence doesn't indicate any sort of disaster?"

"Where you been?" Syl burst out. "Where you been? What—"

"Whoa up, Syl!" Asey yanked at his belt. "Whoa! Yup, Simon, as a matter of fact, there has been a disaster. Stranger named Carson was found dead in Suzanne's kitchen this morning. Garrotted."

"Suzanne all right?" Simon asked anxiously. The

116

dead stranger named Carson apparently held no interest for him whatsoever.

"Yes, but—"

"But you'd enjoy a report from the other side of the fence, I suppose?" Simon said imperturbably. "Probably I was your first thought. Of course, Asey. I'll be delighted to tell you anything. But d'you mind coming home with me? I'm beginning to feel chilly as well as soggy, and I want some dry clothes."

Asey nodded and jerked at Syl's belt again, for Simon's nonchalance had Syl gaping.

"Brisk wind," Simon remarked, "and that bay water is ice cold." He rubbed the back of one damp shirtsleeve against his nose, coughed and then sneezed.

Asey smiled. It was a genuine, hearty sneeze, but there was, as Broody Mary would say, something oily about it.

"Fall in, Simon?"

"After a fashion, Asey. Odd business, all of it. I went out to lock up the hens last night, after mail time, and I saw a light down here off the hill. Fellow in one of those mahogany speedboats. Seemed to be in trouble, so I went down. He was stuck off the beach grass, on one of our old wharf piles. Propeller was smack on a rock. I helped him get off, and offered to guide him to the club wharf to get some gas and do some phoning home to his family. It was his first trip out in the boat, and he was as complete a lubber as I've ever seen. Half way to the club, we ran smack out of gas—would you believe it, Asey, that fellow didn't even have an oar?"

"I've pulled in summer folks," Asey said reminiscently, "that didn't even have anchors, let alone oars. You anchor?"

"We had one, but Withers tossed it over without bothering to see if it was fastened anywhere. It wasn't. In his excitement over plopping a new anchor into the bay, he dropped over his flash light and my sweater, and I can't figure out even now what he did to the side lights."

"Nice wind an' a nice tide last night," Asey said. "Where'd you end up?"

"Way off Truro. One of the Martino's finally had the sense to come out and tow us in. He was on his way to fish, so I had him dump me off below at the point. Easier than waiting for someone to drive me back. I landed in a hole wading ashore. Been a moist night, all in all."

Syl rolled his eyes at Asey.

"Wonder you stayed afloat," Asey said.

"We bailed," Simon said. "And bailed, and then bailed some more. I feel worst about losing my old red sweater, though. I've had that ten years."

Syl said things under his breath. Here was Simon explaining everything slick as you please, without being asked!

"Always keep keys to Sue's on the roof outside your window?" Asey inquired unexpectedly.

Simon stopped and stared blankly at him.

"Do I—no, I know you well enough to know you're

not joking. If such keys exist, they're Abby's—but I doubt it. Asey, where and to what am I being connected, and for what reason?"

"Abby's taken this rather hard," Asey said. "This night out of yours. She's been over to Sue's this mornin'."

Simon's eyes narrowed, and he quickened his step.

"But doc and the nurse," Asey continued, "took her home, an' took care of her."

Simon lengthened his stride. His face was perfectly expressionless, but Asey would have given great sums of money to know what the man was thinking.

The nurse met the trio at the back door of the gingerbread house.

"I'm so glad you're back, Mr. Keith. Your wife's been terribly upset. But I saw you at the window, and told her, and it acted like a charm. She—"

"I'll go right up and see her," Simon said. "Oh, come along, Asey. We'll look into this key business."

Asey followed him up the broad oak staircase along a narrow dark hall to a room at the back of the house. He waited outside while Simon went in.

"Oh," Abby's voice rose shrilly, "Oh, Simon! I thought that Lance had—what! What's that? Keys to that house? Simon, I could kill myself for going there! But I thought they'd done something to you—keys? Of course not! Who —Asey? Send him in here!"

Reluctantly, Asey went into the bedroom.

"What d'you mean by saying I have—"

"Wait, Abby," Asey said quietly. "I never said that

you or Simon owned keys to Suzanne's. Only that a bunch of keys an' a twisted piece of wire was found on your roof."

"Going through my house? I'll have you arrested!"

Simon eventually quieted her.

"Asey, she's telling you the truth, and so am I. If there's been a murder, I know Abby'll understand that any hunting you did here was with—well, probably sound foundation. But I fear, if you found anything that might seem to involve either of us, that—"

"That Lance Howes did it!" Abby interrupted. "I know! I always said that some day those two would—"

"Look," Asey said, "just try to help me here, will you? Just one thing. This handkerchief of Simon's. Is it his?"

Abby looked at it. "Yes. But I put it out with the clothes last fall, and I haven't seen it since. It was the last of a box he had two years ago."

"That's all, thanks."

Simon looked at Asey, and a queer little smile played around the corners of his mouth.

"Folded like that—my guess is that you found it near your stranger, didn't you?"

"Lance Howes, or that Suzanne," Abby's voice was getting shriller. "They—"

Asey held up his hand. "Please. All I want is to get a few things straight, and then—"

Simon took his arm. "I'll call Miss Phillips—yes, yes, I'll be back as soon as I've changed my clothes. Don't worry. I'll settle Asey's few things."

He closed the bedroom door, then swung around and thrust a forefinger on a button of Asey's shirt.

"Get this, Mayo. Neither she nor I had those keys. That handkerchief of mine blew off the line last fall. Now, get out your pad and pencil, and take down some facts. I'd have given them to you and your half-pint shadow before, but it was more fun to play you like the fish you are. The man who owned that boat was named Withers, George Withers. He lived in Brewster. His boat is GC8769. He was going to phone a friend of his named Crossley, in Provincetown, and have Crossley take the boat back to Brewster for him after he got dried out. Those facts you can check. As for Abby, she knows no one named Carson. She has no quarrel with anyone on the other side of that fence except Suzanne and her son. Got that? Good. Now, if there's any more gum-shoeing to be done around here, send a state trooper or the local constable, and let them do it. Got that?"

He jabbed Asey's shirt button again.

"I get it." Asey brushed off the prodding finger and smiled. "You might almost say I got a lot more. Thanks."

With Syl trotting beside him, he started back to Suzanne's.

"Golly!" Syl said breathlessly, "I heard it all, from downstairs! Asey, whyn't you tell him where he got off at? Why—say, slow up, will you? Whyn't you tell him a thing or two?"

Asey waited for Syl to catch his breath.

"Them was his innin's, Syl. Simon was tellin' me a thing or two. First time he ever unbent, as you might say.

I'm pleased to know he can lose his temper. Ain't always so smooth an' oily."

"But he was lyin'! How'd them things git there, if he didn't put 'em there?"

"'Where'd you come from, baby dear, the blue sky opened an' I am here,'" Asey told him. "Let's walk around the fence, Syl. Guess we better call that Withers feller, an' I want to open Carson's suitcase, though I don't expect to find nothin'."

From an upstairs window, Lance watched Asey and Syl as they pulled Carson's case from the rumble seat of the roadster and went into the garage. He heard Joan's door open, listened to her heels tapping as she went down into the living room, and heard her call Levering.

"Did they find Simon? Yes, Asey and Syl are here—"

Lance went out into the hall, put one leg over the banisters and slid down, catching himself just before he caromed out the front door.

"Joan! Hey, Joan!" he shouted with unnecessary vigor. "Asey's back. Come out and—oh. Come along, too, Levering?"

"Asey's got troubles enough," Levering said. "Besides, I'm reading a superb book named 'What Every Youth Should Know, a Dissertation on Rum.' The author's agin it. He—"

"Thousands more of those tracts up attic." Lance stood in the doorway. "Bellamy was agin rum, too. Come on, Joan, I want to hear about Simon."

Levering's indifference made Lance's entirely assumed impatience appear all the more impatient, and Joan hesitated. She'd barely exchanged two words with Lance since the night before, when his comment about Carson had annoyed her so. She was still irritated at the way he had flounced off, into the tentacles of that blonde infant. But she did want to know about Simon.

"I'll come," she said.

But Lance led her away from the garage, down to the boat house.

"It's all right," he assured her with a calmness he didn't feel. "Levering's right. We'll get in Asey's hair. But I want to talk with you. Look, I'm sorry I made those cracks about Carson. None of my business. I told you I was a simple soul, and they always plank both feet into things. Here, sit down. I'm sort of worried about you."

"Me? Why?"

"Asey. Look, Joan, if he hasn't already, he's going to trap you about that phone call from Carson. He did call you, didn't he?"

"Ben? You mean, last night? No. Mrs. Snow told Asey he called someone here, but it wasn't me."

"But you took the call!" Lance insisted. "Of—I mean, who else—look, Joan. I told Asey I answered the phone at nine-twelve, and it was Cummings, so—"

"Lance, you idiot! I didn't talk to Ben, last night!"

"Look here, Joan." Lance got up and paced around the wharf. "We haven't much time, because if Asey sees me talking to you, he'll know something's up. Now, I know you took that call. Why, with your note—"

"What note?"

"This." He pulled a small blue envelope from his

pocket. "It's been burning a hole in me since I took it from Carson's pocket this morning! I saw your writing—"

"How do you know my writing?"

"Looked at the register, silly—"

"Let me see—"

She reached up and took it from his hand, read the single line and then laughed.

"Oh, you almost had me worried for a minute! That's nothing to get excited over, Lance. Just a note I left for Ben last week-end."

"But it says, 'See you tomorrow,'" Lance said with a hint of accusation in his voice.

"Of course it does! I tell you I went away a week ago Saturday to stay with a friend on Sixty-fifth Street, and I left that for Ben."

"There's no date. Asey'll think—"

"Asey won't think anything that's not so. I'll take it to him right now. Honestly, Lance, I wish you'd left it where you found it. I suppose you meant well, but it's going to be silly, explaining now."

Lance caught her arm as she started back to the house.

"You mustn't show it to him, Joan! If it doesn't mean anything, let me throw it away. Then there won't have to be any explanations. You mustn't let yourself get mixed up in—"

Joan pushed his hand off her arm. If Lance had known the Howes temper, he would have given due consideration to the danger signals in her eyes, but he continued hurriedly.

"Honestly, you mustn't. I've fixed things so that Asey's on another tack, and that note'll be fatal! I—"

"Lance Howes! You—you think I killed Ben, don't you?"

"Of course not! But—"

"But I was the only person in the house who knew him, and he called and asked for, or spoke to, a 'Miss' Howes. And my note's in his pocket! Oh—oh, don't be so foolish!"

"Your picture was in his wallet, too!" Lance was beginning to resent being called a fool. First Asey, now Joan! "And—"

"What of it? Lance, you absolutely shall not tear that note up! I won't have it! I'm not going to have you Galahadding around—"

"I'm *not* Galahadding, I tell you! I—"

"Ah," Joan said quietly. "So you're not just being noble and making gestures. You *do* think I killed Ben. You—"

"Joan, don't be so—so damn female! I'm not making gestures, and I don't think you killed Ben, but Asey—"

"You talk of Asey as though he were a six-headed monster who spat fire! What'll Asey think about you, I'd like to know? I saw you scaling the fence, down by the pines, this morning! And 'Mr.' Howes and 'Miss' Howes —Ben might have asked for you, too. And you answered that phone last night more than anyone except Asey. But it would be just as absurd for me to try to shield you as all this stupid nonsense of yours!"

"But Joan—"

"Why *were* you sneaking over there, anyway? Why—"

"Oh, Joan, I was trying to set Asey off your trail! I mean, Carson had your picture, and you were in love with him, and—"

"Fool!" Joan stamped her foot so violently on the wharf that she knocked over a can of paint, but neither of the two noticed. "Idiot—I suppose you think Ben was —oh, get out of my way before I—Lance, give me that note!"

She snatched it out of his hand.

"Joan—"

"Stop saying 'Joan—Joan' in that mournful tone, as though you had a stomach ache! I can't see any reason in the world for your thinking I'm a murderer! No more, anyway, than I could think you were! But if Asey doesn't find Simon, at least I can tell him of your visit—there. There's the car with Marvin and that girl. Go see them, and leave me and my affairs alone. I'm curiously capable of taking care of them myself! And I can mind my own business, too. You—you, of all people, to think—"

Joan swung around and ran back up the hill, nearly knocking Asey down near the garage.

"Here!" She held the note out to him. "This was in Ben's pocket, and Lance took it out. I wrote it last week-end, only Lance thinks I killed Ben and this has something to do with it. Did you find Simon?"

Asey nodded and looked at the note.

"Yup. Take this back. I don't want it."

"You believe—"

"Sure."

"Bates saw me write it," Joan said. "He could—oh, here comes that idiot Lance! What's got into him?"

Asey looked at her quizzically. "You should know. Run along, if you want. I'll see to him. I was on my way to see to him, anyway. Huh. Young love!"

He thrust both hands deep into his jacket pockets, and when Lance approached, he pulled out the bunch of keys and the piece of wire.

"Here, Lance. You may need 'em some day. An' why you picked that roof, an' how Syl landed on 'em is still a myst'ry to me. They say in the papers that the modern gen'ration is sort of queer, an' I'm b'ginnin' to b'lieve maybe p'raps they be."

"How'd you know I put 'em there?" Lance sounded completely crushed.

"Mary said you had duplicate keys, an' they wasn't where they should've been, an' the reg'lar ones was, an' they matched awful nice. Simon'd only had a master key, if he was doin' things. Wouldn't've left 'em out on a roof in plain sight, either. An' that wire come from a coil out in the shed. So that was the way you spent your mornin', huh? Any other bright ideas planted around? 'F they is, just save me time an' tell me now. Found that handker-chief, I s'pose, of Simon's?"

Lance nodded.

"Had a dahlia tied up with it," Asey went on blandly.

"Yup. I found the untied stalk. Your girl friend, Clare, is howlin' for you—"

Marvin, with a broad grin on his face, was lifting small file cases out of the rumble seat when Asey returned to the garage.

"Pleasant trip?" Asey inquired.

"Kind of funny. Say," he jerked his head toward Clare and lowered his voice confidentially, "she's a piece, ain't she? She—"

Mary stuck her head out of the kitchen.

"Asey! Emma Snow just called up. She says it ain't awful important, but she wants to see you some time. Say, is Simon all right? Find anythin' in the suitcase? Get that man in P-town you was callin'?"

"Yup, he al'bied Simon. Nothin' but his clothes in that bag of Carson's. So Emma—guess I'll run up. Where's Joan, Mary? Ask her if she wants to come—"

"Don't you want to see these papers, Asey?" Levering came out. "Maybe together we can cast some light on Bellamy and the rest of it."

"Guess—yup, I guess we'll do that first. I sort of expect Jimmy with Carson's brother, too. We'll let Emma slide."

Levering had spoken nothing but the truth when he said that the Newell accounts were worse than shorthand. It took the remainder of the afternoon to make even a start on them, and it was not until after dinner that Asey had an opportunity to investigate Emmaline Snow's call.

"Come along, Joan," he said. "We'll combine Emma an'

mail. It ain't right that a Cape Codder shouldn't go for evenin' mail, an' you got a lot of years to catch up on. If Jimmy Porter comes, have him wait. Prob'ly won't, though, till tomorrow, if he's this late. Where you two think you're goin'?" he asked Lance, who, with Clare, was climbing into the station wagon.

"Tab's lost a trunk," Lance said. "I thought I'd try to find it. Should I stay here? I'm not going out of town, or anything, and you've got Levering and Marvin and Bob's men—"

"They'll get along without you," Clare assured him. "You can take me home, and I'll send someone for the roadster. Of course your mother's all right! And dad hasn't seen you, and—"

They went off in the station wagon; Clare's little excited shrieks and Lance's hearty laughter echoed back to the hill as the car took the bumps on the marsh road.

"Huh." Asey looked down at Joan. "Why don't you— hm. Got a heavy enough coat on?"

"Yes, thanks," Joan was still watching the station wagon out of the corner of her eye. "Yes, I think so."

Neither of them spoke again until they reached the village.

"This isn't—why, Asey, this can't be Main Street!" Joan said. "It doesn't look a bit the way it did this morning, with all these lights!"

" 'Lectric lights do wonders," Asey answered. "B'sides, the whole town turns out for mail, all four hundred, includin' dogs an' children. I'm goin' to leave you at the far end here, though you'd see more of the goin's on up by the post office. Mind?"

"Not a bit. Do they have to park on both sides of the street?"

"They oughtn't, but the cop don't come on duty till July first, an' they's no one to stop 'em. Our traffic jams is pract'cly metr'politan. I'll be back in a jiffy. If any of those r'porters spot you, blow the horn."

Joan leaned forward and watched him weave in and out of the procession that trouped unevenly in the general direction of the post office. She liked the idea of going for the evening mail. Friendly custom—

Brakes squealed, and she turned around. A provision truck had pulled up directly behind Asey's roadster, less than the proverbial hair's breadth away. The driver stuck his head out and launched a colorful stream of invective toward two men in a small black coupe headed up the Cape.

The driver of the coupe backed up, then shot his car forward.

For the first time in her life, Joan screamed. Then she reached for the horn.

The man beside the driver of the black coupe was Bates.

12

JOAN jabbed at the horn button and slid over behind the wheel.

"Let me get by, please?" she begged the truck driver. "Let—thanks!"

She turned the long roadster around in the nearest driveway and was headed in the opposite direction by the time Asey arrived.

"Want me—what's—"

"Black coupe," Joan wiggled back to her own seat, "hustle, Asey! Just passed—Bates was in it!"

In a flash Asey was in the car, and the car was proceeding up Main Street as though an escort of motor cycle cops led the way.

"Sure it was Bates?" He had to yell above the steady din of his horn. "Get the license number?"

"I didn't notice the plates, but it was him!"

"Any cars pass afterwards?"

"One, but it pulled up in the parking space—"

Asey yanked off his broad-brimmed Stetson, passed it over to Joan and jammed his foot even harder on the accelerator.

"Always wanted an excuse to see what this car'd do," he said conversationally. "Y'know, I used to work for ole Cap'n Porter when he made buggies, an' I helped him fiddle round the first horseless carriage he ever put out. Took us four weeks flat to go to New York from Boston, an' eight weeks to get ready to start back. Who else was with Bates?"

"Dark, stocky man. I never saw him before."

Joan's eyes were glued to the dashboard; there was something fascinating in the way the speedometer needle continued to slant.

"Yessireebob," Asey said, "them was the days—here's— nope, 'tain't neither." They passed a car before Joan saw it. "That was Sam Blair. Know his numbers. Yup, that first car was sort of a lib'ral education, like. Don't know but what I enjoyed it more'n this. This is too dummed perfect—pshaw!" He made an exclamation of disgust. "I told Bill Porter—that's Jimmy's brother, that these cars wouldn't make their best speed 'cept on a straightaway—"

Joan gripped the door and forced herself to turn and look behind. The lights of the village through which they had just passed drew a line of their progress, an up-and-downy line that undulated like a snake.

As she turned back, her beret flew off, and she found herself wondering how it had managed to stay on as long as it had. The speedometer needle was beginning to slant to the left of the dial now. Asey was slowing down.

"Ten miles," he said, "or thereabouts, an' there ain't no sign of 'em, an' nothin' short of Malcolm Campbell'd of got this far—did Bates see you?"

"I'm sure he didn't."

Asey stopped the car.

"Then we'll set an' wait a spell. Mind the top down? It's a bit misty like—"

"I love it down," Joan said. "Asey, where can that car be? We didn't pass it—"

"Might of turned off somewhere. We'll just wait kind of hopeful like."

A truck and two sedans passed up the Cape, and an ice wagon jolted unhappily down toward Weesit.

Asey turned the car around.

"We'll start back, sort of slow an' easy; I'll play with the spot light when a car passes, when it's square long-side. You climb up on the boot an' help."

The third car was the black coupe. Asey again swung the roadster around and shot it forward, but again the black coupe was nowhere to be found.

"Either that lad knows these roads better'n I do," Asey murmured, "or else he's the luckiest feller in this wide world."

"What can we do?"

"Do? Stop again. At least, he's headin' up the Cape. We know that much. We'll stop, but this time I'll draw up so's I can turn either way."

"Can't you let me out, Asey? I could go somewhere and phone. Bob Raymond and his men might help."

Asey smiled. "This strip of plains right here is four-five miles long, an' they ain't half a dozen phones on it an' they're pretty far between. An' s'pose Bates recognized you, an'—nun-no. I guess you'll stick with me. No chance of his gettin' off the Cape, anyhows. If he gets away from us, I can get the bridges warned, an' have the other road watched. If he wants to play hare an' hounds, I'm willin'. Sort of fun—say, I plumb forgot! They's a sand road that runs par'lel to this one, an' comes out again on the main road a few miles up. Not one person—not one native in a hundred knows of it, but I guess we'll do our waitin' at that fork. If this is the feller that's been rompin' around the hill an' swipin' Obed's best milk an' eggs, he might've picked up a little knowledge."

Asey slowed down at the fork, and then speeded on ahead.

"See anything?" Joan peered through the windshield.

"Tail light ahead. We'll invest'gate."

"Asey, it's foggy here—Heavens, be careful! Why, I can hardly see the road!"

"Cheer up," Asey advised. "I once drove this piece blindfolded. Always is sort of muggy an' misty right along on this stretch. Lowlands an' ponds, an' the ocean side cuts in, an' with a good east wind—say, I'm goin' to short cut on him. Hold tight!"

Back on the main road again, Asey drew up and gave a sigh of satisfaction.

"There's a mile'n a half ahead of him. Don't see how he can get by—"

But the minutes passed, and no black coupe appeared.

"He must have gone along," Joan said disappointedly.

"He couldn't of. But I'll tell you what he done. He

seen my lights, an' turned back an' followed us. I'm 'fraid I been kind of underestimatin' this bird."

"I tell you what," Joan said, "you let me drive off, and you stay here, and then you can shoot 'em, or shoot their tires, or something, when they come up."

Asey grinned at her. "Bloodthirsty thing, you! Sure, that's a nice thought, 'cept when I was startin' out, I didn't have no intentions of doin' nothin' but pay a social call on Emmaline Snow, an' I don't usually tote guns around on social calls. Well, 'f he's behind us, an' it looks like he is, he won't come out as long's we're here. I'll turn back toward Weesit on the main road an' do some phonin'. I didn't get the number, did you?"

"I looked, but it was smeared with dirt or dust," Joan said. "But you can describe the two, and the car— Asey, here comes something! They're blowing the horn—"

"Porter horn," Asey said. "Same model as this. That's Warrener, over in Eastham. Has a big place on that turn-off—"

A long open phaeton with its rakish khaki top up sped past them. Before its tail light was out of sight, Asey shot the roadster after it.

"Why—?"

"Happened to r'member," Asey said, "Warrener's in New York this week. His house's closed. He sent me a note b'cause we was goin' fishin'. An' Warrener wouldn't ever of taken that corner at that speed. Grade crossin' here. Nor he wouldn't of gone by without recognizin' this car an' stoppin'. You better hold on."

Joan did more than hold on. She gripped the boot cover with her left hand, and the top of the door with her right, and blessed herself for having changed her pumps for rubber-soled sport shoes before they left the hill. At least she could brace herself with her feet.

She could hear the tires moan as the roadster slewed around what seemed to be one corner after another. Her breath stopped entirely as they skidded half-way around, once, but Asey turned the car and sped on.

"Puddle," he said conversationally.

They were so near the phaeton when they entered Orleans that Joan could read the numerals on the license plates.

"Now we'll see," Asey muttered. "They's lights up here at these four corners."

But the phaeton's driver was stopping for no traffic signals.

He whizzed by the red light, leaving in his wake a bewildered woman in a new car, who blankly surveyed the telephone pole that was suddenly a part of her engine; and sprawled silently on the macadam was a small boy who would never use his bicycle for months to come.

Joan nearly went through the windshield as Asey braked.

"Hey, Peewee!" he shouted to the traffic cop. "Climb in—wait! That Saunders? Get in the rumble, then, you're comin'—no, your motor cycle ain't no use! Stay here an' look after the kid, Peewee! In, Saunders?"

He sped forward again. It had all happened so quickly

that it was several minutes before Joan realized that Saunders was a state policeman.

"Tell him everything," Asey ordered. "Hang on, an' turn around an' explain. Tell him to get his gun out an' get their tires if he has a chance—"

With difficulty, Joan knelt on the seat, gripped the boot with both hands, and yelled to the officer that the man in the Porter ahead had stolen someone's car, and with him was another man Asey wanted in connection with the Carson murder in Weesit.

"And the driver, too—"

"Okay," Saunders said. "We'll get 'em. You better sit down."

But a moment later, he touched Joan's shoulder.

"Tell Asey he better stop an' phone ahead if he doesn't catch sight of him—"

She shouted the order in Asey's ear, and he nodded.

"They're right ahead. I seen 'em a second ago. Get down on the floor, Joan."

Obediently she eased herself down on the floor boards and gripped feebly at the seat. She wanted to crawl back and see what was going on, but it occurred to her that she was far better off where she was if there was any shooting to follow.

The car swerved several times, and twice she heard the horn blare out, and almost felt Asey jockeying the roadster past other cars before she heard the sound of their motors. Once they came to a dead stop.

"Dum fool dog!"

They sped on and on, and finally Asey slowed down.

"Come on up, Joan. I'll go into this stand an' phone. I don't know what on earth Bill Porter put into that car he didn't put into this, but I can't catch it. Beaten by a stock job!" he sounded utterly disgusted.

"They're slowing by the grade crossing, Asey!" Saunders, standing in the rumble, sat down with a thud as Asey started off again. "You can get 'em—oh, step on it! Get down again, miss!"

But the driver of the phaeton had started up again.

"Fool!" Asey yelled, as he stopped the roadster. "Fool, he's going through the bars! He'll never make it in this world!"

Joan could hear the train whistle and the signal bell ringing. Then there was a crash and a shriek, and the screech of train brakes, and what seemed to be an ever-lasting crackling of breaking glass and splintering wood and crunching metal.

13

THE NEXT hour was one which Joan was never able to erase entirely from her memory.

She would always connect the scene with other horrors she had unwillingly witnessed—the hideous face of an armless leper in India who stood outside a shop where her mother bargained for sandalwood boxes; the tenement fire on Fourteenth Street, that awful week before she went to Carson's to work.

All that remained of the gleaming Porter phaeton was a twisted mass of steel and a handful of splinters. She saw just enough to gather that even less remained of the driver, even before Asey took her by the shoulder and pushed her gently back toward the roadster.

"Bates—is Bates—Asey, can't I do anything?"

"He's alive, but he's unconscious, an' they's a doctor on the way, an' there ain't a thing you can do, Joan. He's hurt pretty bad, an' you don't want to see him now, or any of the rest of it."

But it was as awful to hear what went on as to see it.

"My God!" the engineer's voice was shrill, and kept

going higher and higher as he talked. "Look at this! And—see what come into my cab! My God, we was hardly moving! He must of—say," he was crying, "won't none of you clean out my cab? I can't go near it!"

Joan covered her ears, shut her eyes, and waited.

At last Asey came.

"Okay. We'll get along. Bates is still alive, an' they're takin' him over to the hosp'tal. He's still unconscious, an' the doctor don't think he'll pull through. Sure, that cigarette lighter works. Least, *that* works, even if this special job did go an' get licked by a stock car! Next auto I get, I'm goin' to have fewer fancy gadgets an' more engine under me! Say, Joan, ever hear of a feller named James Glotz?"

"Was he the driver?"

Asey nodded. "I found his pocketbook. Had a passport in it. Ever hear of him?"

Joan took a long breath.

She knew that everyone, Asey and Tabitha and the rest, all thought the worst of Carson, but although she hadn't tried to argue with them, she was still firmly convinced that Ben Carson was all she'd thought him for the past three years. Now, it was clear that they were right and she was wrong.

She had never laid eyes on Glotz, but she had made out at least two checks for him every week that she had been Carson's secretary.

"He was an investigator for Ben," she said. "I never saw him or knew him, but," she gulped, "Ben said he investigated his business interests. I—well, I thought he was some sort of efficiency expert. I was never told that in so many words, but—well, I just came to that conclusion. From the—from the way he tore through the light at the four corners, and all, I guess I was wrong."

She lighted another cigarette from the half-smoked one in her hand.

"I guess, Asey, I was wrong about a lot of my guesses about Carson. But truly, he was awfully decent to me, even if—if his investigators seem to—oh, Asey, what an utter fool I've been! I've kicked around enough to know better —how I was taken in!"

"You may be right about him yet," Asey said. "But from his passport picture, I'd say this was the feller that's been harryin' around the hill. He sounds like the one Hamilton chased, an' the one that stole his provender from Obed, an' the thick-set feller that got Broody Mary aroused, an' the one Simon said he seen. Prob'ly he's the one that messed up Sue's house an' went after her. Those is all a lot of guesses, but this short thick-set business sort of ties him up. He most likely took Carson's coupe from Emmaline's this mornin'—huh. Wonder if the car was his, or Carson's. Well, we can find out about that when we get hold of it. It's prob'ly right there at Warrener's."

Joan wanted to know why James Glotz should be doing all those things.

"All the harrying, as you call it."

Asey shrugged. "Just invest'gatin', I shouldn't wonder. Huh. Any more invest'gators you know of?"

"Not a one, Asey. Look, what about Bates? I feel I ought to do something."

"They'll phone," he told her, "an' I'll let you know everythin'. Yup, this is clearin' up some in my mind, but I don't know how sure an' pos'tive it is. Bates'll be able to cast a lot of light, some time, I hope. One thing. I I don't think Bates had anythin' to do with all this willin'ly."

"Why not?"

"He was handcuffed," Asey said simply. "That's how he come out of it alive, I think. Shielded his face, couldn't grab at anythin' or hold on much, an' so he got thrown clear."

"But if this James Glotz was down here, and Bates was in Boston, I can't see where and how they connect."

Asey admitted that he couldn't either. "But it'll clear up some time. I guess we won't stop to call on Emmaline tonight. Honest, Joan, when I asked you to go for the evenin' mail, I didn't have any idea that anythin' like all this was ever goin' to happen! Nosiree, I'd be scared to try any social callin' tonight. No tellin' what'd happen—"

He looked at her face, bit his lip and started in on a series of Cape anecdotes, each funnier than the last, till by the time they arrived home at the hill, Joan was as nearly herself as she could have been. Asey gave an inward sigh of relief as he pulled the roadster up to the door. It was hard to make up funny stories at such a clip when your mind was firmly clamped on at least fifty other things, all at once.

"Gettin' old," he muttered. "What say? No, I just said 'twas sort of cold. Oho—Emmaline! What you doin' here?"

Emmaline, with Mary and Tabitha and Levering, stood at the head of the oystershell walk.

"Do here? I'm waitin' for you, Asey. When I first called, it was just to tell you I thought I seen that car of that Carson man's, an' then I seen it again, an' there was two men in it, an' I think if you tried, you might meet up with 'em!"

Joan and Asey looked at each other and then laughed from sheer exhaustion.

"We already have," Asey said at last. "That's—Joan, go to bed. An' if any of you so much as thinks of askin' her a question, I'll gag you. Same here. No, don't even speak to us. We'll tell all in the mornin'. It'll keep. Neither Joan nor me wants to go through this business again tonight. Say, is Marvin around? Good. I want you. Emma, don't think I ain't grateful, 'cause I am. Marvin'll drive you back to your house, an' then'll you put the car up for me? Thanks. Night!"

The group at the door stared at each other uncomprehendingly.

"Well, I never!" Broody Mary said. "I never in all my born days! The two of 'em's ravin' crazy. An' Asey had spots of blood on his shirt!"

Levering drew his aunt aside. "Joan looked simply worn out—look, take her up my flask, will you, and look after her?"

Mrs. Newell stared curiously at her nephew. He was a much more thoughtful boy than she ever would have admitted in public, but evidences of that thoughtfulness were limited to a choice few.

"If that means what I think it does," she said, "I hope you—hm. Where's the flask?"

He spanked her playfully. "I thought you liked her, aunt!"

Up in Lance's room, Asey lighted his pipe and stretched out on his bed.

The whole thing was beginning to make connections here and there, but there were so many gaps. There was no doubt whatsoever in his mind that Carson had somehow got on the trail of the mysterious something which Bellamy Howes had bought from Newell and Company, and that James Glotz had been hired to delve into the matter thoroughly.

"But I don't think," he murmured to himself, "that even Carson was sure what it was. An' he didn't seem to want anyone hurt. Bet that yellow handkerchief business was just to get 'em scared. An' he didn't kill Sue, an' he called the doc. Just like that magazine said, as crooked as he could be without runnin' smack into the lawr—"

There was a light tap on the door. He sighed, and got up.

"Only me," Mary said, "with some fodder. I'll leave it out here. You looked like coffee."

Asey grinned. "Black," he inquired through the door, "or with cream? Thanks—"

The coffee was good. Mary, he decided critically, put an egg in it. But it disturbed his train of thought, and he had to go back to the beginning again. Old Bellamy Howes had—

There was another knock on the door, and Suzanne slipped in.

"I don't mean to—but Mary said you had shoes on, so I guessed you hadn't really got to bed. Asey, whatever was Lance doing this morning? He tried to tell me, but I couldn't make head nor tail out of it."

Asey explained briefly that Lance had been trying to shield Joan.

"Meant well, but he shouldn't of. Don't worry. He won't again."

"Joan's a dear, isn't she? And so much like that tintype of Bellamy's mother. Asey, what's the matter with her and Lance, glaring at each other in a refined way?"

"Tiff, I guess, about Lance's clew-plantin' on her behalf. An' I think she seen him skip over the fence an' got worried."

Suzanne frowned and lighted a cigarette, in much the same nervous way, Asey noticed with surprise, that Joan had lighted cigarette after cigarette all the way home.

"Surprised at this?" Suzanne smiled. "I know better than to smoke publicly in Weesit. Asey, what about Abby and Simon?"

"An' all this? Wa-el, Simon's got a deep water-tight alibi," Asey smiled at his own joke, "an'—nope, I think they're out of this. Leastways, I think so now. Sue, you gettin' worked up over this flibberty-gibbet of a girl, the Chatfield one?"

Suzanne tapped her cigarette against the side of a ·pewter ash tray.

"About ninety percent of her flibbertyness, Asey, is

purely assumed. She's like her father. From bus boy to streamlined king in twenty years. What Carl Chatfield wants, he goes out and takes. And I'm more than afraid that Clare wants Lance. Chatfield's offered him jobs, you know. And today Lance asked me if I'd mind going to Detroit next winter if he took one. I gathered that you'd been chiding him. At least, he muttered something about Asey's telling him the facts of life."

"Asked you this afternoon, did he?" Asey inquired. Apparently the boy had wasted no time, anyway.

"Yes, and if he takes that job, he'll get Clare thrown in, whether he realizes it or not. And—oh dear! You want to go to bed, and I'm keeping you up. Everything will solve itself, I suppose. It always does."

"Most always." Asey thought of the end of James Glotz. "Prob'ly people always said of him that hangin' was too good. His picture had that kind of face—"

"Carson?" Suzanne asked. "You—"

"Nope, I wasn't thinkin' of him. But in the end, things most usually sort of somehow end by evenin' up, like, seems as if."

"Even with all your qualifications," Suzanne said, "I hope that somehow maybe perhaps they may. Good night."

Asey went back to the bed and tried to figure out how far he had got.

Bellamy had something, God alone knew what, and it was worth money. Carson had, God knew how, found out about it, and tracked down, via James Glotz, both the Howes and the Newell families. About Joan, now. It was entirely possible that Carson had never connected her with the Howes family, though if he had really investigated the matter, he must have come across some pictures—

That time it was Marvin who knocked at the door.

"Car keys, Mr. Mayo. Thought you'd want 'em before I turned in. Say, some class to the room I got over the garage. Fixed up like a ship. Say, that car of yours's got that blonde's beat a mile. Hers is snappy looking, but yours's got what it takes."

"I used to think so too. How was that Boston trip of yours?"

Marvin shrugged and then grinned. "What a dame! Honest, I thought that kind come only in the movies. You know, though," he added confidentially, "she ain't so bad once she forgets who she is and who her father is and how much dough they got. Underneath she's okay."

"Heart matches her hair, huh?" Asey suggested drily. "Huh. How'd you d'scover that?"

"Oh," Marvin's voice was studiously casual, "I told her what a punk she was, and she up and pasted me one, so I laid her over my knee and spanked her. I don't take that from no girl, no matter who."

"You spanked her?" Asey asked with pleasure, "Where—"

"Where? Where you usually—Oh, you mean, where. Oh, in the woods near Plymouth. We made up, though. Say, if there's anything I can do to help in this, let me know, won't you, Mr. Mayo? I been awful worried about this guy that's been trailin' Mrs. Newell. She's a good egg, Mrs. Newell is. She—"

"Say, what'd that guy look like?"

"Him? Sort of a fox terrier with spats. 'Bout a hunner'n thirty stripped," Marvin told him. "Yeah, you let me know if I can do anything. Mrs. Newell's been real good to my mother. 'Course, she does sort of crazy things, sometimes, but she's a good egg. You let me know if I can help."

"I will," Asey promised. The knowledge that Marvin had administered what was probably the first spanking of Clare Chatfield's career would, he thought delight Tabitha Newell's soul.

After Marvin left, Asey lighted his pipe and tried once more to get the business figured out.

Bellamy Howes had—

Downstairs in the living room, something crashed.

Wearily, Asey got up, slid on his jacket and went down to look into the matter.

Clare and Lance, looking very self-conscious, stood at opposite ends of the fireplace.

"Well?" Asey tried not to sound as annoyed as he felt.

"I came back for my car," Clare explained with a winning smile, "and then Lance had to come back while I got John to come back here to come back home with me so I wouldn't have to drive home alone—"

"Did any of that," Asey inquired, "cause the crash?"

"The—oh, that was Rupert. Rupert jumped up on the mantel and knocked off the ship-in-a-bottle. But it isn't hurt. I mean, Lance caught it. The crash was when Rupert jumped into the flower bowl and knocked it over. I'll get another, though. I got Sue that one."

"I'm sure," Mrs. Newell spoke from the doorway, "I'm sure that's very nice of you indeed. It shows a certain spirit. And now, d'you mind awfully if we go to sleep? No, Levering," she turned around, "you can put away your sword cane. It's just—just," she groped for a word, "it's only her."

Suzanne and Broody Mary added themselves to the group. Something in Mary's look set Clare apologizing.

"I'm really frightfully sorry! I mean, we—well, we've been fooling around, and we didn't mean to keep you awake, or wake you up, or anything. Did we, Lance dear?"

Lance, avoiding his mother's face, shook his head and yanked at the end of the marmoset's leash.

Asey thrust his hands into his jacket pockets and leaned back against the mantel. He had a feeling that a scene was on the verge of developing.

"If that's coffee I smell," Levering, in a russet silk dressing gown, walked over and joined Asey at the fire place, "if it is, and there is some, I'd like a cup."

Lance looked at the dressing gown. "Sure you should, Newell? It's not Sanka."

Only Asey caught the expression of irritation that shot over Levering's face as he answered lightly that he'd risk the chance.

"I'll get cups," Mary said shortly. "I—"

"Oh, there's someone at the window!" Clare gave a little shriek. "Oh. Oh, it's only Marvin!"

Lance let Marvin and a state trooper in.

"Nothin's the matter," Asey said. "Just a quiet little evenin' gatherin', as you might say, an'— God A'mighty, Marvin, what you got, brass knuckles?"

"They belonged to a man that knew Capone," Marvin proudly offered them for inspection. "See—"

"Corkers," Asey said. "Hamilton, you an' Marvin can p'trol outside, while I try to get this mob settled. Miss Chatfield, you got a chauffeur waitin' out there? Don't you think it'd be a Christian notion to—"

"It's no use, Asey." Tabitha sat down in the big easy chair. "Now that we're here, we might as well all join in, and possibly we can put an end to it— Lance, d'you mind awfully restraining Rupert? He's up on the mantel again. Levering, go up and see if Joan's asleep. I hardly see how she can be. Ask her if she wants some coffee and explain to her that the din is purely by the way—"

"Mary," Clare interrupted, "have you any of that jam? Oh, and that cake? Oh, how simply swell! Let's have a sort of snack party, and Lance and I'll tell you our secret—"

Asey looked at Suzanne. She knew what was coming, but she was stifling without visible effort whatever feelings she had. She might, he thought, have been waiting for a parade to start. She wore just that expression of eager interest.

"We'll wait for Joan, and—oh, here you are! Now we can tell you all at once! Lance is going to Detroit this autumn and work for father, and we're going to be married after he gets settled in his new job! Isn't that simply wonderful?"

Suzanne smiled as though it were someone else's son, and Broody Mary sniffed audibly. Joan politely thanked Levering for her coffee. Asey pulled Rupert away from the mantel and dumped him unceremoniously on the floor.

"Isn't anyone glad?" Clare sounded aggrieved.

Asey wasn't sure, but he thought he heard Lance's murmured reply.

"*You* are!"

14

Jimmy Porter turned up the next forenoon with Will Carson, who bore not the slightest family resemblance to his tycoon brother, and who seemed not even mildly moved by the murder.

"Ben," he said matter-of-factly, "had it coming to him. Pa used to say so when he was a kid. He stole all Pa's money and run away with it. That's how he begun. Ma wouldn't let us do anything about it. Sure, he had it coming to him. I told him so back last January that he'd go too far one of these days. That was when he come to me and asked me to pump Mr. Porter here about some people named Howes. Well, like I told him, maybe he'd make millions out of his deal, as he said, but if there was that much money lying around Cape Cod, some Cape Codder'd have picked it up long before this."

"Deal, huh? S'pose you tell us the works," Asey suggested.

There wasn't, Carson said, much to tell. Ben made a date to have lunch with him, the first time he'd ever taken any notice of him in ten years.

"He wanted to know if I come to the Cape, ever. I

said once in a while with Mr. Porter, because I liked to fish and so did he. Ben said I could do some business for him, and he'd pay me. He said it meant millions if some one went about it the right way. I told him no. That's all there was to it. Say, Mr. Porter, won't we miss the tides? I—"

"Ever hear of anyone named James Glotz?" Asey asked.

"Glotz? I knew a Sam Glotz from Omaha. Would he be the same?"

" 'Fraid," Asey said, "he wouldn't do."

Carson nodded and wandered off toward Jimmy's car.

"Awful upset by all this," Asey commented ironically.

"The reporters tried to get at him," Jimmy said. "That was a circus. From what he's told me from time to time about his illustrious brother, I'd say that it was pure restraint that Will wasn't hopping up and down, yelling for joy at Ben's untimely demise. He wanted me to ask you to let the murderer get off, if you found him. I promised I'd do what I could."

"That's real nice," Asey said with a grin. "I'll take it into consideration if I ever get to find the feller, which don't seem so very likely right now."

"Learn anything from the New York end?" Jimmy wanted to know.

"Markham phoned Bob. No papers in his house or at his office, but a nice pile of ashes in the office fireplace seemed to show he'd cleaned the place out himself. That's all, an' it ain't much. Oh, they found out a lot of odds an' ends, but it don't 'pear to me that this was the work of any Follies girl. B'sides, she's got a Russian prince now. Keep this feller handy, will you, Jimmy? Try to make him work up some interest."

"The only interest he can work up is over fish," Jimmy said, "but I'll do my best. So long."

Asey strolled over to the garden, where Mrs. Newell was bending over a writing case.

"Lists." She said wearily. "I've neglected them lately. Oh, catch that, Asey, before it blows to Spain—"

Involuntarily he looked at the paper before returning it.

"What is this, Greek?"

The list said: "Hdf. Cdy.Gs. Jn. Ln. Sn."

"Let me see. It's the most recent, and I should be able to—oh. Candy, handkerchiefs, gas, Joan, Lance— I'm sure I don't know what 'Sn' means. Oh,—soon. I know. I wanted to ask you what happened to Joan and Lance. D'you happen to know?"

"Say, Mrs. Newell, have I got bows an' arrows hangin' around me?" Asey asked. "Joan was all right when she routed me out of bed this morning to find out about Bates—"

"How is the poor man?"

"Still alive. Where'd Joan an' Leverin' go, swimmin'?"

"They set out for the shore with that in mind, but I think the east wind will sway them— Asey, I'm trying to work out a list of all that's going on to straighten it out in my mind. Have you got anywhere?"

Asey looked carefully around to see if there was anything or anybody that might interrupt before he answered.

"Wa-el," he sat down in a deck chair and pulled out his pipe, "it's sort of rag-tag an' bobtail, as ole man Blair used to say when the fellers at the wharf used to ask him about his corn beef. Seems to me that Bellamy got somethin' of value from your grandpa in r'turn for his eight hundred thousand. Leverin' an' I worked it out that Cap'n Newell was in Boston all that time, but Bellamy was plyin' b'tween 'Frisco an' China. An' that Bellamy died b'fore anyone on this end knew about what he'd done with his money is certain sure. But the thing never turned up, or if it did, no one had sense enough to know."

"Where's Carson come in?" Tabitha asked. "And, by the way, are we out of range of Simon's binoculars?"

"'Less he can periscope in circles. Wa-el, somehow Carson must've got on the track of this thing. Back as far as last January, 'cordin' to his brother. He hired Glotz to go into this end, an' Glotz, or someone else, to go after you. Didn't mean to murder the lot; the way this feller went after Sue an' then called the doc proves that. Sort of simple, his trailin' you so obvious, but maybe he wanted to get you out of town, or scare you. He done both."

"What about Joan?"

"I don't think he knew she was a Howes. On the other

hand, maybe so. Anyways, I think Bates caught on to somethin' an' come after Joan to warn her. Carson, or your Cockroach, or Glotz, yanked him away b'fore he give the show away. 'Gain, you see, there wasn't any murderin'. They didn't kill Bates, just r'moved him. I think Bates upset the apple cart, an' that's what brought Carson here. Anyway, Carson come, an' got killed."

"Could Glotz—"

A furrow appeared between Asey's eyes. "I don't think so. If he killed Carson, whyn't he kill Bates? Nope, I'm apt to think his dashin' off was caused by findin' out that Carson *was* killed. Bob found that car, the black coupe Carson come in, over at Warrener's. Plates was New York, an' the car was 'parently Glotz's. In his name. But I think Carson come down here in it himself from Boston. Y'see, Bob's men found another car, a sedan, abandoned near Truro. Had a busted axle. That was a New York car b'longin' to Glotz, too. Hamilton says it's the one the feller he chased was in. So I guess Glotz picked up Carson's coupe after that one went. I dunno, really. It's all guesswork."

Tabitha drummed on the chair arm with her pencil.

"But what was Carson after? Surely he wouldn't have gone after something, knowing it was worth money, without knowing what it was! And who killed him? If someone let him in the house here, it must be— Asey, this thought has been practically wearing me to a shadow, but it *must* be one of us!"

"That thought," Asey told her briefly, "also visited me."

They sat there silently for a few minutes, and then Tabitha shivered and buttoned up her coat.

"I don't know whether it's the east wind oozing into my bones, or the conviction that Simon's eyes are boring into my anatomy, but I feel shivery. Wonder how Joan and Levering are enjoying their swim? I should think the two of them would be blotches of goose flesh."

As a matter of fact, Joan was sitting fully dressed on the beach, while Levering's arms flashed rhythmically over the bobbing waves, half a mile from shore.

She was thinking about Bates, and the accident, and Carson, and Lance, and not until the latter spoke did she realize that he was sitting behind her on the sand.

"Pretty swimmer, Levering, isn't he? He was a star at college. Wind scare you? Isn't it a grand day?"

Joan nodded yes to all three questions. Somehow she didn't want to talk to Lance then, but clearly he had every intention of carrying on the conversation by himself, if he had to. He touched on a dozen subjects in half as many minutes and then fell suddenly silent.

"Uh—uh—about last night," he began. "I—"

"I think," Joan got up and started to walk toward the water's edge, "we ought to call Levering. He's been in years, and you told me yourself there were some treacherous currents out there. Won't you yell?"

She wanted awfully to hear Lance's explanation, if it was to be an explanation, of the previous night, and Clare, and all the rest, but on the other hand, she wasn't going to give Lance the satisfaction of knowing that she wanted to hear it.

"I would yell," Lance said, "but he wouldn't hear me in a million years. He'll be in soon, and don't worry about him. He's a good swimmer, and he has more sense than you'd think. I—well, I'll be seeing you. I—well, so long."

Joan poked aimlessly at a horse-shoe crab until Levering came inshore.

"You shouldn't have been so sissy," he told her. "That water's warmer than the air."

"I hoped it would be," Joan said. "Hustle up to the bath house and get dressed. I promised Tab you wouldn't get pneumonia."

Levering smiled. "Isn't Tab a swell? You know, she's spent all my life trying to see to it that I wasn't spoiled, and even now she has doubts. She says everybody thinks I am, which is just as bad. I—"

"Look," Joan interrupted, "would there be an awful rumpus if we didn't go home to lunch? I—well, I—"

"I know," Levering said, "I'd like some perspective, too. Bob Raymond said we should stick around, but he didn't accent it. We'll run down to Provincetown, and let them scold us when we get back. You can phone about Bates, if you want. I've an idea that nothing more can happen, at the hill. It already has."

Levering was wrong.

Asey and Tabitha were just finishing luncheon when the local constable, Elisha Higgins, appeared with Hamilton.

"Hi, Lish," Asey said. "Thought you told me you was too busy gardenin' to come up—"

"Oh, I didn't come about this Carson business, Asey.

Somethin' else. Seems's if someone got into Keith's place last night an' wandered all over it. Didn't take nothin', but Abby got pretty well wrought up. She an' Simon never heard a thing, an' nothin' was missin'. Queer, sort of. Bob said somethin' of the sort had happened here. Where's Lance?"

"So they got looked over, too." Asey had more or less anticipated that. "Huh. Lance went out in the harbor to get a few fish. What's he up an' done that you want him?"

Lish opened his mouth several times, and closed it, and then he scratched his nose reflectively.

"I don't hardly know. Suzanne around? No, I don't want her. Just want to know."

Asey told him she was in the house somewhere with Mary.

"Huh. Well, can I talk to you sort of conf'dential, Asey?"

"Don't you worry about Mrs. Newell, Lish," Asey told him. "She's had her house ransacked, too. One of the s'lect few. What's wrong?"

Lish blew his nose, folded his handkerchief carefully and put it back in his breast pocket.

"Well, Asey, you known me for a long time, an' you know I—"

"So it *is* trouble," Asey said. "Well, sit down, Lish, an' let's get it over with. Always can tell there's somethin' up when a feller b'gins establishin' himself for fifty years, like a grocery store."

"Well, you know I don't like to do a lot of things

I have to do, an' this is one of 'em. Now, mind you, I know the boy didn't do it, just the same's I know my boy didn't—"

"Look," Asey interrupted, "if—oh, I get it. Simon an' Abby is gunnin' for Lance, on 'count of the ransackin', are they? Well, I slept in Lance's room last night, an' he was there all night—"

"It ain't that," Lish said. "It's about the money. An' there's that sneakerprint, plain as day, an' this, too."

He held out a jack knife attached to a lanyard of white tape.

"See, initials an' everythin'. L.H."

Asey examined the knife. It was Lance's, and he knew it.

"But where—say, Lish, where are we, just?"

"Well, you see, Asey, the money went yest'day, Abby found it gone b'fore she went to bed. Only it was too late then to do anythin' about it. Four hundred sixty dollars, in the wallet. In the second pigeon-hole from the left in Abby's desk. So I guess there ain't nothin' for me to do but wait around till Lance gets back. Too bad for Sue. Hurt her trade."

Tabitha and Asey looked at each other.

"Now, Lish," Asey said, "let's sort of work this out, huh?"

"I been tryin' to tell you," Lish said, "that I don't want to do this, an' I wish there was some way out. I—"

"Ham," Asey turned to the trooper, "could you be a one to sum it up, sort of brief an' c'ncise like, just so's I could get an inklin'—"

"Abby Keith had a pocketbook in her desk with four hundred and sixty dollars in it. She discovered last night that it was gone. The knife with the lanyard was there in the room—somewhere near the window. There are sneakerprints out on the porch, and inside on the floor. So they went down to Lish. Apparently they mean to make things unpleasant for Lance."

"But it's perfectly outrageous!" Tabitha said hotly. "Asey, don't you think it's the most utterly absurd thing you ever heard of? Can't you clear this up?"

Asey did, and wanted to clear things up, but he foresaw trouble. Lance had been in the Keith house in the morning, while Simon was away, and Abby out hunting him. That was when Lance had planted the keys. Without doubt the sneakerprints were Lance's. The knife had probably dropped from his pocket.

It would take some explaining. If Lance admitted to leaving the keys— Asey pursed his lips and began to whistle noiselessly.

"Can't I give Mr. Higgins the money?" Tabitha demanded. "Couldn't we settle it that way?"

"That's somethin' on the order of what I asked Simon," Lish said. "But Simon, he said that even if the money was found, that wouldn't matter. Guess he means to be—well, I guess he wants to make trouble."

"Guess so," Asey agreed. "I—"

"It's utter nonsense!" Tabitha interrupted. "Where d'you suppose the money is, Asey?"

"Prob'ly in Simon's safe deposit box at the bank," Asey returned. "Huh. Well, you take this knife, Lish.

Guess I'll get hold of a boat an' go after Lance, an' get him for you. Maybe a chance to settle this. Hey—don't stick that knife in your pocket so careless, Lish! You oughtn't to be so casual with ev'dence. Might lose it, an' then where'd you be?"

Lish blew his nose. "Why, Asey," he said mildly, "how could I ever lose this knife?"

"Might drop it down the well," Asey said.

"That's so." Lish seemed thoughtful. "That's so, ain't it? Well, want me to come with you? We could take Harl's boat. Or maybe I better wait here. Guess I will."

Half an hour later Asey brought the borrowed motor boat alongside Lance's sailboat.

"What size shoe you wear, youngster?"

"Asey, you haven't followed me out to—"

"No foolin'. This is more serious than you think. What size?"

Lance told him, and Asey grinned.

"Fine. Now, listen. Simon's most likely watchin' this. Take off your sneakers, an' toss 'em in my boat when you tack. N'en catch this rope. I'm towin' you in—look after your sheet."

"What's up?" Lance demanded as they walked up the hill from the wharf, later on.

"Nothin', 'cept you sling them sneakers of mine over your shoulder, an' keep 'em slung. Yup, I'm wearin' yours, only they're mine, see? They ain't no time to figger this out with you. It's better for you to act dumb natural than to try to act dumb natural—here's Lish."

"Say, Asey," Lish said, "I went over to Keith's while

you was out, an' by gorry, if Simon didn't throw that knife down the well!"

"Amazin'," Asey said. "Amazin'. How come?"

"Why," Lish said as they walked over to the garden, "why, I was swingin' it round by the tape, an' Simon took it away from me. We was leanin' right by his ole well, there, an' the knife was slip'ry. An' if it didn't pop right out of his hands down that well! I'd been havin' a cup of tea an' a piece of bread an' butter with Mary out in the kitchen, an' seems's if some butter stuck. Simon was real mad. I guess—say, them the only sneakers you got, Lance?"

Lance, utterly at sea, said they were.

"Huh. Well, we'll go over an' c'mpare them prints with the others."

"Compare—where are we going?" Lance appealed to Asey.

"Keith's," Asey said. "Keep your shirt on."

Only Lish noticed that Asey was careful to step on the grass rug, out on the porch, and that he was as wary of the floor inside the house as though he were playing bears with the cracks.

"Now it sort of looks," gravely Lish got up from the floor, "like they wasn't the same sneakerprints, don't it, Simon?" He blew his nose. "I went through his closet, an' there wasn't any other rub'soled shoes there, attall. Mary said these was all he had. Well, now what you think we ought to do, Simon?"

Simon controlled himself with difficulty. "Nothing," he said shortly.

"Oh, but Simon!" Lish said. "You was so sure! What 'bout your money? I got to find that—"

Simon didn't push the three out of the door, but he came as near doing it as he could.

"Now, that's too bad," Lish said half to himself as he, Lance and Asey got into the roadster. "But like I told him, if he's a one to throw ev'dence down a well—y'know, I said we could maybe delve for it, like, but seems's if there was a quicksand there. I don't see—"

"Listen," Lance said, "you two have got me out of something, but what?"

Asey explained, and Lance's jaw dropped.

"And of course I *was* there, and I'd have had to admit it, and *why* I went there, and—say, Lish, you're a swell! Both of you—and with Simon at his binoculars the whole time—"

"Ye-as," Lish drawled. "Simon's an awful looker, he is. Y'know, Asey, I was sort of worried there, for a spell. Wouldn't of 'peared at all right for Lance to come back barefoot an' shoeless, too. Not after the half hour I spent manoeuverin' him round that well. Yup—say, Asey, how'd you know Simon put that money in the bank?"

"Did he?" Asey chuckled. "I didn't know. Just guessed."

"Seems's if he must of. I called up Tobe," Tobias Small, the bank president, was Lish's son-in-law, "an' he said Simon come into the bank this mornin' an' went to his box. Awful little room out there, where they got them boxes. An' since that feller tried that hold-up last year, Tobe's had mirrors stuck around. He said Simon put cash money into his box, real furtive like. Thought he was hoardin'. So I guess—well, lucky Simon didn't want to brood about fingerprints. But I tell you what, Asey, an' you too, Lance. You better treat Simon real r'spectful at a distance for a while. I got a sort of notion he's quite peeved."

"Shouldn't wonder," Asey agreed, "if the air wasn't sort of blue in his 'mediate vicin'ty. Come back to the hill, or shall I take you home?"

"Home," Lish said. "I seem to get my neuralgia if I don't take a nap aft'noons."

"You two," Lance said after they had deposited Lish on his front steps. "You two! Well, I'd expect something like that from you, but Lish! I never knew he had it in him."

"Most folks don't," Asey said. "That's why he's been constable thirty years. Keeps peace real good, an' real unassumin' like. Lance, from now on, you watch your step. Simon's d'clared war in earnest, I'd say, an' this prelim'nary rec'noiterin's prob'ly goin' to touch him off like a sky rocket. He means business. Half of it's Abby regrettin' her weakness in comin' over to your house, an' the rest's sort of the boil comin' to a head. You stick to your knittin', see? An' if I can get Bob to have someone play around with you a spell, I'm goin' to. Simon ain't goin' to carry on 'cordin' to Mrs. Post."

"Why didn't he carry on, even after you and Lish tricked him?" Lance asked. "He knew you had, but his original ideas were still good."

"Sure, he knew it was a put-up job, but so was his.

An' Lish kind of pinned him down when he asked Simon if he was sure he hadn't d'posited that money an' forgot. Don't think Simon ever give Lish credit any more'n you. Ho-hum. Wonder what Simon's sayin'—"

"He's at the window," Lance said. "You can always tell by the curtain. Probably he's frothing at the mouth."

But it was Abby at the bay window of the gingerbread house.

Simon, humming cheerfully, was upstairs in his room, unwrapping a small package that had come in the morning mail. Anyone could track down the purchase of a yellow Windsor scarf in Weesit or any of the surrounding villages, but the country's largest mail order house propably sold hundreds a week.

Simon folded the scarf, stuffed it into the toe of his shoe, and put the shoe back on his foot. The box and its wrapping paper went into the kitchen stove; Abbey was a prying soul, and this scarf was none of her business, yet.

He strolled into the living room and sat down in the Morris chair while Abby delivered a tirade on the failure of her plan to get Lance into trouble.

Simon said sympathetic things at the right time, but actually he didn't care a whit. He had never cared, except in so far as hurting Lance might be a sop to Abby's pride. The point was that Asey was on guard, and Simon wanted him to be. Asey would take excellent care of Lance and Suzanne, and meanwhile— Simon smiled and picked up the Boston paper.

At one time in his career he had successfully run a

pea and shell game. Asey Razor was no different from any other sucker. Point your finger, and they'd all of them stare till their eyes popped. Stare where you meant them to stare.

"I wish," Abby said petulantly, "that you'd stop humming that nursery rhyme, Simon! I'm sick and tired of that spider and his fly!"

"Sorry, my dear." Simon flicked through the paper to the stock market news. "It's been running through my head for some time. You know how bits of songs stick with you. It'll go. Bear with it a few days more, and you'll probably never hear it again."

15

Late that afternoon Asey received cheering news from the hospital about Bates.

"If compl'cations don't set in," Asey told Joan, "the doc thinks he'll pull through. Golly, he must be an iron man, that feller. Busted arm, busted leg, busted rib, an' Lord only knows how many inside bendin's an' bustin's. But barrin' any troubles, we may be able to get somethin' out of him about all this in a few days. Seem sort of nice, it will, to get just one single thing figgered out for certain."

Joan agreed that it would. "You know, I'm sort of —my eye, I'm getting the 'sort-of' habit! But I'm amazed at all this. I thought there'd be inquests, and lots of questioning, and all sorts of bothering about, and reporters—"

"Been plenty of them," Asey said, "only Bob's been handlin' the press d'vision. Had a bunch here early this mornin' takin' pictures. Broody Mary near went mad. As for an inquest, they got thirty days for that. Questionin'? Well, if Bob's real boss, Hanson, was here, you'd have had plenty questions fired at you."

"But I've hardly *seen* Bob Raymond. And you haven't asked about much."

Asey grinned. "Seems to me I don't do nothin' else but ask questions. Oh, I know what you mean. P'petual grillin', like,—where was you at the time Carson was killed, an' why, an' how can you prove it, an' so forth an' so on. Waste of time, don't you think? 'Course, if you feel I ought to, I s'pose Bob an' me could get together an' work up a nice third d'gree."

"But wouldn't it help to know about all of us, and —and all?"

Asey looked at her. "How? First place, the wind was blowin' a gale that night. No one of us in the house could've heard anythin'. That is, anythin' anyone could lay their finger on an' point to. N'en—well, you'n Sue'n Lance, an' Mary an' Leverin' an' Mrs. Newell. Huh. Oh, an' Marvin. S'pose any of you seen any other one lurkin' around? Think it'd come out? Not much. Marvin wouldn't tattle on Mrs. Newell or any of her friends. She wouldn't tattle on him. Mary wouldn't tattle on anybody if you prodded her with pitchforks. N'en I r'call havin' some trouble with you, not so long ago."

Joan sighed. "I suppose you're right. Lance has already got himself into trouble trying not to tattle on me; and he and his mother and Mary would never say a word about themselves or the rest, and I'm sure I shouldn't, and I know Levering wouldn't, and—"

"An' you're right back where you started from. I don't think any of you know anything, anyways, an' you all got too many brains, an' like the others too much to get yourselves tripped up. 'Sides, what motive did any one have for killin' Carson, here? You didn't, an' you're the only one that knew him, 'cept Tabitha from her stocks. An' she wouldn't choke him to death for that, though I can imagine at one time or another, she'd prob'ly have liked to make him eat his purple certif'cates. Nun-no. It don't work out."

Joan lighted a cigarette into the wind, waving aside Asey's offer of assistance.

"You forget I'm a native," she told him. "I can light m't'baccy 'thout histin' up a tent." She mimicked Syl's nasal tones to perfection.

"When you can do him," Asey remarked, "tellin' a tourist that 'them there ain't no clams, them's quohaugs,' with all the proper inflections, I'll buy you a cem'tery lot, an' then you'll be a real native."

"Rather have a wood lot," Joan said. "I always— Asey, what about that phone call Ben made here? Whom did he talk to? Everyone's so sure it was 'Miss' Howes, but— well, I hate to say it, but—"

"Could he have spoke to Suzanne? I dunno. I doubt it. Mary slept in the little room next hers, an' you can bet your boots Mary'd have known if Sue moved as much as an eye winker. She wouldn't of stole downstairs an' killed Carson even if she did take that call. But I'm sure she didn't. Some things you can be mercifully sure of, an' Sue's one."

"Lance, Mary, Tab, Levering and me. But if he spoke to a woman, Lance and Levering are out. And I heard most of Mary's conversation about a church fair, or supper, or something. Anyway, it was all about beans. And Tab— oh, Asey, this is the most circular thing I ever saw!"

"Circular's puttin' it mild. Joan, happen to know how much money Carson carried with him? He had a lot—"

He broke off as Lance and Levering appeared and seated themselves in the garden.

"Been grinding over the Newell papers," Levering remarked. "Can't find a thing more, but I've had a revelation. Just like a minor prophet. I remember where I saw Carson before. Only because I don't connect him and his name, I have a feeling he was using another. It was at an etching auction in New York last fall. Before Thanksgiving. I went over to get some things for dad. November sixteenth. I looked it up."

"Etching auction!" Joan looked at Levering in amazement. "Why, I didn't know Ben knew an etching from a lithograph! Are you sure?"

"Hawkeye never forgets a face. I never knew Lance at school, never even knew his name, but I remembered him at once as the lad who replaced Mark Adams in the third quarter of the Yale game three years ago. Didn't you, Lance?"

"Two plays," Lance said, "and I gave way to that big Swede from Chicago. But listen, Asey, isn't it possible that this etching business may cast a light? Perhaps old Bellamy sunk his fortune in a Raphael or a Titian or something—"

"Maybe," Asey said. "You might go an' peer underneath all the Currier an' Iveses an' the steel engravin's. B'gin with 'My Little Kitten' an' 'My Little Doggie,' will you, at the foot of my bed? If I stare at 'em another night, I'll be feedin' 'em cod liver oil. Either Currier had acute astigm'tism, or else Ives was c'nsumptive. Have to be, to turn out all them anaemic critters—"

"Wouldn't it be a joke," Lance said, "to find a Michel Angelo behind little kitty? After I've torn down the house, all but. Asey, you don't seem to take to this picture notion."

"Fly in the ointment," Asey said. "Wasn't any pictures in the stuff that come home. No pictures come later."

"And let me tell you," Levering added, "that my great-grandfather, esteemed gent though he was, with as fine a crop of whiskers as any Smith brother that ever lived, wouldn't have known a Titian from a Copley or a Stuart, and if he did, even his gorge would have risen at the thought of soaking Bellamy eight hundred thousand dollars for one. His idea of art was St. Cecelia at the organ, or Washington crossing the Delaware. No nonsense. I rather doubt, and I think you do, too, Asey, that Bellamy'd have paid any sort of money for a picture? Lance, just what came home in Bellamy's—what's the proper word? Effects?"

"A chest full of clothes, a few papers of absolutely no importance, his telescope, his gold scales, a few charts, his Bible and his best beaver hat. I haven't put 'em under a microscope, but I've done everything else. Once spent a week just sticking a needle through the beaver hat. Ouch—" He looked at his watch. "I got to beat it. Dinner date."

But somehow, Lance was still there even after Joan and Levering had gone into the house to get ready for dinner.

"Get a wiggle on," Asey said. "Chatfield's a great stickler for folks bein' on time. I went fishin' with him once. He—"

"Say, Asey, I want to ask you something. About last night, I—"

"About you an' Clare? I think you made a fine beginnin' about facin' facts," Asey told him cheerfully. 'Nothin' like marryin' the boss's daughter to sort of get a firm foundation. You'll have a job, an' make money, with a lot more in sight. Sue'll be able to get away from here, an' from the Keith's. Yup, it's a fine idea. Now—"

He was talking to empty air, for Lance was striding away in the direction of the station wagon.

"Did you fall," Asey murmured, "or was you pushed? Huh. Well, if you can crawl out of the twinin's of that flibberty gibbet, you'll come through anythin'. Sue's right. He got into it, let him get out if he wants to, an' can."

Broody Mary uttered much the same sentiments as she and Asey washed the dishes after dinner.

"Worried me some, let me tell you, last night. Then I says to myself, either that boy's no earthly use, or else he is, an' it's his business, either way. Asey, how far you got on this Carson mess?"

"Wa-al," Asey said reflectively, "I'm makin' a dif'rent b'ginnin'. 'Stead of sayin', Bellamy had X, I'm startin' out by sayin' that X is, an' in tracin' X, Carson found Bellamy. Dunno how. He didn't see the Newell papers, that's a cinch, or Bellamy's."

"Lance tell you that one diary of Bellamy's is missin'?"

Mary asked. "Well, 'tis. Last one in his chest is dated six months 'fore he died."

Asey raised his eyebrows. "'Tis? Where is the stuff? Up attic? I'd like to see it."

After the kitchen was burnished and polished and generally tidied up to Mary's drastic specifications, she led him up to the east attic, under the eaves.

It seemed to Asey, as he set down the kerosene lamp, that the place was alive with ships—there were ship models and ships in bottles, ships carved on blocks of wood, ships made of matches, ships made of ivory.

"For the love of Pete," he said, "why—Sue's got a fortune right here! Where they come from?"

"Bellamy an' Eben. Bellamy made lots. See, all his has got name plates, 'Patience.' Lots he got from his crews an' brought home. There's one over yonder that father give him. Rest, all the queer ones out of matches an' all, them's Eben's. His is all named Patience too, till he got married. Then they're Suzannes. She always called this her fed'ral reserve. Many's the time I seen her come up here an' look an' I knew she was figgerin' that just one or two dozen of the fifty odd'd lift the mortgage an' pay another term of Lance's schoolin'. But she never could bring herself to sell 'em somehow."

"Wonder the feller that ransacked didn't get up here."

"He did, in the other side of the p'tition, where there's the stairs. But I guess he didn't understand about this trapdoor end. Here's the chest."

Asey looked through its contents.

"Mary," he said, "somethin's missin' here b'side the

diary. Now, what'd your pa have in his chest that ain't here? I know it was the biggest moment of my life when I saved enough money to buy mine. Had a mermaid on it, an' a wreath of pink roses, an' the nicest little lock. Blind man could open that lock with a piece of putty. I found that out, first v'yage. An' that bosun had two good eyes an' a twist of wire. An' he skipped ship in Liverpool with my eighteen silver dollars an' a silver bouquet holder I was takin' home to my mother."

"Pink roses! Asey, I know what you mean! You mean a little tin money box! Father had one. 'Bout a foot long, an' ten inches wide, an' black—seems to me his had pansies on it. Why, I still got Uncle Ne'miah's to home. Use it for the best spoons. Why, sure enough! Bellamy'd ought to have a tin box. Prob'ly kept his diary in it. Say, I bet someone stole the box, an' the diary, too. Oh." Mary's jubilant tones ended on a dour note. "Oh. But if that happened in China, Carson'd never, never—nunno. That won't do it. Maybe, though, Carson *was* in China—no. Couldn't expect him to pick up that box, an' all, after all these years."

Asey sat down gingerly on a tiny calfskin trunk.

"But he wouldn't of had to find it in China, Mary. Y'know, once I found a sword in an ole Chink pawn shop in Honk Kong, an' it had Elisha Mayo's name 'graved on the back. He was my father's brother, an' the sword'd been stole from him in Wellfleet, when I was knee high to a grasshopper. Stole in Wellfleet, mind you, an' it turned up there! Well, if that can happen, it can happen the other way around."

Crossing his legs, Asey rested his chin on his hand and give himself up to considering possibility, and possibilities.

He enjoyed speculating. Most people were inclined to eye him quizzically whenever he began figuring, but then most people, Asey thought, set themselves up so many and such definite mental bounds that speculation held little pleasure and fewer results for them. People always stopped at some given point and said that the whole business couldn't happen, or, if it could, it wouldn't. People set physical limits based on their own physical capacity or incapacity; you could never really describe with conviction any strange scene to a blind man, although, oddly enough, he always heard things that a person who could see would scoff at. People set mental limitations; this or that had never happened within their experience, or they had never read about it, or even heard it on the radio. Others called themselves broad-minded, and admitted that anything *could* happen, and then set busily to work explaining just why it couldn't.

"Yup," he said, "if uncle's sword could turn up in a Hong Kong pawn shop, I guess Bellamy's box could turn up in a New York pawn shop, or even at a nice auction. S'pose Carson already knew about X, an' he got the box, an' somethin' in that diary led him to connect Bellamy an' X. An' by this last January he's already tracked down the Howeses, an' somehow he gets to the Newells. First step'd be to see if either fam'ly ever had X, or knew about it, or heard about it. They didn't. But Carson must've been pretty sure X was in existence, or he wouldn't of gone to all this trouble. Yup, he knew X was here, or at Tabitha's. Let's see. She has money, but not as much as she'd have if she had X. On the other hand, there ain't no trace of her knowin' or havin' or sellin' X. Howeses never had it, an' don't know. Too poor, altogether. Now—"

"Look, Asèy," Mary said anxiously, "wouldn't you like a nice cup of good hot coffee? Or *some*thin'?"

"I ain't crazy," Asey assured her. "Just broodin'. Now. Carson must have known what X was. Then why this ransackin'? Glotz an' Tab's Cockroach—ain't no doubt they was two of 'em, they must have known what they was after. On the other hand, would Carson of trusted 'em to bring X back to him, if it was so valuable, an' they found it?"

"I'm sure," Mary said, "I wouldn't be a one to know. Asey, you sure you wouldn't like a little coffee? It's wonderful, what a little coffee'll do—"

"I got it!" Asey slapped his knee. "I tell you to hunt for a cherry, say, but for all you know, by the time you hunt for it, the cherry may be inside a tart—I mean pastry tart, Mary. Don't look like that. Or it might be atop someone's spring bonnet. Sure, they knew up to a certain extent. Okay, Mary. Let's go down. I got somethin' figgered out, anyways. Sure. 'Member that line about Carson on the magazine? Millions of ways to make fortunes even durin' d'pressions. Sure they is. You snatch somethin' someone's got they don't know's worth anythin'. Bet he'd prob'ly gone in for treasure on the bottom of the sea, only it's cheaper on land. So—"

"Asey," Mary said patiently, "please, come down an'—who's down there at the foot of the ladder?"

There wasn't a soul in the hallway by the time Asey leaped down, but it seemed to him that the handle of Levering's door was turning.

Had he, Asey wondered, been listening to his half-baked theorizing?

There was a brief click as the door latch slipped into place.

Asey shrugged.

"Nobody here," he told Mary. "Come 'long an' make my coffee. The whole business is screwy, an' I sometimes wonder if I ain't, too."

They had been in the kitchen only a few minutes before Joan came in.

"Asey, you asked me this afternoon about the amounts of money Carson carried with him."

"Yup. His wallet was jamfull. I wondered if he always had a lot, or if this was a special occasion."

"He always carried ten one hundred dollar bills in his wallet. He had the same ten bills for years and years, —I think he even saved them from a shipwreck once. Then after this gold business, he had to turn them in. As he said, if he proffered ten gold certificates in some emergency or other, people would probably arrest him on the spot for being a kidnapper. We always sort of joked about them. The last thing I said to him before I left was 'Be sure to keep your mad money safe.' He said I could bet that he'd come back with it intact."

Asey lined up five lumps of sugar on the table, then pushed them into various formations.

"Sure of that?"

"Sure? Why, Asey, of course I am! I got to thinking about the bills, and it occurred to me that maybe, if they were missing, robbery might be a possible motive for killing him."

"True," Asey said thoughtfully. "True."

"Well," Joan sounded annoyed, "that's all. I thought I'd tell you."

"Thanks," Asey said briefly.

Joan surveyed him for a second, watching him fiddle with the sugar bowl, then turned on her heel and left.

She had nothing but the utmost admiration for Cape Codders, but there were times when Cape Codders proved just a little too much for her.

Asey lined up five more sugar lumps on the table, ranged all ten in pairs, then made a triangle with four at the base and one at the top. Then he reached into the sugar bowl and brought out five more.

Mary watched him, and the cream bottle nearly slipped from her fingers.

"Land's sakes!" she said. "You ain't goin' to use all them in one cup, are you? An' I'm sure no one wants to use sugar lumps after you been buildin' d'signs with 'em. P'ticularly after you just come out of the attic, where Lord knows I ain't had no chance to do any cleanin' this year!"

"Well," Asey said slowly, "it's a sort of a problem, as you might say."

"What's a problem, I'd like to know?"

"Whether to get you on pins an' needles, takin' five lumps at a time out of this sugar bowl, or to dump all the sugar out real dr'matic, an' wave them two hundred dollar bills that's in the bottom at you, an' ask you how come, an' why you put 'em in there, an' all."

16

Mary set the cream bottle noiselessly on the table, stood back, and folded her arms over her chest. She didn't want Asey to see her fingers shake.

"Two hundred dollar bills in that sugar bowl? What you mean? What makes you think I put 'em there? Asey, I never heard the like!"

Asey tipped out the sugar lumps that remained in the bowl, unfolded the two bills and spread them out on the table before him. From his coat pocket he produced a small red notebook, consulted a page in it and nodded slowly.

"Yup, that's them," he said. "I guessed when I seen the num'rals showin'. Ain't many bills that size wanderin' loose around this part of the world. They b'longed to Carson. Serial numbers trail along with those he had."

"What makes you think I put 'em there?" Mary's voice was steady, but it had lost its defiant note.

"You b'gun fiddlin'," Asey told her, "the second I touched that bowl. An' your eyes near popped out of their sockets when Joan begun talkin' about Carson's money. Mary, do I have to play act, or will you tell me the works, right now?"

"Play act? What you mean?"

Asey tilted back in his chair and rested his feet on the old pine cricket.

"Well, I can edge round an' round, an' work you into a hole till you have to tell me. I can talk about the p'lice, an' I can tell you what'd mean to Suzanne to have you taken off to jail, an' I can tell you how I'd feel if I had to have Bob—but I don't want to do any of that, Mary. I don't have to go at you the way I would at Simon Keith, or any of these boarders or summer folks or tourists. I don't have to make up any yarns to bring home to you that honesty's the best pol'cy, an' that in a thing of this sort, you might's well be honest first as last. You got sense enough to know all that."

He could see the whiteness of Mary's knuckles, and her folded arms rose and fell with her rapid breathing.

Asey fumbled for his pipe. He hated to talk like that to Mary. Outsiders and off-Capers, they were for the most part fair game. Their minds worked differently, and you had to bait them just so much before they'd break down and tell the truth.

But it was different with people like Mary. With them he was even surer of his ground, surer of the proper strings to play on to get results. Cape Codders were as clannish as any Highlanders, and it was partly that same clan feeling that made him dislike having to penetrate a reserve he respected and a pride which he shared himself.

He thought irrelevantly of Tabitha's summing up of Lance. Without doubt the boy would have marched jauntily to meet the Roman lions, and the whole business would have been one magnificent gesture. Mary would have set her mouth, gritted her teeth, and walked doggedly out into the arena—anticipating no miracles, singing no hymns, desiring no sainthood, but firmly convinced that—what was the way that poem went? "My own convenience counts as nil, it is my duty and I will—"

His involuntary smile had a curious effect on Broody Mary.

She sat down suddenly at the other end of the table, buried her face in her hands and burst into tears. Great racking sobs shook her angular body; it was almost, Asey thought, as though all the things she had wanted to cry about all her life, and hadn't, had come to her mind in one devastating whole.

She stopped as quickly as she had begun, and wiped at her eyes with a red-checked napkin from the table.

"First time I done that," she said ashamedly, "since I was ten years old, and father took me aft—it was on the schooner 'Albert G. Sekells,' in Kingston Harbor,— an' told me mother'd died. Never forgot that harbor. Water was just like pale blue glass, an' the blue mountains risin' up out of the mist, an' a bugle was blowin' like sixty on a British warship 'longside." She blew her nose on the napkin, shook her head as though to clear her thoughts. "Asey, I never done nothin' like that in all my life. Takin' that money, I mean. It's burned a hole in my pocket ever since, an' t'night I stuck it there in the sugar bowl, thinkin' it was the last place you or anybody else'd ever think of lookin' into. You don't hunt things in front of your face, like that letter—what's the name of that book?"

"Purloined letter, or somethin'," Asey said. "I know what you mean."

"Yup. Well, I'm awful glad you found that money, Asey. I—I'd of put it back, only I didn't have no chance. Lance was here, an' then the doc an' everyone, an' all— I'd of told you myself, only I was so awful ashamed that I just couldn't. I don't know what got into me. I come down that mornin'—seems like years ago, somehow,—an' I seen that man lyin' there, an' I went over to him an' looked to see who he was, an' seen his wallet in his inside pocket, where his coat was unbuttoned—oh, I'm so blessed ashamed to tell you, Asey!"

"You won't," Asey said wisely, "feel half so bad now you have told, Mary. After all, you was upset an' not yourself. Ain't just a casual thing, findin' a dead man in your kitchen in the mornin'."

"I hope," Mary said fervently, "I hope I never find another! Asey, I pulled out his wallet, thinkin' it might have his name, an' there was all that money—why, I don't know's I ever seen a hundred dollar bill b'fore in all my life, let alone ten of 'em to once! I don't know what come over me, but I took two of 'em. It was certain sure he had enough, if he carted all that round with him, an' it was just's sure he'd never need it. An'—why, Asey, I work here all summer for less'n two hundred dollars, though last year I got more b'cause of big tips. All my life I've thought how nice t'would be to have just a hundred dollars to spend. Not on things you need, but things you didn't need. An'—well, there it was, an' I took it. An' I'm glad to get it off my mind an' out of my hands! If just two hundred dollars makes you all the unhappiness that made me, I feel awful sorry for millionaires. Poor fellers, no wonder they always look so sour, in the newspaper pictures. Like they had indigestion. Land's sakes, I should think they would!"

Asey threw back his head and laughed.

"I mean it," Mary said. "I feel sorry for 'em. Why, it's a wonder they can eat anythin' but sody—when," she changed the subject abruptly, "when you goin' to have me arrested, Asey?"

"I'm 'fraid," Asey grinned, "that if you think your face's goin' to be smeared all over the papers as—as an arch crim'nal, you're goin' to be awful disappointed. Don't be silly! Money's back, ain't it?"

"But—why," Mary's eyes opened wide, "why I thought, why—when you found this money, I thought you'd say I killed him for it!"

"Know the Meth'dist church?" Asey inquired.

"Why, of course I know it! What's it got to do with this?"

"I'd just as soon think," Asey informed her, "of the Meth'dist church rearin' itself up on its hindlegs an' dancin' a good rollickin' rhumba, all by itself, as I would of you killin' Carson. I—oh, h'lo, Mrs. Newell."

"This tête-à-tête," Tabitha said, "has gone on just about long enough. People are beginning to talk, Mary. Asey, wander out and cast a few pearls before us."

"Sure," Asey pretended to pull at Mary's nose as he

left the kitchen. "I'll have my coffee later, Broody Mary. Stick it on the stove. 'Member what I said about the church, too."

Levering, who was playing Russian bank with Joan in front of the fire, waved a card at Asey.

"Don't ask me why I'm not at those papers. I've passed the buck to Suzanne. She's taken the whole lot to bed with her. Probably have perfectly ghastly nightmares. Check, Joan. Two of hearts—"

"I can see that boy," Tabitha remarked, "fifty years from now, draped in a wheel chair, and squeaking 'check' to the two of hearts. If the games of Russian bank I've been forced to play with my nephew were laid end to end, and buried, it would suit me beautifully. It's the only thing he ever learned from his first tutor except an Oxford accent, but he outgrew that."

"I can swim," Levering returned, "and I can play Russian bank, and I can look and act decorative. You mustn't blame me if I try to appear at my best, pitiful as it may be."

"You're a pretty good buckpasser, too," Asey said. "I don't think you give yourself full credit. Think of poor Suzanne, an' that shorthand!"

"I give myself plenty of credit," Levering said honestly, "but my aunt doesn't. She likes spectacular people and she finds me curiously drab. I resent it, but I can't do anything about it now. Got you again, Joan. King on the queen."

Tabitha sighed. "Come into the alcove, Asey, and tell me all."

Briefly Asey summed up his ideas about the possible tin box of old Bellamy's, and the possible diary, and its possible passing into Carson's hands.

Tabitha nodded as he concluded.

"It would work out that way, I think. You know, I've a book collector friend who spends half his life hunting around his friends' attics for a copy of 'Tamerlane.' I've often thought he makes friends only with people who have attics. Anyway, he spends the other half of his time wondering what he'd do if he found one. He thinks he'd deliberately filch it. Well, it's something of the sort with Carson. He knows, or knew, that something of value existed, he got on the trail, and landed here with the Howeses and me. And as you say, the only connection is Bellamy, and the only possibility of anything valuable that we don't know about lies in what he paid that money to grandfather for. Carson might have come here about that himself. But I wonder why, if you think he had men working on it? And if no one knows about this thing, why was Carson killed? Don't you feel the fine Machiavellian hand of Simon Keith in here, somewhere?"

Asey said frankly that he didn't know.

"Bob's men are workin' like dogs tryin' to find out all they can about Carson, an' this Glotz, an' they're lookin' pretty hearty into the lad that followed you, an' about your house bein' ransacked, an' all the cars Glotz had. They're lookin' into Simon. Found out a lot about him, by the way. Found out about how he learned his lip readin'. Seems he was a small time gambler. Pea an' shell games an' fair c'ncessions, an' all. Sort of a pre-war racketeer, small time. I can see how lip readin'd come in handy to him. They're all at work, anyways, an' we may get somewhere with the things they find, an' let me tell you, they're thorough. I got nice little tidbits about you an' Leverin' an' Joan. I didn't know you was a Newell that'd married another, though I might of figgered it out, an' I didn't know you'd lived in China. Lots of things I found out."

"Anthony was a remote cousin," Tabitha said, "and we were in China while he was in the oil business. We left years—what's that noise?"

"Rain." Asey got up and closed the windows. "Just a little rain."

"I don't call it a little rain," Levering remarked. "I call it a torrent, with thunder and lightning. Hope Lance isn't out in it."

"Lance is probably enjoying it to the hilt," Tabitha told him. "He loves storms. I suppose anyone brought up on this hill would either have to love storms, or die young. Personally," she winced as a clap of thunder seemed to envelop the house, "I'd prefer an early death. I'm going to bed and pull the covers over my head, and chew the pillow, which is the way I've managed to live through thunderstorms all my life. Good night!"

Levering and Joan continued their amiable bickering over the cards, and Asey amused himself by reading the newspaper accounts of Carson's death, wherein Carson was referred to as a Banker-clubman, a Millionaire-playboy, a Wealthy-New-York-Tycoon, and he himself was described as a Hayseed-detective, a Sailor-sleuth, a Picturesque-Cape-Sherlock.

"Poor hyphen," he murmured. "Huh, you know, Joan, you're a tycoon-dash-secretary, an' Leverin's a socialite-dash-playboy, an'—deary me! Wonder what Mary'd be? Brooder-maid sounds like somethin' for settin' hens. Comin' to bed, you two, or are you makin' a night of it?"

Joan yawned. "I'm sleepy as a pig, but I hate the thought of going to my tower room. I don't mind thunder and lightning so much, but that wind drives me to distraction. It also scares me to death. It moans like a sick cat, and rattles like a burglar, and crawls in the window like a snake, and—oh, I *am* sleepy if I can't describe the way that wind goes, and the way it makes me feel!"

Asey observed that she had given them a rough idea.

"Don't you worry, Joan. Hamilton's around, an' with Lance an' Leverin' an' Marvin an' me, you needn't get scared about the wind. We can't stop it, but we can see to it that nothin' dreadful goes with it. I wish," he peered out the window, "that Lance'd come back. Bad drivin', an' a storm like this last year tore up a lot of trees an' scattered 'em all over the road."

Lance, on his way back from the Chatfield house, was enjoying the storm as fully as Tabitha had predicted, but when he heard a tree crash behind him on the shore road, he prudently stopped the car in a clearing and waited. There might well be more trees down on the road ahead, and his car lights made little impression in all the downpour.

Pulling a blanket over his shoulders, he lighted a cigarette and leaned back and watched the lightning as it zigzagged over the bay. Before one flash ended, another was on its way. He could even see the buoys of the sail boats anchored off the club. He made out the lines of Chatfield's cruiser, and wrinkled up his nose.

There, he thought grimly to himself, was a mess he'd got himself into. Childish, that was what. He'd been a damn fool, blithering around, letting his mother support him, letting this Simon business go on, waiting around for Heaven to toss a job at him.

Asey had been right. It was high time he snapped out of it and looked at facts. But when he broached the job question to Chatfield, he hadn't for one instant dreamed that Clare went with it. And Chatfield had thrown the job and the girl at him at one fell swoop. He couldn't very well say "I'll take the job and thanks, but please, sir, I don't want your old daughter!" Of course he should have thrown the whole business over right then and there, and said just that, but Joan's barb about Carson and his opportunity-grasping, and Asey's scorn—he'd so wanted something to toss in their faces! So he'd stood and goggled, and look what came of it!

"Hell of a way to face facts, Lancelot," he told himself.

There was one fact he was sure of. He didn't want Clare Chatfield. Yet he had. He freely admitted that. He had wanted Clare, until he laid eyes on Joan. Levering, the old smoothie, had seen at a glance what an empty half pint Clare was, and made a dash at Joan. It had taken him longer, but he'd grasped the thought by degrees. Only it wasn't until Chatfield handed Clare to him on a silver platter that he realized it all. Playing around with Clare was like romping with a puppy. She always made him feel sort of big and he-man. But any girl that could look at a news-reel picture, as Clare had the night before, of a dog herding sheep, and hear the dog bark, and then say she didn't know that sheep barked!

A nice mess, that was what. Clare—why, he couldn't remember what the wench looked like. Lots of hair, and all. But he could shut his eyes and see Joan's face, and the curve of her chin, and the way her hair grew at the back of her neck, and the way her smile started, sort of slow. And the way her nose tilted, and the way her eyes shot sparks when she got mad. And her stocking seams— it occurred to him that Clare's were always crooked.

He began to laugh.

Tied for life to a girl whose stocking seams were crooked?

He laughed till the tears ran down his cheeks. It was good to laugh again. The last two days had been drab. No other word for it. Seeing Carson lying there, with those hideous eyes! He hadn't been lying when he told Asey how that affected him. Not one bit! And then worrying about Joan, and all that fool to-do about the keys, and barging into this Chatfield business. Made a fool of himself, and the wonder of it all was that Asey hadn't spanked him.

It came over him suddenly that no one had read any lectures to him. Probably all of 'em figured he could paddle his own canoe. Well, now that he could see how damn funny it was, maybe he could. Here were some facts, and now to face 'em.

Two more cigarettes, and he started the car. There was a sort of plan that might work. He chuckled as he drove up the shore road. Old smoothie Levering had a good thought about buckpassing. He'd look into that.

The lightning was still playing around the bay, but the rain had stopped. Even so, he had to go at a snail's pace along the marsh road, for the ruts were filled with water, and the moist soil underneath had turned to a gluey combination of mud and clay.

Half way across the marsh the station wagon skidded out of the ruts, lurched almost all the way back, then slewed to a stop with the rear wheels spinning. Lance, swearing fluently, tried to coax the car back, and then forward, but it stuck obstinately in spite of all his gentle manoeuvering and his violent words.

Opening the door, he peered out at the mud and really aired his vocabulary. He knew from bitter experience the routine he would have to go through to make the car budge an inch. He would have to go up to the house, and fetch burlap bags, and ashes, and an axe to cut down some bushes, and it would all entail considerable pushing and pulling and tugging and yanking. It took at least half an hour in the day time, with luck. Now—well, he'd just leave the damn car there, and set to work on it the next morning. Asey, or Hamilton, or someone, could help. Maybe they could tow it out. Odd, Lance thought, that Hamilton hadn't challenged him, for it was a part of his duty to scrutinize everyone who came anywhere near the hill. Probably out in the garage, out of the rain.

Lance stared at the mud. Nothing to do but plunge through it, still—he hesitated and surveyed his best white buckskin shoes. No sense ruining those, even if the space between the ruts was filled with blackberry vines. Iodine, as Broody Mary had informed him severely on similar occasions in the past, iodine was cheaper than a new pair of shoes, any day in the week.

He took them off, tied the laces together, slung the shoes around his neck and stepped out of the car just as one terrific bolt of lightning shot out of the sky and seemed to remain suspended over the bay; for a long second every detail of the whole marsh, and the hill, and the bay on either side was revealed as plainly as though a spot light had been turned on. He could see the fretwork on the gingerbread house, and the weathervane on his own garage, and the grill around the top of Bellamy's old light.

Lance blinked, looked again and leaped into the mud as though a pack of raging tigers had suddenly started to nip at his stocking feet.

His best white shoes splashed into a puddle, but he paid no attention to them. Blackberry vines ripped at his socks and tore the soles of his feet, but he ignored those, too. He had only one thing in mind, to get up to that hill just as fast as his legs could carry him there, mud and vines and thistles notwithstanding.

For in that flash, as he looked at the lighthouse, he had seen the unmistakable figure of a man, clinging to a rope just under Joan's window.

17

IF LANCE HOWES had ever displayed in any stadium just one fraction of the speed and dogged endurance that he showed on his mad sloshing across the marsh, no coach in creation would have yanked him on the second play. His name would have appeared on a dozen all-American lists instead of among the third-string backs.

Going up the hill itself was worse than crossing the marsh. The ground was sandy and humpy and covered with treacherous hog cranberry vines that came so near tripping him a dozen times that he took to the road, whose surface of crushed oyster shells slashed into his bare feet—his thin socks were behind somewhere in the marsh mud.

A hundred yards from the lighthouse, he stumbled over something—someone—and fell flat on his face.

His groping fingers came in contact with buttons, brass buttons, and the smooth outlines of a leather belt.

It must be Hamilton, lying there.

"Ham! Hamilton—"

But there was a knotted gag in Hamilton's mouth, and heavily-knotted cords bound both his wrists and ankles.

Lance lumbered to his feet and went on. No time to undo those, no knife to cut them—and Ham was either dead, or out cold. No time to find out now.

Underneath Joan's window Lance tripped again on a pile of rope. Something else there, too. Silk.

Joan's silk dressing gown. Lance felt cold all over.

The fellow had made off with Joan.

He never knew where he summoned up the breath to bellow for Asey, but he did, and pitched a rock from the rock garden at his own bedroom window.

The satisfying crash seemed to give him insight.

There hadn't been any car on the road, and his own beach wagon was effectively blocking that, anyway. Fellow had a boat. Must have. Snatching Joan off on a boat somewhere.

He picked up speed on the downhill slope to the beach. Unconsciously he left the wellworn path and took the short cut through the beach grass. One thing, he knew every inch of the hill. Fellow didn't. That would help some.

His legs wobbled as he crashed through the tall grass and came out on the sand.

For a second he stood still and listened. Boat was pushing off, to the left.

Lance raced toward the sound, plunged into the water. His outstretched arm grabbed the bow of a boat; he could see the bare outlines.

"Joan!"

Something swished through the air, and he automatically ducked. An oar glanced off his shoulder and splashed into the water. He groped for it, just caught it, and lunged at the figure in the bow.

The man grunted and fell back, and Lance clambered into the bobbling boat.

A merciful flash of lightning showed Joan on the stern floor boards, yanking at a gag with her fingers. Her wrists, like Ham's, were bound.

"Okay!" Lance sang out. "I'll get him—"

But the fellow was small and wiry, and wriggled out of his grasp like an eel.

"Stand still, damn you!" Lance yelled. "For—"

He planted his feet and rocked the boat, and then went for the fellow as he lost his balance; and suddenly Lance's own right thumb was caught in a vise-like grip, and he staggered back, yelling with pain. Jui jitsu, or something, the blasted shrimp—

The shrimp laughed pleasantly at Lance's summing up of his character and ancestry, and slid over the side into the water.

"Get him!" Joan finally worked the gag out of her mouth. "Get him! Get the brief case! Don't mind me—get that case!"

Wearily Lance dropped over the side and started after the fellow, but his feet wouldn't work. He landed flat on the water line, with his face in a bunch of wet seaweed.

Then he heard voices coming from the path, and saw flashlights darting and cutting through the beach grass.

They could follow the man, Asey and the rest. He was all in.

"Asey!" Joan added her cries to his. "Asey! Get the guy! Going up the beach! Up—get the brief case! Brief case! Don't mind us! Get him and the case!"

Asey yelled back some indistinguishable affirmation, and the flashlights turned up the beach. Lance watched them, and put his face back on the seaweed. It smelled like the devil, and there was a crab in it somewhere, and a dead squid, but its smells and clamminess didn't matter. It was cool.

"Lance!" Joan knelt down beside him. "Lance, are you —Lance—"

He forgot that his head was beating like a drum, and that his feet—there just wasn't any word to describe those feet. But he forgot them.

"I'm okay. Just—Joan, did he hurt—are you all right? You—you're shivering!"

"I'm sort of wet," Joan said in a small voice, "and sort of torn, what I do have on. Lance—oh! I'm still scared, and—"

Lance peeled off what was left of his white linen coat and draped it around her.

"There! You—you are sort of coming apart, too, aren't you?"

"It was sort of a—a skimpy nightdress to begin with—"

"Here, stick your arms through. I'll give you my shirt—"

"Can't stick my arms anywhere." Joan. said. "My hands are tied. I—" she sat down suddenly. "I'm going Victorian on you. I'm going to cry."

"No, you're not!" Lance took her in his arms. "You —oh, Joan!"

"I knew it was you before I—oh, Lance!" She pulled away from him and stood up. "Lance, you—ugh! Fish! Where *did* you—why, you sm—"

Lance threw back his head and laughed till he cried. After a minute, Joan joined in.

"There," he said at last, "that shows you the difference between fact and fiction. In fiction, there'd have been a tender interlude, and then I'd have told you all about my B.P. plan—"

"Your what?"

"B.P. plan. The Howes theory of recovery. And we'd have everything all ironed out and settled, and instead, a couple of dead squid come between us. Look, you sit down again, and we'll begin where you were going Victorian, and I'll whisper in your ear, and you whisper in mine— oh. Oh, for Pete's sake! Levering. Well, well. Hullo, Levering. Look, undo Joan, will you? She hasn't any hands. And then let's have your light. I want to look at what were my feet, once."

Levering cut the cord around Joan's wrist, and then focussed the flash on Lance's feet. Both he and Joan yelled at the sight.

"Lance! How on earth! Lance, don't they simply kill you? You can't walk—"

"No, Joan," Lance said resignedly, "I don't think I

can. I mean, there's a point beyond which feet will not walk, and mine got there years ago. This is another point in the fact-fiction problem, too. In fiction, Joan, I'd have carried you back triumphantly in my arms, and as it is, you and Newell'll have to make a chair."

"But Lance, however did you—"

"All for you," Lance said. "All for you. I didn't catch your snatcher, Joan, and I couldn't undo your hands, and I didn't put up much of a battle for you, and I can't walk home, but I meant well. My intentions were of the best. Lancelot Howes, thinking only of you."

In the end, he rode piggy-back on Levering's shoulders all the way to the house, but even that ignominious return didn't dampen his spirits. Joan had known he'd come— it sounded like the first line of a popular song.

He remembered Hamilton about the time Dr. Cummings was summoned to attend to his feet. Levering and Mary went out and helped him in.

"Not hurt," Hamilton said, "but mad as hell! He got me from behind, and then came back and sat on me as I was coming to, the punk!"

"I was the punk," Lance said. "Sorry, but you were in my way, Ham. I didn't really want to sit on you. Look, shall we try to explain this now, or wait till Asey gets back? And what about a brief case, Joan, and why were you being snatched?"

Joan, with one of Tabitha's jaeger dressing gowns draped around her like a tent, set down her glass of brandy.

"Well, I hadn't got to sleep. The wind was awful. And I kept saying that Asey was there, and all the rest, and still the wind sounded like someone coming into the room—how'd he get through the screen?"

"Cut it," Tabitha said. "I dashed up to your room when the window smashed. Who was that?"

"Me," Lance told her proudly. "That was me, spreading the alarm o'er every Middlesex village and farm. I was the window smasher—"

"Anyway," Joan interrupted, "first thing I knew the covers flipped off my bed and a gag went into my mouth, and my wrists and ankles were tied. Very deft, business-like job, all in the dark. Then he slung me over his shoulder and tossed something out the window—my brief case, and went down that rope like Dracula, with me dangling like a bag of meal! He undid my feet when we got to the ground, and jammed a knife in my back till it pricked, and told me to get along. I didn't argue. I got."

Hamilton nodded. "I know," he said feelingly. "This lad got me from behind—zip, one, two, three! And there I was. Quick as lightning, and sinister—"

"Don't," Joan said, "or I'll cry. Anyway, he got me in the boat, and then Lance appeared—"

"Chugging like Peter Cooper's first locomotive," Lance said, "but practically lousy with spirit. Unhand her, villain, said Lancelot, breathing fire—"

By the time Asey and Marvin returned, Suzanne and even Broody Mary, had begun to look on the affair as something pretty funny.

"Lost him," Asey informed them disgustedly. "Had him in clear sight, and my flash went dead, and he ducked into the bushes an' lay low, an' by the time Marvin got there, we was sunk. I got a good look at him, though, an'—"

"You know who it was?" Marvin broke in. "It was your man, Mrs. Newell! I mean, it was that one you used to call the Cockroach—"

"So Archie has come back into our life, has he?" Tabitha remarked. "Hm. You—dear me! You don't suppose that he thought, by some rare chance, that he was kidnapping me, do you? After all, if he'd started down any rope with me draped around his neck, it would have been his funeral, and very good riddance!"

Dr. Cummings, panting and red-faced, burst in on the entire company.

He was speaking his mind when he entered, and it was apparent that he had been speaking it for some time.

"And whoever had the audacity, the downright, forthwith nerve, the consummate gall, the—words fail me. But the next time you rout me out of a comfortable bed—at least, a bed with which I personally have found no active fault in all these years—the next time, I say, please see to it your damned road isn't full of abandoned cars! Tend someone's feet, forsooth! Tend my own, that's what! Look, will you? Cast your eye on my footwear! Look at me. Look at me, I say! It's my private opinion that every one of you has spent days—days? Nonsense. Years. Centuries. Centuries, just sprinkling that hillside with glue. Glue for old Doc Cummings to crawl up. Give the kiddies a laugh. Pull the old boy's leg—leg? Damn near had 'em pulled out of me! I tell you, I'm speechless! I never was so—for the love of God, Lance, at least I had the wit to keep my shoes on!"

After he got through, Lance looked, as Tabitha said, like a gouty uncle out of an English novel.

"All but the rest of your person. Now, if everyone's been aided and succored, let's get this settled."

"Let's," Asey agreed. "Let's get the 'sentials down. The lad that caused all this to-do was Archie the Cockroach, the one that p'sued Mrs. Newell up an' down an' round the narrow streets an' alleys of Boston. The handkerchief waver, number one."

"Why'd he want my brief case?" Joan demanded. "And me?"

"Well," Asey told her gallantly, "anyone might want you, but why they'd want your case is a dif'rent thing. What's in it?"

"That's what's so entirely incomprehensible," Joan said plaintively. "It's a mess of odds and ends I was going to take my time about straightening up this summer. There was a list of charity contributions to make out for income taxes, a couple of old routine reports to type. Not even to type, really. Just to make copies of. There was a bunch of bids for sandblasting the house. They came the day I left, and I never had the time to open 'em, even. Wasn't going to be done till fall. All the house bills to budget out, and expenses to list. Lists of sheets and pillow cases—we needed lots of new linen. That's all there was in it."

"Looked into it since you come?" Asey inquired.

"No." Joan shook her head. "I tossed it on the floor

of my closet the day I came, and it's been there ever since. Haven't so much as glanced at it."

"Did you so much as glance at it, ever, after you left?"

"Why, no, Asey. I just caught it up when I left New York, and carted it up to Boston, and down here. There really wasn't a single thing of value or importance in it."

Asey lighted his pipe.

"Did Carson have a brief case?"

"Half a dozen. We—oh! Asey, d'you think I might have his, or one of his, by mistake? Oh, but I couldn't, possibly. Bates gave it to me himself."

"Aha!" Asey crowed. "Bates did, huh? Now—now, Joan, we're gettin' somewhere. Go through it step by step, will you?"

Joan had come downstairs and gone into the library, the day she left, to say good-bye to Carson. She had brought the brief case down herself, and Bates and Beulah had carried the rest of her things to the hallway.

"Ben was sitting at the desk," Joan said, "and I wished him a pleasant vacation, and said all the things you usually say when you're going away, and joked about his mad money, as I told you, Asey. Then he asked for something —I think it was a carbon of a letter to some official or other in Washington, and I had some trouble finding it in the files. My filing system isn't so hot. By the time I found it, I had to rush. Bates hailed a cab for me, and put my luggage in, and then I remembered the brief case. I'd left it in the library. Bates dashed in and got it and brought it out."

" 'A,' " Asey said. "One. Some brief case, but not 'it.' That's the way it must've gone. He brought out Carson's instead of yours, an' that's why Carson started after you, an' why Bates tried to tell you somethin' the next mornin'. Huh. I wonder—"

"Undeniably," Tabitha said, "that's how that all went. Bellamy's papers were in it, I'll wager— Asey, you make things sound so simple that they have a certain lilt to them. But supposing that's so, where does Archie come in? How? Why'd he take Joan? How'd he know? And did he have anything to do with killing Carson?"

"Seems likely," Hamilton said, "considering the way that Archie rushes around with handkerchiefs and gags and all. And—"

"And jiu jitsu," Lance added. "He all but rent my thumb and body, with one tweak. Next time I lay hands on Archie, I'm going to rend him limb by limb, just for spite. Don't you think Carson's murder was some of Archie's work, Asey? Same technique?"

It was the same technique, and certainly, Asey thought, if Archie was one of Carson's henchmen, like the unfortunate Glotz, he would have more occasion for a motive for killing Carson than anyone at the hill.

"Just as slick," Hamilton went on. "All this business tonight. Waited for rain and wind and storms, too. Say, what about the boat? Maybe he'll get away in it—"

"Not," Asey said, "unless he paddles with his feet. That tender on the shore b'longs to—what's the fat friend of Chatfield's, Lance, the one with all the teeth?"

Lance blinked at the mention of Chatfield. Somehow

in the past two hours he had completely forgotten the existence of the Chatfield family and all his problems.

"Tubby Something—sort of like Smallbones, but more like Lawrance. No, begins with a B—"

"Tubby Shaw," Dr. Cummings said. "Sort of like Smallbones! Nonsense. Did he swipe Shaw's boat, Asey?"

"Uh-huh. Anchored off by the point. He come in to shore in the tender. Marvin an' I beached that—"

"But he can swim out."

"Oh, I sculled out first, an' jammed it up some. He'll p'form miracles, Archie will, if he ever gets that boat goin'. I called Bob, too. He'll carry on with the scourin'. Archie's a long ways from his car, I shouldn't wonder, an' he'll be plenty lost out back of the islands there. We'll pick him up."

"You sound very confident," Tabitha remarked, "and I've no doubt you will pick up Archie eventually. Only, if you don't mind, Asey, just see to it that he's picked up before he carts anyone else off, or garrots anyone else, or generally cuts loose. It appears to me that thus far, he's just been being playful with us. I'd hate the thought of his really getting mad. What with this screen cutting, and rope sliding—it's not human!"

"Oh, it's diabolical!" Suzanne said. "You might conceivably do something, if you were confronted with a man bearing a gun. At least, you know what to expect. But these soft-footed souls who slide around and grab you from behind! I know what it is, Ham."

"Take Carson," Ham said. "No bullets left to dig out and find out about. No knife wounds to say, 'This blow was struck by a left-handed man six feet tall, and the knife was thus and so.' Not a clew, not a trace of anything. Nothing for us to work on. Why, you could pick up the bandanna he gagged me with at any five and ten!"

"Thoughtless thing!" Asey murmured. "Not a clew!"

"Fiddlededee!" Tabitha said. "Perhaps you've found clews, Asey Mayo, but no one else has! And you've got to admit it's pretty infernally clever, this garrotting."

Asey had long since admitted that fact to himself, and he said as much.

"Nifty, takin' it all in all. I always thought a nice bash was the neatest way to kill anyone. Pick up somethin' an'—whang! Somethin' at hand, like a candlestick, or a book, or a vase. In a room full of things, someone'd have a hard time even figgerin' out what you used. But this business is quicker, an' surer, an' quieter, an' just as hard afterwards, an'—"

"Bloodthirsty buccaneer!" Tabitha said. "Don't look that way at that candlestick, as though you—uh! I'm going back to bed, and I'm going to lock my windows, and push a bureau against the door. If I wasn't thoroughly scared before, I am now, with all your talk! Come along, Sue. You too, Joan. If you ask me, Deathblow Hill is beginning to live up to its name!"

Levering helped Lance to the couch, and with Asey and the doctor assisting, made a makeshift bed and got him into pyjamas.

"This is the life," Lance said. "Three valets. I'm coming up in the world. When can I walk again, Doc?"

"Few days. Asey, I want to talk to you—"

"How exact he is," Levering remarked when he and Lance were alone. "Talk *to*, not *with*. No one's told you, Lance, but you did a pretty swell piece of work tonight. I mean it."

"Seemed noble at the time," Lance admitted, surveying his bandaged feet, "but I got my doubts, as Mary says. Damn fool. I should have waited and told you all what was going on, instead of dashing after Archie myself. You and Marvin and Asey'd have made quick work of him."

"Maybe. But you got Joan back. That—well, good night. Tell Mary to let me know when you want to get up. Maybe I can help."

"Thanks," Lance said.

So Levering was only interested in getting Joan back. That wouldn't do.

"Oh," he added, as Levering left, "Clare asked for you tonight. Seems to think you're sum'pin'."

"Too awfully divine," Levering returned coolly. "I know. She's told me ten times."

Lance lay back and sighed. The B.P. plan wasn't going to be anywhere near as easy as he had hoped. But something would turn up. It had to.

"Aren't you," Dr. Cummings asked Asey, out in the kitchen, "going to have the common decency to offer me a bed for the night? If anyone thinks I'm going to batter this body of mine down that hill—of course, I could always sit in a dishpan till I got to the marsh, but even so, I wouldn't plough across that marsh tonight if all six of my prospective confinement cases were howling on the other side. And my car's stuck worse than Lance's. Where are you going?"

"Gettin' the roadster to take you back."

"But you'll—"

"Nope, I shan't get stuck. I got them silly soft tires, an' they'll get through. They got through worse'n that marsh last fall when I went duck huntin'. I'll stop an' see Ham an' Marvin. They got to keep their eyes peeled. I don't think Archie'll come back, but he's slick enough to figger we wouldn't expect him."

"What d'you really think of all this?" the doctor asked as Asey successfully crossed the marsh.

"I'm hopin'," Asey said, "that Bates'll come to soon enough an' long enough to do some clearin' up. I'm countin' on him. If he don't, we're sunk for sure. That feller don't know the prayin' that's goin' on for him. An' if he's the game little feller I think he is, he'll pull through just on purpose to help."

Whether it was his prayers or Bates's determination, somehow he did pull through.

Asey yodelled at the message that came from the hospital the next noon.

"Bates wants Miss Joan. Says it's important."

18

Joan involuntarily wrinkled up her nose as she and Asey entered the hospital later that afternoon.

"Scared," Asey inquired, "or what? I know this ain't goin' to be much fun for you—"

"It's not that at all," Joan returned. "It's that elusive institution odor. You know, disinfectants and cooking and faded flowers. It varies from place to place, but I always seem to smell it, and it reminds me of one of the most hideous months I ever spent. In a London nursing home with a broken leg, while mother scoured Spain for something or other. Shawls or needlework, I forget which. That home had the steamiest cooking and the fadedest flowers and the starchiest nurses— Asey, does Bates know?"

"About Carson? I think he must, but we'll find out for sure before we go in to see him."

Bates's nurse, a fat friendly little soul, pounced on Asey and led him away, and Joan commented on it when he returned.

"Thought you said you didn't know a person here, you big fraud, and that woman greeted you like a long-lost brother!"

"Never set eye on her till I come in that door," Asey answered, "but it seems her name's Dyer, an' her mother's father's brother married a kind of aunt of mine—oh, well, we won't get all 'nvolved with Cape r'lationships at this point. Just put her down as a sort of fourth cousin couple of times r'moved. She says Bates knows all about the murder. Knew before he come here. Doctor's with him now. We'll—here he is. We'll get to Bates after we seen him a few minutes."

But the few minutes lengthened into half an hour. The doctor, it seemed, was a Paine on his mother's side, and Asey's great grandmother was a Paine, too. At least, that was Joan's impression, but she wouldn't have been sure. These casual genealogical intervals, during the course of which people reeled off the names of their great-great-grandfathers' fourteen brothers and sisters without once hesitating, baffled Joan completely. Most of her acquaintances, she reflected, spoke but little of their parents, barely mentioned their grandparents, and further data couldn't probably be wrung from them at the point of a gun.

"Well," the doctor said, "that's settled. Must have been either the second Isaiah or the other Ezekiel. Don't excite Bates any more than you can help, you two, but let him relieve himself of whatever it is he's got on his chest. He's burning up with things to tell Miss Howes—you a Weesit Howes, by the way?"

Asey explained hastily that Joan was only a recently discovered Howes, and not really up on her family tree.

"Where is it we go, Doc?"

"Second floor, second door to the right."

Asey took Joan's arm and propelled her out the door before the doctor had time to ask if Joan were a Neck Howes or a back-of-the-Islands Howes.

"Right on the tip of his tongue," Asey whispered as they mounted the stairs, "an' he looks real disappointed to've lost his chance. Like we'd interrupted him in the middle of a good sneeze. Here we be—"

Joan's startled cry at beholding what was visible of Bates under the miles of bandages and adhesive tape was more or less drowned out by Bates's exclamation of joy.

"Miss Joan, Miss Joan! Oh, thank God you've come! And you're all right! Oh, it's been awful, not knowing and not being able—" he looked at Asey and broke off.

"That's Asey Mayo," Joan reassured him, "and he's been awfully good to me, and to you too, if you only knew it. He got you here, and took charge of everything—"

"Asey Mayo, the detective? Glotz said you were the one that followed us. He'd been told of your car and knew. Oh, Miss Joan, I've worried so, since the day you left. And then—"

"Look," Asey drew up two chairs, "look, we got all the time in the world, an' so of you, an' they's about fifty million things I want to know about, an' we been ordered not to rouse you too much. S'pose you let me ask you questions, an' you answer, an' that'll make it easier all 'round."

"That's a fine idea," Joan chimed in. "I know you have a lot to tell me, Bates, but you let Asey ask questions and then you can sum things up or correct his impressions."

"Yes—but the brief case! Did they get it, Miss Joan? Did they hurt you? Did—"

"Now we're gettin' somewheres," Asey said with satisfaction. "They got the case, Bates, but—say, what's in the blessed thing, anyhows?"

"Why, a small tin box full of papers all about a sea captain, and some papers of Mr. Carson's, all about what he was after on the Cape."

"A tin box! An' papers!"

Asey leaned back in his chair.

A tin box. His guess had been right, but to think that the tin box and the papers, and the solution to the whole business, had been in that brief case on the floor of Joan's closet even before he'd thought of Bellamy Howes and the tin boxes and the rest! Everything, right there in their hands, all the time!

"An' Archie's got it," he muttered. "The—"

"Archer?" Bates said eagerly. "Is Archer down here? He got it? I—"

"Is his name Archer?" Asey demanded. "Honest? Joan, won't Tabitha howl! Just a typ'graphical error, that's all she made. Bates, this is goin' too fast for you an' us. Look, you took Carson's case, an' give it to Joan, thinkin' it was hers. An' then Carson found out—how soon later?"

"About half an hour. He—oh, I never saw anything like it, Mr. Mayo! He was—why, I thought he was going to burst like a balloon! He kept saying 'House, House, and I never guessed! That face and that name!' I thought he'd gone crazy."

"Her name's Howes," Asey explained, spelling it out. "Not House. Huh. Carson must of said it outloud, that Joan House had the Howes papers, an' guessed, b'cause all the dope about ole Bellamy was in the brief case. He thought she'd got wise, an' swiped the case an' skipped. N'en what?"

Then Carson had grabbed Bates and shaken him till his teeth rattled, and demanded Joan's address. Bates knew, but he didn't tell.

"I just said I thought it was New England she was going to, or maybe Canada, but he yelled that it was Cape Cod, and he knew it, and he pushed me away so hard I fell on the floor. I honestly thought he'd gone mad. Then he went to the phone and started making calls to Boston and Cape Cod, and sending telegrams, and those gave me the creeps."

"Who was they all to, the calls and the wires?"

"Archer, and Glotz. They worked for him, you see, and—"

"How dumb I was!" Joan interrupted. "There I made out two checks every week to Glotz—probably one was for Archer! If I'd an ounce of sense, I'd have guessed, or at least seen through some of it, but I never did!"

"There were a lot of things you didn't know about, Miss Joan! Beulah and I often worried for you, for fear you might find out more than was good for you."

Bates couldn't remember the telegrams exactly, but Carson's instructions to Glotz and Archer were much alike. They were to get hold of Joan's brief case, at any cost.

"What got me," Bates went on, "was the end of those wires. He said they weren't to use force unless they had to, but to get her and that case, and that he was coming up to see to it that they did."

The violence of his fury struck terror into Bates's heart. He liked Joan, because she reminded him of his daughter, and because she had always been kind to him, and it seemed to him that it was his own fault that she was in any danger.

He tried to explain to Carson that the switching of the brief cases was his mistake, that Joan had no intention of stealing the case, but Carson knocked him down and told him to shut up.

"He said it didn't matter if she stole the case on purpose or not. He yelled at me and said she'd know all right the minute she looked inside, because of the picture. I still don't know what he meant."

"Prob'ly had a picture of Bellamy's mother," Asey said. "Joan looks like her. Yup, I can see where he'd of hit the ceilin', after havin' Joan in front of him for years, an' never recognizin' her looks or her name either. But after all, why should he? No reason for c'nectin' her, a Western girl named House, with a Cape sea cap'n named Howes. Then what?"

Then Bates had talked the matter over with Beulah, the cook, and both thought that Joan should be warned. Both knew all about Glotz and Archer, and knew they would carry out their orders to the letter.

"I wanted to wire her at Miss Atterbury's," Bates said, "but I was afraid she'd never understand, or that she'd get curious and look into the things in the brief case, and her knowing what was in it would make it just as bad, if not worse. So I slipped out and took the midnight to Boston. I told Beulah where I was going, and Carson must have bullied her into telling him."

Asey nodded. Joan had thought that was how Carson had got her address to send the wire Monday night.

"I'd never been in Boston," Bates said, "and I had a hard time finding the address. And I was sure I saw Archer at the station, and that made me cautious."

"Carson prob'ly posted him to watch for you," Asey agreed. "Maybe he was there himself, too, for all we know. N'en you went to Atterbury's? Sneaked in the back way? Yup. An' then, just as you found Joan—whoof!"

Whoof, apparently, was the word to describe what had happened.

Bates had come to in the room of what appeared to be a boarding house on the Boston water front. Archer was there, and so was Carson.

"Just what," Asey inquired, "what was your r'lationship to Carson, anyway? You seem to of took a lot from him, an' took it awful easy. Why?"

"Matter of a check," Bates confessed. "He had several of mine. At least, several I'd happened to have signed. I—I was occasionally of use to him in that way, I'm sorry to admit."

Joan opened her eyes wide. Bates was a forger, was he? What kind of a place had she been living in the last three years?

Bates proceeded to enlighten her.

"Glotz was just a thug, a paroled gunman," he said. "No brains to speak of. But Archer's a different sort. There's a dangerous man! Never even had his name on the blotter. Clever. Probably more dangerous with his scarves than Glotz was with a Tommy gun."

Joan swallowed hard.

"We gathered Archer was a handy lad," Asey said. "Huh. Wonder if he—huh. Why yellow handkerchiefs, Bates? Why not pink or blue or candy striped?"

"Yellow? Oh. Why, Beulah used to buy his handkerchiefs, Mr. Mayo. Those handkerchief scarves. She liked yellow. I guess that's why."

Asey leaned back and laughed till the fat little nurse poked her head in the door and waggled an admonitory finger at him.

"She liked yellow!" Asey said weakly. "Liked—why'd she? Oh, I get it. Archer liked a special kind of handkerchief, huh? One that'd fold easy. Silk. Good an' strong. Was they like this?"

He pulled from his pocket the yellow scarf that Broody Mary had found on the hill and given him Tuesday morning.

"That's it."

"Then he and Glotz used the same kind of handkerchiefs? But I thought Glotz was a gunman."

"He was, but Archer showed him all his tricks. They both had the same kind of scarves. Carson thought it was a clever idea. Quick and quiet, and left no clews. Anyway, so Beulah got the handkerchiefs for them. She knew a place downtown and it was safer for her to buy them."

"Huh," Asey said. "An' I was almost thinkin' of lookin' up in the 'ncyclopaedia to see if yellow handkerchiefs meant anythin' special! Go on about when you come to."

"Carson didn't hurt me," Bates told him. "Just said to be myself and keep my mouth shut, and I did. But they handcuffed me. Carson knew very well I'd warn Miss Joan if I got the chance. Glotz had his own car down on the Cape, but he had another in Boston, so Carson took that and me, and we drove down Tuesday. He gave me over to Glotz after we got here. I don't know just where."

"Carson'd followed you to Boston by plane, of course," Asey said.

"Yes. Archer, he stayed in Boston—"

"Ransackin' Tabitha's house. Yup. Say, what would of been the idea of brandishin' them scarves around? To scare folks?"

"Perhaps. They wanted to get into someone's house in Boston," Bates said. "I don't know whose. Anyway, Glotz tied me up, Tuesday night, and went off. He came back with enough drinks inside him to be very talkative. He bragged to me that he'd gone through a house earlier in the day—"

"Clears up Sue," Asey said. "Go on. Didn't mean to cut in again. Say, where was you, by the way? What place?"

"In a shack, I think it was in Weesit."

"Good. Then everythin' that went on down here was done by Glotz. He was the feller that Mary seen on the hill, an' the one that ransacked the place, an' went for Sue, an' stole Obed's stuff, an' all. Archer did the dirty work in Boston, with Tabitha, an' he took you last night, Joan, an' cleaned out Simon's house. Must have. Go on."

"Glotz told me he was going back the next day to do the job right, in the house he'd been in. He said Carson and Archer were fools, that if there was so much money in all this, they might as well get the people out of the way. He said Carson's orders weren't to kill anyone, and it was all nonsense. I gathered, Mr. Mayo, that he and Archer were sick of doing Carson's dirty work, and they had some plan of their own up their sleeves."

"Double crossin' him, huh? Well, I don't wonder at it."

"Neither do I. Well, Glotz slept for a few hours, and then got up and took the sedan and went off. It was noon before he got back, and he was in the coupe Carson and I had come in. He said he'd started for Provincetown and the sedan broke down, and he'd picked up a truck, and seen the coupe in a barn, and got out and taken it that morning. I asked what about Carson, and he said the hell with him, he'd decided to ditch Carson and play this game his own way. He fed me and then went off again, and when he came back that afternoon, he was nearly as crazy as Carson had been. He bundled me into the car and drove off. Didn't seem to know where he was going or why."

Finally Glotz stopped the car and poured out the story of what he'd discovered; that Carson had been murdered, early that morning, on Deathblow Hill.

"He said Archer was in Boston, and too clever to get mixed in it all, but that was the place he'd been the day before, and where he had to grab a woman. I asked if he thought Archer had killed Carson, and he said there wasn't a chance of it. Glotz had called Boston, when he first heard, and Archer's landlady told him Archer had come in at two in the morning, and went out around six. He said he knew her, and she wouldn't lie to him."

Glotz had raved around for an hour or more, and then he started up the Cape.

"By then he didn't dare let me out," Bates said. "He didn't want me, but he didn't dare dump me or kill me. He decided to start back to New York, and then he changed his mind. Then a car started after us. I recognized you, Miss Joan, and Glotz said the car was Asey Mayo's. That was the last straw, for him."

Asey wanted to know if Glotz knew the roads, or had simply enjoyed a streak of dumb luck.

"Luck, I think. He was all to pieces. He thought he was safe when he got that Porter, and when he found that didn't help—I tell you, he went for that train on purpose. I never expected to get out of it alive."

"Well," Asey said, "that's cast considerable light, that has. Now the big thing is, what was in the brief case? I know 'twas papers an' all, but did they tell what Carson was after? Do you know?"

Bates shook his head.

"Carson and Glotz wouldn't tell me. Carson just laughed when I asked, but I got something out of Glotz. He said the reason they were ditching Carson was because they were tired of pawing around vases and jugs and boxes to find one that was heavy when they didn't know—"

"Vases and jugs and all!" Joan said. "What in the name of all that's—"

"They're as sensible as pictures," Asey remarked. "Well, it's makin' some sense."

To him, at least, it was.

Carson, on the trail of something valuable—perhaps it was a vase or a jug or a box, but Asey recalled his reasoning about the cherry and doubted it. A piece of bric-a-brac that was unusually heavy might well mean one that had something valuable imbedded in or attached to it. Anyway, Carson had landed on Bellamy's tin box and diary, had set Archer and Glotz to work to discover if either the Newell family or the Howeses had the slightest knowledge of this valuable thing, whatever it was. Finding that they obviously hadn't, he had set his two men to work ransacking. In some form or other the valuable thing must still exist. Carson wouldn't have continued, or taken such risks, if he had not been positive. Then the episode of Joan and the brief case had shot everything sky high.

"So you don't think Glotz killed Carson, Bates?"

"No, sir! That was what got him so. That the one murder, as you might say, that he wasn't responsible for, should be the one in which he had the greatest chance of being involved. He was afraid they'd spot some clew where he'd been prowling around things, or else spot the coupe as Carson's. He hadn't a chance. He kept saying that over and over, that he hadn't a chance. He didn't know anyone who could get him off, up here, and he couldn't have explained anything, like hunting for vases and so on. Don't you really know what Carson was after?"

"What he was after," Asey said, "an' who killed him, an' what for, they seem to be the only things we can't piece together. You're sure it wasn't Archer, either, who killed Carson?"

"Glotz was sure."

Asey nodded.

The murder did look like some of Archer's work, but after all, it had been someone inside the Howes place who had made a date to meet Carson, and who let him in. He said as much, but Joan disagreed.

"Look at the way Archie—Archer, or whatever he is, crawled into my room last night!"

"But," Asey pointed out, "he had to cut the screen. There wasn't a trace of anythin' like that, Wednesday mornin'. Nope, it all boils down to who took that call, an' who let him in. Anyways, we know who 'tis we're up against right now, but blessed if I know what they'd get him for if they caught him. Can't 'rest him for trailin' Tabitha, or messin' up her house, 'cause we ain't got any proof of either, though we know it was his work. No prints at Simon's, Bob says. An' even though he started to kidnap you, Joan, he didn't. An' I doubt kind of s'vere doubts about our ever findin' that brief case. Well, we'll be gettin' back."

Bates protested that there were many more things to tell.

"I don't doubt it. They's dozens of little odds an' ends left. But that's enough for today. Save the rest. I got to get home. Think it's goin' to be a good plan to pepper the hill with men. Brother Archie seems to be the sort of feller you could take pains with. I—"

The friendly nurse opened the door and poked her head in again.

"You stayed long enough," she announced cheerily. "Besides, someone wants you on the phone, Asey."

It was Levering on the other end, speaking from the hill.

"Asey, did you just call us?"

"Call you, in Weesit? No. Why—"

"Well, someone did. Suzanne answered. She thought it was queer. Said the fellow didn't sound a bit like you. But it came from Hyannis. He said he was you, and wanted to know how many of us were on the hill, at that precise moment, and who—"

"Tell him?"

"No," Levering said. "She was pretty suspicious of the whole business. But she did ask if Bates had told Joan anything, and then he cut off. I had an idea that it might be the Cockroach trying to take another whack at Joan, and thought you ought to know."

"How long ago this all happen?"

"Ten minutes or so. We had to hold a parley to figure out what to do."

"Bob there?"

"No, but Ham's sitting outside with a sawed-off shotgun on his knees, and Marvin's striding around, gripping his brass knuckles, and there are a couple of other troopers wandering around. Oh, and dear Clare's here, with Rupert."

"You hold the fort," Asey said. " 'Bye."

The top of his roadster was up. It was possible that Joan wouldn't have been seen leaving with him, or at least, couldn't have been recognized.

Asey turned back to the telephone and fished in his pocket for a coin. It would be just as well to call the local police and see if they'd give him an escort for the trip home. Perhaps Archie had done some figuring, decided that if Joan were a Howes, and if the other members of the Howes family knew nothing, possibly she might. And as Bates had remarked, once Archer had his mind made up, he was a hard man to sway.

And while he was about it, he decided as he fitted a nickel into the slot, he'd ask for someone to stay at the hospital with Bates. He'd told Bob to see to it, but apparently Bob had forgotten.

His requests were instantly granted. An officer in a car would be delighted to see that Asey and his passenger reached home safely, and another man would come to the hospital at once.

"Thank you—" Asey never finished the polite little speech he had ready.

From upstairs came Joan's voice.

"Asey—Asey—quick!"

19

Asey flung back the half-open door of Bates's room with such force that he had to throw up his hand to keep it from slamming in his face.

Joan—Joan was all right. Asey sighed his relief. White and scared, she was, but no more so than Bates.

"What—for Pete's sakes, what's wrong?"

"Archie!" Joan began.

"Archer!" Bates said.

They both began to talk at once.

"Wait up!" Asey ordered. "Whoa—now, Joan, heave ahead. Archie was here."

"He knocked!" Joan said. "Knocked at the door! We thought it was the nurse and said come in, and he did, and it was Archie! Asey, go after him! Go—"

Asey sat down on the arm of an easy chair and grinned.

"Archie knocked at the door p'lite like, did he, an' come in? Brandishin' hankies, or scarves, or—"

"Nothing at all! He was smiling! Asey, see if you can't get him!"

"Look," Asey said, "I chased that bird two hours,

more or less, last night. I ain't so young as I used to be, an' after that war whoop of yours, he's prob'ly miles an' miles away. That yell'd of scared the dead clean out of their graves. Where's the nurses?"

"Oh, they're chasing him, and an interne is—"

"Well, then, no sense my chasin' too. So, just let me get this straight. Archie come in here, peaceful an' p'lite—make any passes at you?"

"No. He said hello to Bates, and then I yelled—"

"Just," Asey observed, "just dropped in for a neighborly chat, I s'pose. Maybe he wanted to know what time it was. Huh. Well, see where he went?"

Three breathless nurses crowded into the room.

"He went down the fire escape and over into the next street, and away in a car! We think he was in the empty room next door all the time—"

Asey nodded. If Archie had followed him and Joan to the hospital, that was highly possible. He could have slipped down stairs and done his phoning—after all, Joan had said little, her voice was low, and Archie might not have been sure she was in the room. They had slipped in the hospital by a side door.

On the other hand, maybe Archie had tracked them by Asey's car parked outside, and had not actually seen their entrance. That seemed more logical.

"What d'you make of it?" Joan demanded. "Bates, tell him what you said. What you thought—"

"In Boston, Tuesday morning," Bates said, "just as I was coming to, Carson and Archer were talking about Miss Joan. Carson said he was going to try to explain things to her, at least, as much as she'd need to know, and he thought she'd be reasonable. Archer said Glotz told him the Howeses were poor, and he thought they might get them to trail along, if it worked out."

"I get it," Asey said. *"That's* why Carson phoned the hill the other night. 'Madame, I got somethin' of int'rest to tell you'—uh-huh. An' Archie, here, has come round to the same c'nclusion, that after failin' with his snatchin' last night, it might be nice to try m'lasses. More ways of killin' a cat than chokin' it t'death with sour cream. 'Miss Howes, I got a vital message for you.' Yup, that'd do it."

"That's it!" Bates said eagerly. "I was going to tell you about that, and forgot, with all the rest. I think Archer was going to try and compromise. See what Miss Joan knew, and split with her if she'd help. That morning, Carson asked what about the Newells, and Archer said there wasn't any chance of working with them, or her. And Carson said he had a feeling that his name wouldn't help with Mrs. Newell."

"Not exactly." Asey chuckled. "Not after them purple an' mauve stocks. Yup, Archie's thought it over, an' is goin' on another tack. Huh. Wonder if he's gone after Simon. There'd be a case of two of a kind. Huh. Guess we'll be runnin' along, Joan. I sort of hate to think of any Simon Keith an' Archer combine. An' I been havin' thoughts about Simon, too. I got ideas about him, an' I don't want 'em to spoil. Bates, there'll be a feller here to look after you. We'll see you t'morrow. Hop along, Joan."

They set off for Weesit, with the police escort trailing along behind. His car was no match for Asey's.

"Then you think Archie won't try to kidnap me again?" Joan asked.

"If he didn't try when he had the chance, it seems unlikely. As I said, I think he's guessed again."

"What about Simon?" Joan wanted to know. "It's seemed to me all along that that yarn of his about being out on some boat was awfully fishy."

"Fishy but true, more's the pity," Asey slowed down to give his guard a chance to catch up. "I double checked that, an' so's Bob. Nope, it all comes back to who took that call from Carson, an' who let him in."

"In all of which I figure so prominently," Joan said. "Asey, who but me had a motive for killing Carson, in that house? Not that I did, to be sure, but I'm the only one who knew him, except for Tab, through her old stocks. You'll have to go through us one by one, Asey, and find out. Somehow the thought makes my blood run cold."

"Uh-huh," Asey said.

He knew perfectly well the futility of trying to check on the occupants of the Howes place from the time they went to bed Tuesday night until Wednesday morning. The storm and the wind and the rain had any such a thought beaten right from the start. He knew Lance hadn't left the room. Suzanne and Mary checked each other. Marvin was out, anyway. Levering—no, that wouldn't work. Nor Tabitha. He believed Joan.

There just wasn't any way of getting anywhere by the where-were-you-from-two-to-four method. And as he had said before, they were all nice intelligent people, and would lie like mad to keep any of the others from being involved. There wouldn't be any sense in trying to stir up a hornet's nest and get them mad at each other; they wouldn't tell then, either. They'd see through the trick before he had his plans organized.

And that phone call. That was almost more puzzling than who let Carson in.

"How were the fingerprints in the kitchen erased?" Joan wanted to know. "Have you gone into that?"

"Bob has. Someone used a damp cloth. Carson's own white linen handkerchief, I think he said. There's a bottle of bicycle oil on a shelf there, an' that's what someone rubbed over the bolts. Nope, no matter where we go, we come right back home again with our tail b'tween our legs. Who let Carson in, an' who took that call? When an' if we find out them, we may find who killed him."

They found Syl Mayo sitting out in the kitchen when they reached the hill.

"Slacker," Asey greeted him. "Where you been?"

"Jennie made me finish my Eastham job," Syl said plaintively. "She—well, you know how she is, Asey!"

Asey chuckled. Syl's wife was built like a brick house, and towered over him by a good eighteen inches. She had been known to pick Syl up bodily and enforce her wishes with a razor strop.

"It's no laughin' matter, Asey Mayo!" Syl thrust out his chin. "Let me tell you, I done the work of twelve men t'day! How's things comin'?"

"They ain't."

Briefly, Asey caught Syl up on what had been going on. Near the end of his recital, Tabitha came out into the kitchen.

"Finish up," she said. "Don't leave Syl hanging in mid-air because of me. I've nothing to contribute."

Syl allowed, after Asey was through, that he didn't know as he had any suggestions, either.

"Seems to me though," he said, "that we ought to find somethin'. Ain't nat'ral, not havin' any clews attall. Ain't right."

He sounded so aggrieved about it that Asey and Tabitha laughed.

"It's like that pie Jennie made from that radio crooner's recipe," Asey told him. "It wouldn't of happened in a book. This wouldn't. It's got a sort of charmin' simplic'ty about it, like that cast-off Russian count over Orleans way said about fishin' for flounders. He'd got ready with more rods an' flies'n I ever seen, an' it kind of got him when Bill Porter handed him a piece of line an' some clams. Well, Syl, hunt if you want to. I'd like real well to get that brief case, but I sort of think that's even b'yond you. Come outdoors an' I'll point to you where we lost Archie."

Syl looked over the territory, got the route defined to his liking, and disappeared down the hill.

"At that," Asey said to Tabitha, "it wouldn't s'prise

me if he did find somethin'. I wonder what Simon knows. I'm dis'pointed in Simon. I thought he'd crash through with somethin' b'fore this."

Tabitha agreed. "What about Archie?"

"I think we got to let nature take its course with him. Bob's goin' up to see Bates, an' get a good d'scription of him, an' see if he can't get some dope on him, an' pictures an' all. He'll have a job tryin' to get off the Cape, anyway. 'Less he goes by boat, an' I give him credit enough for thinkin' of that. Now—is Simon at the window?"

Mrs. Newell turned around and looked, and then faced Asey again before she answered.

"I'd say yes. Either he or Abby. Someone's been glued to that window all afternoon. Clare got out Lance's binoculars and sat out in the garden and stared back, which amused Lance for the first time today. His feet have been giving him awful twinges. I—wait," she looked around again. "Yes, Simon's just come out on the porch. He's got the glasses. Probably wants a better view. Why—"

Asey swung around so that he faced the gingerbread house.

"I hope," he said, forming the words carefully with his lips, "that Archer don't go to Simon. They might fall for him, the Keiths might, but I think Simon's got more sense. Archer'd just find out what he wants to find, an' then go for Abby or Simon, or both, an' that'd be the end of 'em."

He turned around again.

"S'pose the ole weasel got that?"

"He should have. But why?"

"Don't want Archer an' Simon teamin' up. If they did d'cide to band t'gether to get this unknown quant'ty, like as not they'd launch poison gas at us. Huh. I'll have another go."

He faced toward the gingerbread house.

"So I think, Mrs. Newell, that Archer killed Carson, an' I'm awful scared he'll go for Simon, too. He's keen on this business, an' he's got somethin'—"

The dinner gong sounded, and he and Tabitha turned back to the house.

"I hope," Asey said, "that got over. Simon values his life. Shouldn't wonder if his life wasn't the only thing he did set much store by. An' yet," he stopped short. "Huh. I could of said that better."

"I can't see how," Tabitha remarked. "I thought it was a miracle of conciseness and lucidity. And— Asey, Simon's goin in! You've started something!"

"I got an uneasy feelin'," Asey returned, "that I started more'n I want."

Tabitha looked at him curiously as he held the door open for her.

"What d'you mean?"

"Hard to explain," Asey said gravely. "Kind of— well, ever buy a coat, say, after a lot of thinkin' an' figgerin'? An' you get one the right color, an' the right size, an' the right cut, an' weight, an' price, an' all? An' then, after someone's started to cut the sleeves off a bit, an' you can't turn back, you b'gin to worry? Like, if you'd looked more, you'd done better, an' maybe you'd ought to of bought that other? I don't often feel this way, but I feel it now. I thought that was an awful nice plan, I did, an' now—huh. I could kick myself from Dan to Beersheba, I could, an' for the life of me I couldn't tell you why. Just feel it."

He was gay enough during dinner, but Tabitha suspected that his thoughts were miles away from the group at the table. Probably he wanted a chance to think quietly, she decided. Well, she'd try to see he had one.

"Would it be safe for Marvin to drive us to the mail?" she asked as they went into the living room. "I've been on this hill, just sitting here, so long!"

"Take the bunch," Asey said, "except Joan. An' have Ham an' a trooper string along. I think Joan better stay home. She can amuse Lance."

But Joan made no attempt to amuse Lance other than to turn on the radio, just loud enough so that conversation was impossible. Asey would have dearly loved to turn the thing off, but he knew that if he did, he'd only have to talk to Lance, himself, or answer more of Joan's questions. Ordinarily he shouldn't have minded doing either, but he was still worried about Simon.

Why had Simon made all that fuss about Lance? To get Lance into trouble. Why had he given up so easily? Clearly because—Asey pulled out the three typewritten pages which Bob's men had compiled on Simon's past, and glanced through them. He'd given up because—oho. He hadn't either. Fair concessions, small time gambler, circus barker. Pea and shell stuff.

Maybe—Asey got up and paced around the living room, maybe that was Simon's idea. Make him and the rest think he simply had a good mad on toward Lance and Suzanne. Camouflage, while he carried on something else. But what?

Unconsciously he made an exclamation of annoyance as the radio blared forth the raucous notes of some Harlem band, and just as unconsciously he snapped it off and continued to pace around the room.

Lance and Joan exchanged inquiring glances, but there was something about Asey's manner that kept them from asking any questions. Even after he settled down in an easy chair and lighted his pipe, neither of them broke the silence, though Lance wanted to, terribly.

His own plans weren't going so well. Every time he tried to thrust Clare off on Levering, Levering neatly thrust her back again. And a blind man could tell that the old smoothie was gone on Joan. Not that he *did* anything about it, Lance thought. Levering never did much about anything. But you could tell.

Lance wiggled his toes experimentally and tried to catch Joan's eye, but she had found another volume dealing with the Howes family, and Weesit, and refused to be bothered. Lance sighed, and wondered if he'd told anyone to bring him back some cigarettes. He'd meant to.

He hadn't, but Levering remembered that the supply was running low, and stopped in one of the little Main Street stores on his way back to the car from the post office. Someone jostled him, and the pile of letters and papers under his arm scattered all over the floor.

Levering suppressed his annoyance. Weesit had taken altogether too much interest in him just on his trip to the post office, and this scavenging of mail from a none too clean floor was just a field day for them.

No sense in hurrying—he'd only fumble the things and make it last just that much longer. So, with a deliberate indifference that held Weesit in spell-bound fascination, he knelt down on a newspaper and picked up the letters, one by one. Fourteen. That was right.

"Here's another."

Levering looked up, and his automatic "Thank-you" died on his lips. He'd never seen Simon near to, but he recognized him from his grey felt hat and light suit. He'd watched Simon chasing that hat after a gust of wind had blown it off earlier in the evening.

"Mine?" It was addressed to Suzanne. "Oh, thanks. Yes, that magazine's mine, too. Right-oh. Thanks."

He got his cigarettes and escaped from the barrage of eyes. It was one thing to be pointed out at the opera, or at the races, or something like that, but this Weesit process of identification was more searching and more personal than anything Levering Newell of Beacon Street had ever encountered.

"Your ears!" His aunt said delightedly. "They glow like a bonfire! How simply splendid! Was it your coat that roused them, or your voice?"

"Neither." Levering was just sufficiently annoyed not to divulge his brief encounter with Simon. He didn't mention the letter, either. He'd thought there were fourteen, but there might well have been fifteen, and if he told about his confusion in the store, Tabitha would ride him unmercifully. "Here's the mail. All yours, aunt, at least all the important looking ones. At least two dividends."

Tabitha put the mail away in her handbag.

"I've lost interest in dividends," she said, "and I don't mean to make a bad pun. After I've deducted two sets of income taxes, there's nothing left but a nice looking piece of colored paper. Shall we drive to Provincetown, just for the ride? Ask Hamilton if we may, Levering. I've always wanted a police escort, all my life, and this appears to be the only opportunity I'm likely to have."

It was late when they got home, and Tabitha forgot the mail until after she was ready for bed. She found two letters for Suzanne, and a post card for Levering. That could wait, she decided, but she'd best give Suzanne hers.

"Sorry about these," she apologized a few minutes later. "Levering misled me. What's the matter?"

Suzanne looked at the second envelope.

"That's Simon Keith's writing. I've—thanks, Mrs. Newell."

Mary came in with a glass of orange juice.

"What's wrong?" she demanded. "You look—"

Suzanne held out the letter. "Mary! Read this!"

"Huh! Simon, the oily thing! Huh! Wants you should meet him outside your house, on your side of the fence, does he? Tonight if you can make it. He'll be on *his* side. Oh, he will, will he? Somethin' important. Suzanne, you take that straight to Asey Mayo, this instant minute! Don't you let that man worry you! You give that letter to Asey, an' let him take care of that skunk!"

"I intend to. Oh, Mary—I—there's one thing to be said in favor of Lance's plans. At least I shan't be here next winter! I love the hill and everything on it, and I love this house. I'll be miserable away from it, without the marsh and the bay to watch. But to know that Simon Keith will be hundreds of miles away—it's almost worth the price! Let's go get Asey."

Asey read the note through and frowned.

"Now what's he up to? He knew you'd bring this straight to me! No postmark. That's funny. Stamped, but not mailed. Leastways, I never knew 'em not to cancel a stamp up to that office. Well, we can go into that later. Huh. So Simon wants—this is curious, this is. Two-thirty, he says, an' if not t'night, t'morrow, or the first night it can be pos'ble. Huh, he knew it'd be t'night! An' he don't say nothin' about your comin' alone, does he? Well, at two-thirty, you'n me'll march out an' int'view Br'er Simon. You run up an' nap, an' I'll wake you when it's time."

"Can't I come?" Mary demanded.

"Nope. You see to it that Lance stays put, if he wakes up. See that everyone in the house stays put. I'll get Bob's men posted."

At two twenty-nine, Asey, with Suzanne gripping his arm, sallied forth from the house.

They heard the church clock strike the half hour, but there was no sign of Simon.

"Wh-where are your men?" Suzanne asked in a whisper.

"Here'n there an' round 'bouts." Asey, mindful of the pea and shell game, had stationed Marvin downstairs in the house, and the others at the back. If Simon wanted all the attention to be focussed in one spot, he was going to be unpleasantly surprised. Asey could take care of Suzanne, Marvin and Mary could take care of the house, Levering was sitting on the tower stairs, half way between Joan's and his aunt's rooms.

The minutes passed.

At three o'clock, Asey took Suzanne's arm.

"Back we go," he said grimly. "I don't know what his game was, but it didn't work. Well, maybe the ole fox'll turn up t'morrow night."

But Simon Keith would never keep another appointment.

He was lying on the floor of the woodshed of the gingerbread house, killed as Carson had been killed.

Hamilton, summoned by Abby's frenzied cries the next morning, marvelled at the dead man's horrified expression of surprise.

20

"I DON'T understand you, Asey," Bob Raymond said after the two of them had examined Simon's body. "You don't seem even mildly surprised at this murder."

"Ain't s'prised at the murder," Asey said slowly. "It's that it's Simon."

"Wh—you mean, you thought Abby might be killed? That Simon—"

"Sort of. I done some figgerin'—"

"Then, if Simon was going to kill Abby, and he's dead, she killed him?"

"Don't go so fast, Bob. I was thinkin', last night after he didn't show up to meet Suzanne, why he'd go to such lengths to be somewhere at a certain time, with at least two people knowin' it an' seein' him? Come to me he might be tryin' to set an alibi. He'd of left Sue an' me, then come back bellowin' that Abby'd been killed, that she'd been all right when he left, an' all that. An' if she was killed the same way as Carson—yup, Simon was all set to grasp op'tunities. Cagey ole op'tunity grasper, Simon was, but this time his reach sort of got ahead of him."

Bob thought a moment. "But if that's so, Asey, why'd he try to make us think he was out to get Sue and Lance?"

"Pea an' shell game. That's what he wanted us to think, but 'cordin' to my figgerin', his plans was aimed somewheres else. He liked Suzanne. Craved her, as you might say. When I told him about her house bein' ransacked, an' someone grabbin' her, an' all, an' later when Carson was killed, he was real anxious to know if she was all right. He thought too much of Sue to do her any harm. Let's save the rest till the doc's done his work. I want to have a look around."

The woodshed of the gingerbread house was a drab, dark little entry way, connected to the barn by a flight of narrow steps, and leading directly into the kitchen. In addition to a miniature coal bin whose capacity couldn't have been more than half a ton, there was an untidy pile of oak logs, a dented kerosene can, a battered saw horse, a bag of shavings, and piles of stained berry boxes.

"Mess." Bob summed it up. "Nasty hole."

"Uh-huh," Asey agreed. "Tell me about that kindlin', Bob, there in the corner. Ain't that odd?"

Bob glanced at the precise little pile of edgings.

"What's odd about it, Asey? Seems to be the only tidy thing in the place."

"That's just it." Asey walked over and peered into the kitchen. "Why? They's kindlin' in the kitchen, but it's just flung down any which way by the stove. Now—"

"Asey," Bob said impatiently, "what difference does kindling make? Who cares?"

"I do. Offhand, I'd say someone caught Simon from b'hind, an' some time or other, that kindlin' fell. Maybe he was carryin' it, maybe it was just in the way an' got strewn around, but—yup. Just space enough. Look careful, Bob. If Simon fell this way, an' that kindlin'd been there, it'd be all scattered around, not piled up neat. See? It got piled up afterwards."

"D'you think it's a clew or something?" Bob plainly didn't.

Asey went to the other end of the entry and surveyed the steps leading down into the barn.

"Some pictures he had for dec'rations. My, what a mind Simon had! Say, that's funny, too. Why're them calendars on this wall here all crooked? This is—"

"Cookoo," Bob said. "I'm going outside and help Syl scavenge, Asey."

Asey shrugged and sat down astraddle the saw horse.

"Poor ole Mayo," he murmured. "Ole boy's nuts. Balmy. Huh. Ole man Mayo's gettin' somewheres for the first time in days, brother, if you only knew it. An'—h'lo, Doc."

"Morning," the doctor said cheerfully. "Simon, this time, eh? How's Abby?"

"Sue's with her. Didn't you bring the nurse?"

"Sent her around front. Abby in a dither?"

"Nope, seems to be stunned."

Asey watched the doctor at work.

"What," he inquired after a few minutes, "what—"

"Time? Two-thirty or so, if you mean when he was killed. Same thing as Carson, Asey. What d'you make of it? Not the same person, of course—what about Abby?"

Before Asey could answer, Syl and Bob called to him.

"Got something. Come look!"

Syl was triumphantly waving the yellow Windsor scarf which Simon had received by mail.

"So-ho," Asey said. "Where?"

" 'Twas crumpled in a ball in the bushes by the side porch. Guess this is the work of Archer, huh?"

"Not his kind of scarf, Syl. Bob, I do think I'm on the right track. Simon watched us through the glasses when we was talkin' about yellow scarves, an' d'cided to cash in. We didn't always call 'em handkerchief scarves, just scarves, an' he got the wrong idea. 'Member, Bob, Archer's was more of a square. S'matter, Syl, swallow your 'baccy?"

Syl pointed to the scarf.

"Say, you know, Asey, Jennie sent to Boston for one like that last week, only red, for her niece at camp. Tried everywheres down here, but they only had short ones. That's long. Say, if you think Simon got that—say, cousin Bertie—you know, Ella May's son, he works up to Sears. I bet we could find out."

"Scoot in," Asey said, "an' get cousin Bertie an' see if they shipped a yellow scarf to Simon. He'd never of bought one round here, for fear of its bein' traced. Mail order house'd of been his choice."

"You really think the scarf was Simon's, and someone used it on him?" Bob asked.

"I do. I'm c'nvinced Simon meant to kill Abby, Bob. He knew just enough about this scarf business to see how nice it would be if he could kill her with one, an' then claim it was someone else."

"And he got killed with his own scarf—but Asey, if he tried to kill her and failed, then didn't Abby kill him? It sounds crazy, but what else—got anywhere, Doc?"

"Killed around half past two. Strangled. Yes, that scarf's a good bet. Keep it for your men at the lab. They'll know."

Levering joined the group in the backyard.

"Asey, Mary's just told me about this. Look, about Simon's letter to Suzanne. I never had a chance to explain about that last night. Simon gave it to me."

He described the scene in the store.

"I'm embarrassed that I didn't explain about it before, but—"

"All right," Asey told him. "Letter itself is the important part. Simon was establishin' an al'bi. If Abby was killed like Carson was killed, then it'd seem the same person killed 'em both. Simon had an al'bi you couldn't beat for Carson's death. Here he'd have a motive, but if he was al'bied for the first, that'd pretty much of let him off the second, an' b'sides, he could pretend it happened while he was talkin' with Sue. There'd be the time el'ment, but as the doc'll tell you, you can't split seconds on that. Have to take Simon's word. Toss-up."

"Why should Simon have given me the note?" Levering inquired.

"Too late for the mail, he was, an' he wanted her to get it in a hurry. I'm scared my talk inspired him the wrong way, like I told Mrs. Newell." He explained briefly what he had tried to say for Simon's benefit. "So—"

"Asey," Bob made a gesture of despair, "I don't get this!"

"Well, Simon always thought there was Bellamy's money hangin' around. That's what he married Abby for. Then he got the idea Sue had it. Things goin' on there lately made him sure. He also wanted Suzanne; that's somethin' you don't give due credit for, Bob."

"But she never gave him any encouragement, Asey! Had to drive him away, you told me. What chance would he have had of getting her?"

"None."

"Then it doesn't hold water, Asey! It doesn't work, this idea that Simon was going to kill Abby, and then march over to get Suzanne and her money, if she had any!"

"Asey's absolutely right, Bob," the doctor said unexpectedly. "Simon's the sort of man who'd feel that he was conferring an honor on a woman just to pick her out. He wasn't the sort to feel hurt by being driven away, or by any succession of noes. He probably thought that with Abby out of the way, Suzanne would fall on his neck. I know. I've heard his braggings about town, and I know of several of his affairs, and I know several he attempted, and got squelched on, that were all hushed up. The man had a simply colossal conceit, as far as women were concerned. Asey's right. If Simon thought Bellamy's money was coming to light on the other side of the fence, he'd think nothing of killing Abby and setting out for Sue, entirely convinced that he had only to crook his little finger, and she'd come, and the money with her."

"It's—oh." Bob broke off as Suzanne appeared around the corner of the porch.

"Syl asked me to tell you, Asey, that he'd got hold of Bertie, whoever Bertie is, and that they were going through records—look, I couldn't help hearing something of what the doctor was saying. About Simon and—and me. I— well, that is—"

"You could help us," Asey said. "My idea here is that Simon was all set to kill Abby, an' got his instead. I— honest, I hate to ask you, but in any of your 'ncounters with him, did he ever—well, mutter anythin' about Abby?"

Suzanne put one hand against the corner post of the porch.

"Yes. It was in February, while Lance was away, and Simon was drunk. I got in the house and locked the door, but he hung around outside and yelled—things about getting me, and getting the money, and getting rid of the old woman—it, well, it was pretty hideous."

"That sort of thing even happen b'fore?"

"He insinuated as much, many times. He—"

Syl bustled out importantly.

"Yessiree, Simon bought that scarf this week! They got the papers. Killed with his own scarf, he was, the one he was plannin' on usin' on Abby, an' then someone got him!"

Suzanne gripped the post a little harder.

"Asey, do you know who?"

"Abby, 'course," Syl said. "Who else? Ain't that so, Bob? I—"

"Abby? I—I don't know anything, of course," Suzanne said, "but truly, Bob, I should think that Abby was the only person in this world who'd mourn Simon and feel that his death was any loss to the world. She—she's just sitting there, staring, not saying a word. I—oh, Bob, I don't think it could have been Abby, possibly!"

"Then who—" Bob began.

Asey laid a hand on his shoulder. "Let's try to figger this out more, first, b'fore you do anything. There's still Archer. This ain't his kind of scarf, but that don't mean he couldn't of picked up Simon's."

Bob started to argue, and the doctor and Syl chimed in, and Levering began on his theories. Asey let them all talk, and proceeded to think things out in his own mind.

Beyond any doubt, Carson had been killed by someone inside the Howes place, by someone who had taken his phone call, made a date to see him, and let him in. That couldn't have been Archer.

Simon had been killed in exactly the same way, around two-thirty. If it was after that time, it was no one from the hill. But before two-thirty—well, Asey and Lance had been downstairs, but that didn't mean that anyone in the household couldn't have slipped out.

"Asey," Bob said wearily, "why *not* Abby? And who, if she didn't—"

"One," Asey said, "why'd she kill him now, if she's borne with him all these years? Two, takes an expert to do a garrotting job like was done on Simon. True, Abby's frail lookin', but she ain't no weaklin'. She's strong enough. But this business needs experience more'n strength, an' I shouldn't say Abby'd had none. Three, Simon'd of been wary of her. He wouldn't let her get near him. Four, she wouldn't of dared. Five, like Sue says, she's the only one that seemed to care for him. Six, if she'd killed him, she'd killed herself, too. Seven—"

"That's enough," Bob said, "but—just the same, I want to see her."

"Let me, will you?" Asey asked. "Alone? I promise you I'll find her guilty if I can, but if she ain't, an' I'm sure of it, I want you to take my word for it. Leastways, I don't want her bullied."

Bob hesitated.

"I'll take the doc with me," Asey said. "She likes him, an' she's used to him, an' whereas she don't waste no love on me, I know—well, I've lived in these parts a long time, an' I—"

"Can manage the native," Bob said. "All right."

The nurse opened the door to Abby's room.

"I don't know what to do with her," she said helplessly. "She just sits there. Doesn't say anything, doesn't do anything, doesn't want anything."

But Abby turned around as Asey and the doctor entered. She had never, Asey reflected, seemed so worn and old.

"I know," she said, "what you want. You want to know if I killed Simon. I've been waiting for you."

"No," Asey said quietly, "I wanted to know if you knew Simon wanted to kill you."

Abby looked at him, and a puzzled expression came over her face. She slumped back in her chair and leaned her head against the crocheted tidy.

Asey had been prepared for an outburst, but none came. He was amazed to see tears on her cheeks.

"I've known it," she said, "for years. I've made a will he knows nothing about. Elisha's son-in-law, Tobe Small, has it at the bank."

The doctor and Asey looked at each other.

"Last year he tried to poison me," Abby went on in a tired voice. "I guessed, though, and it didn't work. The year before he made me take out another insurance policy—I was sure, then. Sure that he—but I was too careful. Except for that time—"

"Your leg!" Dr. Cummings shouted. "That time you fell downstairs and broke your leg—was that his work? Woman, for the love of God, why didn't you give me a hint? Why—"

"If anyone had known," Abby said with perfect truth, "or even guessed, that would have been the end."

"But why didn't you get away?" Cummings stormed. "Why? Why—"

"I have no money of my own" Abby said. "Every

cent I had was turned over to Simon long ago. He had all the money. What could I have done if I went away, Doctor? I'm an old woman. I've no friends. No relatives. I've no way to earn a living. Simon had money, and he would have found me."

"My God!" Cummings said. "My God—for once in my life I'm speechless, and I'm—I give you my word, I mean it! How long has this been going on?"

"Since we were married," Abby said quietly.

The bright morning sun showed every wrinkle on her face. The Howes face, Asey thought as he turned away; a Howes who'd taken thirty odd years of a beating that—

"Look," he said suddenly, "that was why you kept up the feud, huh? Long's you could keep alive some hope in him that there was Bellamy's money, somewhere, you felt safe?"

"Partly," Abby said. Her long thin fingers rubbed over the chair arm. "And for a long time, Asey, for many years, I loved Simon. I believed the things he said and told me. Then, when I finally realized that everything Eben said about him was true—well, there wasn't anything I could do about it then. And—I honestly don't think I would have if I could, in those days. I—" she looked out of the window. Suzanne was crossing the lawn. "She's been kind," Abby went on. "She was kind the other day. I saw the police cars there Wednesday morning. I thought Simon might have—have bothered Suzanne—"

"You knew about that?"

Abby closed her eyes. "I've known about that, Asey, and all the others. He—he used to talk a lot when he was

drunk. Anyway, that was why I went over. I thought
Simon might have hurt Sue, or that he might have been
hurt. I was frightened to death when I found out Simon
wasn't there. That's why I wanted to come home. I knew
what he'd do if he found me there. As it was, I managed
to convince him that I went there only because I was
worried about him."

"Are you glad," Asey asked after a moment of silence,
"that he's dead?"

"Yes," Abby answered. "I feel rather dazed, Asey.
When I was a girl, father brought me home a canary in
a cage, once, from the Azores. I remember the day we
opened the cage to let it out in the room. It just didn't understand. I don't, either."

"Oh," Cummings said. "Oh—oh, by George, Asey,
we've got to *do* something! Abby, isn't there any way on
earth you can prove you didn't kill that—that fellow? You
didn't, did you?"

"I didn't kill him," Abby said honestly, "but I can't
prove it. I just didn't."

Cummings stood up.

"Well, if worse comes to worse, I'll write you certificates saying you couldn't lift a hand above your waist.
Arthritis might do it. Or if need be, you can have a couple
of sprained wrists. Abby Keith, what on earth are you
crying for, now?"

There was a look of old Captain Bellamy, Asey
thought with a start, in the twinkle that suddenly appeared in Abby's eyes. Blue eyes—he'd never noticed their

color before. The way she tossed back her head, too. That was like her father.

"Probably," Abby said, "you'd weep at the first kind word anyone'd given you for— Asey, if Suzanne is downstairs, d-do you suppose you could ask her if I could see Lance?"

"Huh?"

"Lance," Abby repeated. "Even the other day when he was here with Lish and you, I didn't really get a good look at him. And when you've watched what amounts to your nephew through binoculars all his life—d'you suppose she'd let him come over and see me? I—"

Syl burst into the room, his eyes nearly popping from his head.

"Asey—say, Asey! Hamilton's found Archer!"

21

Asey lingered at the gingerbread house just long enough to call to the nurse and to Suzanne.

"See to Abby, please—"

He gripped the doctor's elbow, ran him to the roadster and bundled him in without any ceremony.

Syl hopped on the running board as Asey started the car.

"Asey, where you goin'? Why—"

"Ain't he at the house?"

"Why, Asey, he's where Ham found him, down on the marsh. He—"

"Syl, are you tryin' to tell me that Archer's dead?"

"Why, yes, Asey. You see, that new trooper with the long face, Turner, he come over to the house an' told Ham he found some footprints, an' that Ham'd better come, an' Ham went, an' thought he seen somethin' movin' in the water by the bushes, an' fired, an' it was Archer. He didn't know—he thought it was a muskrat or somethin'—you better come down. Bob's already left."

Asey circled the hill, drove the roadster along the solid ground by the beach, wove around soft spots with as much assurance as though he were on a main highway.

Dr. Cummings winced.

"I suppose you know what you're doing, and I suppose this miracle car with its miracle tires'll get you there and back, but I wouldn't risk this trip in my old crate—where is he, Syl, in the main bog?"

"Guess so. That's what I thought from what they said. Yup—see, Bob come round the long way. There they be! Asey, you'd better leave her here!"

"Guess you're right. Take care of your footin', Doc. This is soggy—"

They circled around to where Bob, Hamilton and Turner stood by a limp, muddy body.

"I wiped his face off," Bob said. "Archer all right, from Bates's description. Some papers in his pocket with T. Archer. Blurry, but—well, what now, Asey?"

"No sign of the brief case?"

"Not a trace."

The trooper named Turner was biting his lip.

"Gee," he said, "I feel—honest, I didn't know it was—"

"Aw," Hamilton said, "I was the one that fired that shot that—you see, Asey, Turner found some footprints, and he thought he saw someone dodge around the bushes—"

"I went back to the hill," Turner said, "and asked Ham to come down. This brush is thick, and if this was the fellow that did all that garrotting, I wanted someone with me. Ham and I looked, but we didn't see anyone, and then—"

"Then I saw something move along the edge of that pool," Ham said, "and I took a pot shot, and then we saw a hand—"

"Prob'ly," Asey said, "he tried to short cut it across that pool, an' got caught."

"He was down in the mud almost to his waist," Hamilton said. "We nearly popped getting him out."

"Must of got stuck while Turner went back—that's awful stuff. One hole over Wellfleet way I r'member, b'fore they had proper roads, an' I once seen a horse go down in five minutes. More Archer tried to get up, prob'ly the more he went down."

"What I saw," Hamilton said, "was probably his last thrashing about, and my bullet finished him. Well, I—"

"Don't," Asey said. "If your bullet hadn't finished him prob'ly another would, an' under the circ'mstances, I guess—huh. I told Joan we'd better let nature take its course with Archer, an' seems's if it did. Him an' Glotz, they kind of had the cards stacked against them. Well, Doc?"

"I'd be inclined to think," the doctor said, "that he was gone before you shot, Ham. After all, I couldn't say for sure without considerable delving, but it would have taken Turner twenty minutes to walk back to the hill, and certainly twenty minutes more for him and Ham to get back—plenty of time for him to wear himself out. What's your idea, Asey? What about the brief case? And all the rest?"

"It was round here," Asey said, "that me an' Marvin

lost him the other night. I wonder, huh—I bet that's it! I bet he lost his brief case here!"

"You mean you don't think Archer ever got to see what was in the brief case he stole?" Bob asked.

"That's it. I think that's why he went for Joan yesterday aft'noon, all so friendly like. I think he lost it, an' figgered that since she had it, she knew what'd be in it. N'en this mornin' he come back again to try to fish for the case, an' found you wanderin' around, Turner—an' tried to git it while you was away, an' that was that. They was someone wanderin' around here most of yest'day, durin' daylight, so's he didn't have much chance."

"You don't think we'll find the case?" Bob asked.

"I don't," Hamilton answered. "We've been over every dry part, one or another of us, and if it went into any of the boggy spots, it's in China now. Don't you feel the same way, Asey?"

Asey nodded. "I had a kind of prem'nition from the first that we'd never get to look at them papers. Bob, you better come back to the hill with me. You only got two fellers there, an' if Markham was to drop in, you'd get merry hell. Sure, I know one's with Simon an' one's at the Howes place, but you better come back—you can send someone down here. Stay, Doc? Okay. You sup'rintend."

Outside Suzanne's house was a car; Bob looked and then whistled.

"This," he said, "is worse than Markham. That's Leary, Asey. Hanson's pal Leary. Probably Markham sent him in all good faith, to help us out. But you know how he'll help—whee! I—where you going, Asey? Come help me with that guy—"

"You cope with him," Asey said. "I got somethin' I want to do, first."

He disappeared around the corner of the house and slid into the kitchen before Bob had a chance to say anything more. He had no desire, at that point, to haggle with Leary, and he knew Leary well enough to know that the only way to escape haggling was to escape the man.

His ascent of the backstairs was so quick and so quiet that not even Levering, who was just coming into the kitchen, heard him. Asey paused for a moment and grinned. Levering was calling him—yes, so was Bob. And in the distance he could hear the peremptory tones of Mrs. Newell. Let 'em call. He had things to do.

Pushing up the trap door, Asey swung himself into the attic, then replaced and hooked the door in place. Then, waiting a few moments until his eyes became accustomed to the dim light, he walked carefully on tiptoes to an old cobbler's bench, sat down and lighted his pipe.

Back to the beginning once more.

Carson knew of some valuable thing, of which in all probability records were complete to a certain point, and then fizzled out. Somehow he had come into the possession of the tin box and diary of Bellamy Howes, and those apparently gave him the idea that this valuable thing had been bought by Howes from Newell. But if this valuable thing was not recorded as belonging to either family, if they knew nothing about it, perhaps it existed without their knowledge. That, Asey felt, was the way Carson had gone at it.

Glotz and Archer had been sent to look for it. Glotz hadn't really known what he was after, in one sense, except that it was worth money. Archer knew no more. He'd never seen the inside of the brief case. Even if he had, it was no use to them now.

They hadn't known what they were after, but Carson had. That sounded odd, but worked out nicely. Suppose it were a jewel. Carson wouldn't have told those two, anyway. Besides, if a jewel were not concealed, or hidden, or a part of something else, clearly the Howeses and Newells would have found it themselves. Therefore, if the object still existed, it was hidden, or a part of something else. Vase, jug, something.

Asey ran over quickly in his mind the problem of Joan, Bates and the brief case. Carson had come to get that back. And he had decided, en route, to take at least Mrs. Howes—Suzanne—or Miss Howes—Joan—into his confidence to a certain extent. He had telephoned someone at the place Tuesday night. That person had made a date to see him later. That person had let him in and killed him.

Emmaline said Carson had spoken to "Miss Howes." Not Mrs. But Miss. Carson would have called Joan just "Joan." He would have talked to Suzanne as Mrs. Howes. Could he have asked for Mrs. Howes, been told that this was Miss Howes, and gone on with his story? At any rate, Asey reflected, Carson talked to a woman, or of course, it might have been someone who pretended to be a woman. Not Lance, certainly, with that deep voice of his. Mrs. Newell? Levering? Mary? Or—Joan, disguising her voice? It was all crazy. It—

"Asey!" Bob was yelling in the hall beneath. "Asey, Mister Leary wants you! Asey, they're taking Simon and Archer, are you through with 'em? Asey, for Christ's sakes!"

"Yah," Asey murmured comfortably. "Yah. Do your own copin'."

Now for Simon.

He'd been killed around two-thirty. Before that time, Asey himself had been busy getting Hamilton and the others together, and assigning them to places that they were to take before he and Suzanne marched out to see Simon.

As for the people in the house, Tabitha and Joan and Levering, before two-thirty, had all been downstairs. Lance was on the couch. Suzanne and Mary had been upstairs.

Everyone, as he remembered, had been everywhere.

"An' that," Asey said, "is that."

Of course there was Abby. But Simon's death wasn't any of her work. He sat up straight. Perhaps Leary would —no. Bob and the doc would keep him off Abby.

That letter of Simon's to Sue. Certainly he had planned it as part of an alibi. But it was odd, the way he shoved it at Levering. Odd that Tabitha should take so long in giving it to Suzanne.

Sue. She'd been pretty breathless during that wait out in the dark by the fence. To his knowledge she was the only person besides Abby and Lance who had a really good motive for killing Simon. But Abby was out of the thing, and Lance couldn't walk. He'd told Sue to go back and take a nap before they went to meet Simon, but with all that hurly-burly going on, she could have walked to town and back, had ample time, and no one would have missed her.

He didn't think she took that phone call. Yet, after all, it was possible that she might have. But why would she have had any motive for killing Carson?

Asey slapped his thigh. Suppose Suzanne had taken that call from a strange man who said he was Carson, and wanted to see her alone as soon as possible? Would she have swallowed it? Of course not! As far as she knew, Carson was romping around on freight boats. Sue—of course she'd have thought it was Simon, with more funny business!

Suppose she had made that date—

"Come, come," Asey chided himself, "come, come, Mayo. Sue Howes might of done all that, but not the rest. She don't fit in with the couple things you *do* know about this. Sue's short, an' she ain't—"

She didn't fit.

There were just a couple of things he did know, and they'd stuck in front of his nose, and you couldn't get away from them.

It was half an hour before he unlocked the trap door and swung down into the hall, nearly knocking Tabitha over in the process.

"Hm," she said. "Brush those cobwebs off your nose! Fine how-d'you-do you've caused, Asey! Mr. Leary's going to slaughter you. He's fit to be tied. He's phoned Markham, Mr. Leary has, and according to him, Markham's sending down a regiment, and all the experts he owns, and they, with Mr. Leary, are going to show you incompetent souls how things should be run."

" 'Bout time," Asey told her cheerfully. "It's their business, not mine anyhows. I don't pretend to be nothin' but a reas'nbly good mechanic, an' the only job I got here was to see who was heavin' yellow hank'chiefs at you. An' I did. These bypaths is Markham's an' Leary's, an' not mine. That's that."

Tabitha's eyes narrowed at Asey's finality.

"You mean, you're giving this up? But Asey, you can't—oh, dear Heaven! There's that creature and her beast! Listen—"

Clare's shrill tones penetrated the hallway.

"Something about that voice," Tabitha said, "that brings loudspeakers to mind. She doesn't talk, or converse, or chatter. She broadcasts. Listen—hear that? Rupert's knocking things down again. I simply cannot bear—Levering, will you come here?"

"Yes, m'am?" Levering's head was visible from the stairs.

"Levering, please do something about that child. Remove her. I want to come downstairs."

"Yes, m'am."

"There," Tabitha said. "Now come down, Asey, and tell me why you look this way, and why you're so curiously content to have Markham's hired men do your work. Why's the blue room being opened, Mary?"

Broody Mary set down her broom and dustpan, and planted a double fist firmly on either hip.

"I been told," she said coldly, "that Abby Keith's comin' over here to stay a spell. Abby Keith ain't goin' to find no fault with this house! Not if I have to lick the carpet to make sure it's clean! I cleaned this room thorough yest'day, but I'm goin' over it again!"

" 'F you're goin' to do any carpet lickin'," Asey advised with a chuckle, "sprinkle some tea leaves first. Easier on the tongue. By golly, Leverin's got her out, Mrs. Newell. Hear that?"

"I'd say," Tabitha remarked, "that Levering was carrying her out bodily, and she was loving it. Come down, Asey. I want to grasp all this up to the very hilt. Sit down here in the hall—"

"Just a sec," Asey said. "I got to wash off cobwebs. Can't do any hilt-graspin' with cobwebs on the brain."

"Now," Tabitha said when he returned, "let's get down to business. You've settled this, and—"

"Lance! Oh, Lance!" Joan stood by the screen door and called in. "Lance, Clare says she wants to go to Hyannis, and will you come if we get you in the car."

"Ask Levering," Lance roared back. "He'd love it."

"Levering," Joan relayed the message, "Lance says you go—"

"That would be too, too divine!" Levering's falsetto brought Asey to his feet. "No! Besides, we can't leave. Asey said so."

Asey sat down again quickly. "Gee," he said, "he had me fooled there."

"Russian bank," Tabitha said, "the backstroke, and a nice falsetto. His only accomplishments, as far as I can make out. Asey, you've made Lance grow up in the last few days. How much would you charge to set a rocket off under my nephew? This infinite incapacity for action, or capacity for inaction— Asey, will you pay some attention to what I'm saying? That's only Rupert, in there, and Lance can tend to him! What—where are you going now?"

"Ask Mary somethin'. Just be a minute."

With growing irritation, Mrs. Newell watched him mount the stairs. She prided herself on her ability to sense a change of mood, and Asey had changed his no less than three times in fifteen minutes.

"Well," she said to him when he returned, "if you're done with asking questions, what about—"

"Too, too divine!"

The shrill voice came from outside, but Asey didn't know whether it was Clare or Levering, until the latter added in his natural voice, "Too, too my eye! You—"

"Land's sakes," Mary said as she came down the stairs, "was that him? Don't it beat all? Well, that room's cleaned fit for the King of England, an' I guess it ought to do Abby Keith. I'm goin' up to town if it's all right, Asey. Want to go over to the church about the fair—"

"I can't tell you yes'r no," Asey said. "Ask Bob, if you want, or Leary. If I was you, though, an' really wanted to go, I'd go an' ask when I come back."

"And if it's anything to do with the fair," Tabitha said, "be sure to save me all the white handkerchiefs with hemmed hems—not the rolled kind, and about five aprons. My cook loves 'em, and she won't wear the kind you buy in stores. Now," she added as Mary left, "now, Asey, tell me. You've found out about all these things, haven't you?"

Asey screwed and unscrewed his pipe stem.

"You have," Tabitha persisted, "haven't you?"

"Oh—"

"Come, come! Haven't you?"

"Yes, dum it!" Asey said explosively. "I have! An'—an' for the love of Pete, don't ask me anythin' more!"

22

TABITHA leaned back in the wicker chair and studied Asey's face.

He had been on the track of something when she met him in the hall. Since he had come downstairs he had made up his mind. During the interval, something had startled him.

Tabitha folded her hands in her lap. Looking down at them absentmindedly, she was amazed to find that the knuckles were white. Her nails—why, it was she herself who was digging those nails into the backs of her hands!

"It—it's not Levering." She made a statement. She almost didn't dare ask questions.

"No," Asey said morosely. "It's not. Oh, don't ask me any more! I'm goin' home, an' Leary an' Bob can do the rest, if they an' their bunch ever dope it out. I'm through. I wash my hands of the whole works."

Unconsciously his eyes went to the staircase.

Tabitha, following his gaze, felt her mouth open.

She had to blink to keep her eyes from staring out of their socket.

Levering had dutifully told her Bob's version of Asey's thoughts on Simon.

"Asey's murmuring about crooked pictures and a pile of kindling—"

The framed ship pictures on the stair wall were crooked. They'd been even when she and Asey came down. She had straightened one just a sixteenth of an inch, herself, and had admired their symmetry.

"Asey—you mean Mary? You don't mean Broody Mary? You don't mean—" she caught herself up before she parrotted it again. Of course he meant Mary, that was why he was going home. Of course.

"Asey—why? Why? W-how?"

"Carson called, and she took it, and thought it was Simon," Asey said dully. That worked out for Suzanne, all right, that business, but it'd worked better for Mary. "Made a date to meet him, an' did. Killed him, n'en found out it wasn't Simon. Who else but Mary would of neated the kitchen up afterwards?"

Tabitha nodded. Who else but Mary would have piled the kindling up? That was why Asey had gone out and pretended to wash off cobwebs. He'd been out staring at the kindling in the kitchen wood box.

"Planted those hundred dollar bills on herself," Asey went on as though Tabitha weren't there. "Only plant in this whole business, one way or another. She admitted it. An' Broody Mary wouldn't steal, an' she wouldn't burst into tears if—if lions chawed her."

Tabitha nodded again. Mary knew about the letter of Simon's. She—

"Person who tipped them pictures had to be tall," Asey said. "Angular like. All for Suzanne. Looked after her so long, got to feel that Sue's happiness was all that mattered, an' Simon was the thorn in Sue's flesh, an' Mary set out to r'move it."

"If you asked her, she'd admit it," Tabitha said.

"Uh-huh."

"If you gave her guns, or ropes, or knives, or dynamite," Tabitha went on, "she'd never use 'em!"

"That's right."

"She—oh, Asey, if one gangster killed a couple of others, and you read about it in the papers, you'd just say it was good riddance. You wouldn't care."

"Yup."

"And Carson wasn't much better than a gangster, and Simon—well, he was just a civilized slug. Nothing more."

"Less," Asey said briefly.

"Asey—look, you've got to do something so they don't find out! We—we couldn't have her go to trial! Why, she'd go through with it!"

"An' she wouldn't," Asey observed bitterly, "take to black, an' claim she was a poor b'nighted orphan, or let anyone say she didn't know what she was doin', or that her great-great-grandfather had hallucinations, an' that's why she done it. She didn't an' it wasn't. Her grandfather was a bit queer," he added, "come to think of it. But she'd go through with it, to the last scene."

Mrs. Newell toyed with her lorgnettes.

"Do we have to do anything about it, Asey?"

"A murder," Asey said, "is a murder, an' two murders is just another added onto the first. That's why I'm goin' home. I can pretend to kick up a row with Leary, an' that's all there'll be to it. I shan't offer any advice or any ideas. But when they get them bright boys down—well, they're good. An' it's poss'ble they might make it worse instead of better—"

"Let me tell you," Lance observed from the doorway, "that no one's going to get Mary, if she did all this for me and mother, or mother! Yes, I'm walking, and my feet hurt like hell, but I heard just enough of this to come if my feet fell off during the process. No one can be let know! You, and Tab, and I, Asey—that's—oh, Mud!"

Suzanne was standing at the screen door.

"Lance," she said matter-of-factly, "you'd better sit down. I—"

"You know?"

"I half guessed, and I heard the rest just now. It's lucky that Joan and Levering are out in the garden, and Bob and that Leary off somewhere. I half guessed, but I didn't believe it. Yet it had to be one of us, and Mary is so deft!"

"An' the only one," Asey said, "who'd've been able to garrot. She thought out why that first yellow scarf was knotted, just in a flash, soon's she found it. Oh, boy!"

The four were still grouped around the hallway when the first detachment of Leary's reinforcements arrived.

Leary himself, a tall loose-jointed man in plain clothes, favored Asey with a curt nod.

Asey smiled. He remembered other times when Leary had followed him like a shadow, eager for any pearls Asey cared to drop. This was different. Here was where Leary intended to do his own pearl dropping.

"Glad to see you," Asey said pleasantly. "'Fraid I've kind of been no help, this trip. Gettin' old, I am."

"Well," Leary shrugged his shoulders, "you can't always expect to hit on a lucky break, and you've had a lot of breaks, Asey. This is the sort of thing where our methods are really needed. Can't always go at this sort of thing hit or miss. Now," he pulled a notebook from his pocket, "I want—let me see. Mrs. Newell, I'd like to talk to you. This your nephew?"

"That's Lance Howes," Asey said. "Levering's outside. Want him?"

"Hammond wants him. Just see he connects, will you? Oh, and if you're going out, Asey, just bring in my bag, will you?"

Lance drew a long breath. Who was this bald scarecrow to order Asey Mayo around like an errand boy? He'd tell him a thing or—but Asey caught his eye and shook his head ever so slightly.

"Sure, I'll get Leverin' an' fetch your bag. Sort of a nice aft'noon, but sort of hot, too. Like a nice glass of iced tea?"

Asey's irony slid over Leary's bald head.

"Yeah. Thanks."

For the next twenty minutes, things, as Asey said, hummed.

Tabitha, coming out from her conference with Leary, overheard him and sighed.

"Hum, Asey," she remarked, "is one of those beautiful understatements at which you so definitely shine. You know, I personally feel like a slab of shredded wheat. But doubt seriously if Mr. Leary got much from me. On the contrariwise."

"Did you 'My-good-man' him?" Asey inquired.

"I 'My-good-manned' him, and I 'The-very-idead' him, and I come-comed till I was fairly ashamed. Asey, Leary's got his mind made up about Suzanne."

"I had a feeling that might happen," Asey said. "I thought—"

"Here's the nurse," Tabitha interrupted. "Dear me, I hope nothing's happened to Abby?"

"It's not Mrs. Keith," the nurse said, "but Mrs. Howes promised me that someone would bring a big car over and drive her back here. I'd have asked one of the state police, but they seem so occupied, and they've taken the body away, and we were there all alone, and Mrs. Keith's getting impatient."

"I'll run her over," Asey said. "You come along with me."

Suzanne came into the kitchen, looked at the nurse and sighed.

"Oh, I meant to look after getting Abby here, and with all that's gone on, I forgot entirely! And there's the phone ringing—"

Asey went into the hallway and answered it.

"What? Oh, h'lo, Emmaline. No, no, Mary ain't here. She's gone to town. Something about the fair, she said. To the church. Why, I don't know. What—what's that? It—you sure? I—"

Asey slammed down the receiver, dashed to the back door and howled for Bob.

"Bob! Ham! Quick, I want you! Leverin', you'll do! Hustle, Syl, get that ladder! Here, gimme the end, an' hop to it!"

Leary, with two of his shock troops, came out to see what the uproar was all about.

They made no effort to help Asey, with Syl and Levering, as he set the ladder against the fence, ran nimbly up it and dropped over on the other side. Levering followed, stopping only long enough to catch Syl and set him on the ground. Then they dashed after Asey, who was running with long loping strides toward the gingerbread house.

Leary laughed shortly.

"Crazy," he said. "Just crazy. I told Markham, he might have a few lucky breaks, and then he'd peter out. I—"

"Why, my good man," Tabitha raised her lorgnettes, "why, instead of wasting your time on general comments concerning Mr. Mayo's ability, or lack of it, why can't you bring yourself to a point of finding out what he's after? Or possibly—mind you, I say possibly,—aiding him in whatever he may be doing?"

"Waste of time," Leary looked at Mrs. Newell as though it would be no chore for him to indulge in general character comments regarding her, either. "The old man's crazy. I always thought so, and after the way he's wasted his time on this affair here, I finally convinced Markham I knew what I was talking about. He's just putting on a grandstand play. His pride's taken a beating. Come on, Sam. Let's us get on."

Levering caught up with Asey as he reached the porch of the gingerbread house.

"What—"

"Just keep comin'," Asey said, and reached for the door.

The door was locked.

Levering ran around to the side door. That, too, was locked.

"'K out," Asey said, and swung a rocker through a porch window.

He was in the house even before the glass had finished falling.

Levering followed, and Syl, panting loudly, crawled in after them.

Asey went up the stairs two at a time, and made for Abby's room.

That door was locked, too.

"C'mon, Leverin'. All t'gether! Nope, that won't do—"

"Can't you shoot the lock?" Levering pointed to the handle of a revolver which showed above Asey's belt.

"Don't dare. Syl, get into the next room an' go out the window. Start in when you hear us. Climb 'long the gutter. Beat it! Get that oak hat rack! Leverin'—get it! There, now—"

Using the hat rack as a battering ram, they lunged against the door. A bullet tore through the panel and thudded into the wall behind them.

"My—my God!" Levering turned white. "That—that went between us—"

Asey shoved him away from the door.

"Git out the way—"

Standing on the other side of the door, he reached out and banged the panel. Two more shots splintered through. Then one ripped the plaster on the wall, an inch above Asey's head.

"Down," Asey said quietly to Levering.

A split second later, another shot crashed through the wall. Just, Levering thought dazedly, just about where his face had been.

"One more," Asey whispered, "n'en—"

"Is—who is it? What?"

Asey motioned for him to be still. As he lowered his hand, the sixth bullet spat through the door, less than a foot above the floor.

Levering saw Asey wince. The top joint of his little finger had mysteriously disappeared.

Asey got to his feet.

"Okay. Gimme your hank'chief. Now—"

"But—"

"That's all there'll be of that. Come on."

On the third lunge, the door crashed open.

Broody Mary, her gun in hand, stood in the center of the room. Her face was distorted, and her eyes—

Levering felt the cold shivers run up and down his spine.

"Put it down, Mary," Asey said conversationally. "Put it down."

She was either going to jump him, or try to dart

past, or make for the window. Syl—ah! Syl was behind her.

"Come on, Mary. Put it down."

Mary looked down at the gun and gripped the barrel; without looking up, and with a motion so quick that Levering barely saw her, she swung the butt at Asey's head.

He ducked just as Syl grabbed her shoulders from behind.

"Hold her, Syl," Asey said. "I've—Leverin', get round—here, take your hank'chief back. N'em mind my finger. Hold here while I get at her wrists. There. Syl, open the closet door. S'matter, Leverin'?"

"I can't—"

"This," Asey said, "ain't no time to r'member 'bout layin' hands on a lady! She's stark, starin'—there!"

With his free hand he yanked off Levering's neck-tie.

"There, ease her down till I get her feet. Hold still, consarn—"

One of Mary's heels caught him squarely in the face.

"Down, Lev'rin'. There, she got you that trip. Abby in the closet, Syl? She all right? Good. There." Asey knotted the necktie around Mary's ankles. "That's—see to her, Leverin'."

He got up off the floor and went over to the corner where Syl was busy over Abby's still figure.

"Get some water," Asey said, "an' then phone the doc,

Syl, an' get them others. She's still alive. She's goin' to come to—"

He carried Abby in his arms over to the open window. Levering, catching sight of her purple, mottled face, turned back to Mary and renewed his efforts to keep her still.

Syl returned with the water just as Mary began to kick and scream and writhe again. So engrossed were all three men that they failed to see Tabitha appear in the doorway, or hear Leary's dazed question.

"For—what's this?"

"Just," Tabitha said quietly, with a note of relief in her voice, "that it wasn't Asey who was, as you remarked, crazy."

"Just," Bob Raymond's face appeared over Tabitha's shoulder, "just that Asey's done it again, Leary!"

23

"But where," Tabitha asked, "is Asey?"

It was late that afternoon, and for over an hour the five of them, Joan, Lance, Suzanne, Levering and Tabitha, had been trying to clear up loose ends.

Levering shook his head. "Asey just upped and offed, as Syl put it. Left us to put Leary in his place. Syl did, all right. He strutted up to Leary and said, 'Say, run over t'Howeses, will you, an' fetch Mr. Mayo's pipe?' Leary fetched it without any argument. He seemed almost glad to."

"I'm proud to say," Tabitha remarked reminiscently, "that I had my innings. I tapped Leary's vest button with my lorgnette and said, 'Come, come, my good man, let this be a lesson to you!' He said it would, but I doubt if it's any lasting reformation."

Suzanne broke the uncomfortable little silence that ensued. All of them were thinking about Mary, but none of them wanted to think about what had happened after Mary left the Howes place that afternoon.

"It's awful, but we couldn't have gone on, knowing about her, and after all, she—Dr. Cummings said there wasn't a thing we could do. Mary knew I was frightened to death about Simon. It was Glotz who came around the house Monday, but she thought it was Simon, and she thought Carson was Simon. I don't blame her. I should have, if I'd taken that call. And she went for him, thinking he was Simon. And last night I told her how I loved the hill, and wouldn't dream of going away this winter if it weren't for Simon. And then, when she found out I intended to have Abby stay here, for a while, that was more than she could bear."

"I should have known," Tabitha said, "this afternoon when Asey and I were talking upstairs, and she was putting the finishing touches on the blue room. She was so bitter about Abby's coming. I thought she was putting it on. No one could have seen Abby this morning and still felt bitter about her. But she must have—how lucky Emmaline called, and told Asey there wasn't anything going on at the church, and it wasn't even open! Asey got it in a flash— he must have followed the doctor up to the hospital with her, to see everything was all right. For Abby, I mean."

Tabitha bit her lip. There she'd gone and brought that issue up again! There was a vast difference between the hospital where Abby had been taken for treatment and rest, and the institution where Broody Mary had been carried. And there was nothing to do about it. The doctor had given it all a name, but Asey's summing up was easier.

"Just stark, staring mad. Prob'ly somethin' that was comin' anyway, whether any of this'd happened or not. But killin' them two men, an' then findin' Abby was comin'

here, after all her efforts to save Sue from the Keiths—
that was the last straw. Been a lot of odd ones in her
fam'ly. I didn't realize till the doc counted up. He had
names for all of 'em. Seems those we thought was just
freakish or queer, like, was more'n that. Chances is one
against a million of her ever bein' herself again. It's pretty
bad, but it'd been so much worse—"

"Oh, dear!" Tabitha said. "Where is that man? He
should be here, now! Levering, didn't he give you any
hint at all?"

"I hoped he had some idea about the brief case and all
that, but apparently nothing's come of it."

"Nothing'll ever come of it," Lance said gloomily. "I
could have told anyone that before they started. Haven't
I spent the better part of my life, hunting—what's that?"

They all jumped as the marmoset Clare had left behind
knocked a book off the table.

"Give me that leash," Tabitha said, "or there won't be
a whole thing left in the house. I wish that girl would
return my chauffeur! I want to go up town. Marvin is going to get a piece of my mind, in my best manner, for
dashing off to Hyannis with her, and Asey was furious
about it."

"She's probably feeding him chocolate sodas in St.
Clair's," Levering observed, "and telling him he's too, too,
divine."

"His hair is rather nice," Joan welcomed the opportunity to think of someone other than Mary. "So curly."

Levering agreed. "Only you couldn't call that left ear
very divine. It's pure cauliflower. I hope she doesn't spoil

Marvin for the simple pleasures of life, aunt. He's not used to the likes of Clare."

Lance sighed gloomily. He'd almost forgotten about Clare. It was awful to let your fiancée slip your mind completely, but he couldn't seem to help it. And the B.P. plan, the buckpassing plan, that wasn't getting anywhere. Levering was too wary a lad to be caught by Clare. Besides, he was crazy about Joan. Clearly, Lance thought, he'd aimed this campaign at the wrong man.

Only thing to do was to go see Chatfield, and return both the job and the girl at one fell swoop. He could find another job, somewhere, even if he had to dig work relief ditches.

"Wonder if you could help me out to the car, Levering," he said suddenly. "I want to—well, I guess I'd better wait for Asey. He'll tell me how—you know, this household seems to go out like a light, with Asey away!"

Asey would be more of a moral support with Chatfield than Levering would be, and then, too, perhaps Asey did have some clew about old Bellamy's fortune. It was a feeble hope, but Asey had something up his sleeve.

The phone rang, and even Lance started to his feet.

"Asey!" Tabitha said. "It's got to be him!"

She returned from the entry almost at once.

"It's only Carl Chatfield. He wants to see you right away, Lance. What'll I tell him?"

"Say I'll be over later."

Tabitha had hardly replaced the receiver before the phone rang again.

"Asey!" All five of them yelled out his name at once.

"It must be Asey," Suzanne said. "I—I still hope he's got—"

Tabitha's scream of surprise brought the whole group out into the entry.

"Marvin! What's that?" Tabitha snorted. "Well, you'll undeniably feel worse. Yes, do!"

She turned around and faced the others.

"Marvin, and what d'you—in his most sheepish tones, he announced that he and Clare were eloping! And—"

"Eloping?" Lance nobly restrained his impulse to perform war dances and throw the furniture around. "They've eloped?"

"He said he felt awful about leaving me in the lurch, and—oh, my! I'll never find such a good chauffeur, never in this—"

"Levering," Lance interrupted briskly, "get me out into the station wagon, will you? If I can get hold of Chatfield while he's still sorry for me, and before he gives this job of mine to Marvin! Come on, I want to nick him while the nicking's good. Reach me my cane—"

"I'll put you in the car," Levering said, "but I refuse to drive any jilted fiancé to cadge a job off his ex-prospective father-in-law. It's not decent, and besides, I want to go into the Newell papers some more. Can't you wait and let Asey—"

"Buckpasser!" Joan said. "Help him out, and I'll drive him! It's obvious, Levering, you never had to hunt jobs—"

Lance looked at her, and his grin broadened. It wasn't possible that she could seem so cheered over just snaring a job. Why, she looked as though she wanted to dance war dances and ring bells, too—

Suzanne and Tabitha watched their departure.

"Asey told me," Suzanne remarked, "that things most usually evened out in the end. And—"

"And as usual," Tabitha said, "Asey was right. In his remorse, Chatfield'll probably give Lance a much better job than he'd have got otherwise. Poor Marvin! Or maybe it's poor Clare! Yes, I guess it's poor Clare. Marvin wasn't nearly middleweight champion, or something, for nothing. He'll make her toe the mark! Sue, go up and lie down."

"But dinner—"

"Fiddlededee! We'll go out for it. Sue, I know how you must feel about Mary."

"I don't think you can, really. She's looked after me so many years, ever since I came, and Lance was a baby. I suppose—oh, I did hope Asey could find—but I suppose there's no hope for that, either."

Levering came back a few minutes later.

"What," Tabitha demanded, "are your plans, Buck?"

"The Newell papers again. I thought Asey had some ideas—"

"Whatever ideas Asey had," Tabitha said succinctly, "about Bellamy's fortune, ended forever with Carson and Glotz and Archer. If that case went into a sink hole, I'd say the papers were well on their way back to Hong Kong by now. Levering, I don't like to proffer advice, particularly after the opportunity for following it has passed, but the papers were not that important—oh, no matter!"

She walked back slowly into the living room. The little

marmoset, its leash tied to the door handle, was chattering around.

"Poor beast," Tabitha said. "Come on out. Probably you want to be fed, too, but I haven't the slightest notion of what your diet consists. Asey would know, if he were here. It's high time he were here, too!"

Rupert seemed to find a banana entirely acceptible; after he finished his meal, she took him outside and let him play around the lattice. Then she went back to her favorite chair before the fireplace. Rupert curled up at her feet, and both of them dozed off.

A step in the room wakened her.

"Levering, hasn't Asey got back yet? The fiend—"

"It's the fiend himself. Huh, seems to me like you'n Rupert struck up a friendship—"

"Touch of the chameleon in him," Tabitha retorted. "He reacts to polite society. Asey, you must hear about Marvin and Clare—"

"Already have." He pulled a small bottle from one pocket of his canvas coat, and a ball of twine from another.

Tabitha looked at him curiously.

"Asey, what've you been up to? What *are* you up to?"

"Wa-el," he drawled, "Leary an' his pals went an' said such nice things to me that I sort of got excited an' went to thinkin' in earnest, an' the more I thought, the more I—"

"Asey Mayo! You've found out what Bellamy—what Carson was after? Let me call Sue, and Levering, and—"

"Whoa up!" Asey removed his coat, and rolled up

the sleeves of his flannel shirt. "Don't call 'em now. I don't want no more anti-climaxes. This is enough of a one as 'tis."

"Asey—"

"You p'ceive I got absolutely nothin' up my sleeves, ladies an' gents. This is all to make it look harder. No, you don't, an'mal!"

He grabbed Rupert just as the marmoset leaped on the mantel after the ship-in-the-bottle

"No, you don't! That's what I want!"

He removed the bottle from its wooden stand, and put it on the table before him.

"Asey—"

"See 'f it works first, Mrs. Newell."

He cut off a length of string, and dipped it in the bottle.

"Alcohol," he explained. "Now—"

He tied the wet string around the bottle, lighted a match, and applied it to the end of the string. The flame ran around the string, the bottle cracked, broke neatly in two.

"Asey Mayo, Sue'll ruin you! That's her favorite object—Asey, what's it got to do with—"

"So far," Asey didn't seem to notice her, "so good."

The ship inside the bottle, a five-masted schooner, was intact, and the putty in which it lay still stuck to one half.

Asey took his knife, inserted its tip just below the deck line of the ship, and twisted the knife ever so gently.

"It—it's coming off!" For the second time that day, Tabitha screamed.

"Yup. Hollow inside. Deck an' masts are the lid, an' the hull's the box. Seven inches long, an' an inch wide, an' near an inch high—hold out your hands—"

"Asey!" Tabitha said incredulously, "you—it—oh, my hands are trembling! Oh, Asey, diamonds! And—"

"An' a couple of pearls." Asey's voice trembled just a little, too. "An' though I ain't no gem expert, I got no reason to b'lieve these is fakes."

"And if they were worth all that when grandfather sold 'em, they're worth it now. That's the advantage of—and that ship and the bottle've been here for years, staring everyone in the face! Oh, call Sue, and call Levering, and tell them. Hurry! No, wait. Tell me first how you knew. I'll never get the chance to know later."

"It was simple," Asey picked up one of the pearls, "after—y'know, I'm kind of prideful of all this—"

"Stop! Tell me—"

"Well, Bellamy was a fool for ships. Everyone knew that, an'—"

"But he didn't send this home from China! It wasn't among the things that came home later!"

"Nope. That's what I asked Mary this aft'noon, when you an' me was in the entry. Where this come from. 'Member Lance was playin' with Rupert, an' I thought of how he'd most likely bust this b'fore he was through, an' then I wondered why, with all them really good ships up attic, they kept this one on the mantel. Kind of a punk ship.

Punk bottle. Too big an' clumsy. Proportions is bad. Anyway, Mary said it was the last ship Bellamy ever made. He sent it home from Boston by someone or other before he set out on his last v'yage. That's why they kept it out."

"But—"

" 'Member Leverin' said he seen Carson at an etchin' auction? Well, he give me the name of the place an' the date, an' this aft'noon I called up. It wasn't—'course, it was an etchin' auction to Leverin', 'cause that was what he was after. But it was mostly china an' ole jewelry. Jewelry fit in. An' then there was the name business. All the other boats Bellamy made was named 'Patience.' But looky this—"

He held up the hull, and Tabitha made out the tiny letters.

" 'The Golden Shell'—"

"Just so. That kind of struck a r'sponsive note, so I went to the lib'ry this aft'noon, too, an' done some readin'. That was the name of a pirate ship that got wrecked off the coast here in seventeen somethin'. So I just figgered it was jewels Carson was after, an' this seemed where."

"So I thought," Tabitha remarked, quoting Syl, "if I was a horse what I'd do, and I went there and it was— or however that famous line goes. I—oh, here's the station wagon with Lance and Joan. I'll get Levering to help Lance in—"

She went to the front steps and called.

"Levering! Come, please, and help Lance! And tell Sue to come down. Knock on her door, and tell her it's important. Hurry, both of you!"

"Asey'll have to, if he's there," Levering's muffled voice came back. "Sorry to pass the buck again, but I'm in the tub—"

"I'll go," Asey said, "n'en we'll get Sue an' have a grand showin'—"

Tabitha followed him outdoors.

He stopped short on the millstone that served as a step.

"My, my," he observed mildly. "Young love."

He waved a hand toward Lance and Joan, firmly and unashamedly gripped in each other's arms.

"Movie influence," Asey added judicially. "Even plunked themselves 'gainst the sunset. Huh. I try to wake Lance up, an' that's what I get!"

"That," Tabitha told him, "is not what you get. It's what my nephew gets, for passing the buck just once too often."

Mysteries available from Foul Play Press

The perennially popular Phoebe Atwood Taylor's droll "Codfish Sherlock" Asey Mayo, and "Shakespeare lookalike" Leonidas Witherall, have been eliciting guffaws from proper Bostonian Brahmins for more than half a century.

Asey Mayo Cape Cod Mysteries
The Annulet of Gilt, $5.95
The Asey Mayo Trio, $5.95
Banbury Bog, $5.95
The Cape Cod Mystery, $5.95
The Criminal C.O.D., $6.00
The Crimson Patch, $6.00
The Deadly Sunshade, $5.95
Death Lights a Candle, $6.95
Deathblow Hill, $6.00
Diplomatic Corpse, $5.95
Figure Away, $5.95
Going, Going, Gone, $5.95
The Mystery of the Cape Cod Players, $5.95
The Mystery of the Cape Cod Tavern, $5.95
Octagon House, $5.95
Out of Order, $6.00
The Perennial Boarder, $6.00
Proof of the Pudding, $6.00
Punch With Care, $5.95
Sandbar Sinister, $5.95
The Six Iron Spiders, $5.95
Spring Harrowing, $5.95
Three Plots for Asey Mayo, $6.95
The Tinkling Symbol, $6.00

Leonidas Witherall Mysteries (by "Alice Tilton")
Beginning with a Bash, $5.95
Dead Ernest, $6.00
File for Record, $6.00
The Hollow Chest, $5.95
The Iron Clew, $6.00
The Left Leg, $5.95

Available from book stores, or by mail from the publisher: The Countryman Press, Inc., P.O. Box 175, Dept. APC, Woodstock, Vermont 05091-0175; 800-245-4151. Please enclose $2.50 for 1–2 books, $3.00 for 3–6 books,or $3.50 for 7 or more books for shipping and handling. Prices are subject to change.

Margot Arnold

The complete adventures of Margot Arnold's beloved pair of peripatetic sleuths, Penny Spring and Sir Toby Glendower:

The Cape Cod Caper	*192 pages*	*$ 5.95*
Death of a Voodoo Doll	*220 pages*	*$ 5.95*
Death on the Dragon's Tongue	*224 pages*	*$ 4.95*
Exit Actors, Dying	*176 pages*	*$ 5.95*
Lament for a Lady Laird	*221 pages*	*$ 5.95*
The Menehune Murders	*272 pages*	*$ 5.95*
Toby's Folly	*256 pages*	*$ 5.95*
Zadok's Treasure	*192 pages*	*$ 5.95*

Joyce Porter

American readers, having faced several lean years deprived of the company of Chief Inspector Wilfred Dover, will rejoice (so to speak) in the reappearance of "the most idle and avaricious policeman in the United Kingdom (and, possibly, the world)." Here is the series that introduced the bane of Scotland Yard and his hapless assistant, Sgt. MacGregor, to international acclaim.

Dover One	*192 pages*	*$ 5.95*
Dover Two	*222 pages*	*$ 5.95*
Dover Three	*192 pages*	*$ 4.95*
Dead Easy for Dover	*176 pages*	*$ 5.95*
Dover and the Claret Tappers	*203 pages*	*$ 6.00*
Dover and the Unkindest Cut of All	*188 pages*	*$ 5.95*
Dover Goes to Pott	*192 pages*	*$ 5.95*
Dover Strikes Again	*202 pages*	*$ 5.95*
It's Murder With Dover	*192 pages*	*$ 5.95*

"Meet Detective Chief Inspector Wilfred Dover. He's fat, lazy, a scrounger and the worst detective at Scotland Yard. But you will love him."   —*Manchester Evening News*